CRIMEUCOPIA

One More Thing To W— bout...
A Murdero— gy
****

Dear Debbie,

Hope you enjoy my story!

Best wishes,
Asterix
#HandMade

Murderous—Ink Press

CRIMEUCOPIA
One More Thing To Worry About...

First published by Murderous-Ink Press
Crowland
LINCOLNSHIRE
England
www.murderousinkpress.co.uk

Editorial Copyright © Murderous Ink Press 2023
Cover treatment and lettering © Willie Chob-Chob 2023
All rights are retained by the respective authors & artists on publication
Paperback Edition ISBN: 9781909498440
eBook Edition ISBN: 9781909498457

The rights of the named individuals to be identified as the authors of these works has been asserted in accordance with section 77 and 78 of the Copyright, Designs and Patents Act, 1988

All rights reserved. No part of this publication may be reproduced, stored in or introduced into a retrieval system, or transmitted in any form, or by any means (electronic, mechanical, photocopying or otherwise) without the prior written permission of both the author(s) and the publisher. Any person who does any unauthorised act in relation to this publication may be liable to criminal prosecution and civil claims for damages.

Every effort has been made to obtain the necessary permissions with reference to copyright material, both illustrative and quoted. We apologise for any omissions in this respect and will be pleased to make the appropriate acknowledgements in further editions.

This book and its contents are works of fiction. Names, characters, places and incidents are either a products of the authors' imagination or are used fictitiously. Any resemblance to actual people living or dead, events, locations and/or their contents, is entirely coincidental.

Acknowledgements

To those writers and artists who helped make this anthology what it is, I can only say a heartfelt Thank You!

And to Den, as always.

Contents

Every Mind is a UXB….	vii
Last Night – Gerald Elias	1
Pillowcases – Bob Ritchie	13
Driven Over the Edge – Michele Bazan Reed	17
Murder at the Aragalaya – Terry Wijesuriya	27
Chinese Submarines – Aran Myracle	47
The Taxidermist – Alexei J. Slater	53
Bad Apples – Nikki Knight	73
The Black Glove – Issy Jinarmo	125
Danger at Death's Door – N. M. Cedeño	143
Tears of a Clown – Wendy Harrison	159
Terrestrial Timeslip – Andrew Darlington	173
The Ultimate Serial Killer – Larry Lefkowitz	179
The Gathering Puddle – Jesse Aaron	185
Not the Dog – Madeleine McDonald	203
Ashes, Ashes – Joan Leotta	209
A Missing Piece – H. E. Vogl	217
Killer on the Loose – Vinnie Hansen	225
The Usual Unusual Suspects	235

"Gerald Elias is a maestro of mystery"
(Gabriel Valjan)

A packed house at London's famed Royal Albert Hall. Gustav Mahler's monumental 6th Symphony, with its three massive hammer strokes of Fate. The first and the second go by uneventfully. But then, the third! Will Mahler's third hammer stroke of Fate claim another victim?

Gerald Elias's riveting eighth installment of the critically acclaimed Daniel Jacobus mystery series will keep readers on the edge of their seats. Blind, curmudgeonly violinist Jacobus and his devoted companions, Yumi Shinagawa and Nathaniel Williams, join forces with Englishman Branwell Small, a questionably trustworthy partner in crime solving, and officious DCI Christopher Mattheson as they follow every baffling twist and turn in a truly classical whodunnit.

Paperback 9781685122386
eBook 9781685122393

https://geraldeliasmanofmystery.wordpress.com

Jefferson Dance is a prototypical cowboy with a philosophical bent, a man willing to entertain newfangled concepts, like climate change and women's rights. Nevertheless, he is etched with a set of traditional Western values, including using a gun when necessary; and self-deprecating modesty, talking about himself in only the most humble terms. I thank him for his contribution, nevertheless.

Simmering just under the surface of the levity of Roundtree Days, an annual festival celebrating the sensational hit television series, Roundtree, a clash of cultures between traditional and progressive values threatens to tear apart a proud Western town surrounded by an unforgiving desert environment. In a single day, Jefferson Dance, acting sheriff of Loomis City, Utah, confronts a suspected kidnapping, a surreal hostage situation, arson, and murder, while fending off his popular fictional double, who the public perceives as a real life hero. In a setting in which fantasy and reality become blurred, Dance unearths the town's dark secrets as he brings the culprits to justice in the course of twenty-four hours.

Paperback 9781685121709
eBook 9781685121716

Every Mind is a UXB…
(An Editorial of Sorts)

One of the things about a Free-4-All anthology is that, in theory, every piece can be the total opposite of the piece before, and the piece after.

Fine.

However, one of the things we do here in the world(s) of Crimeucopia, is to look for bridges – even the very slightest or tenuous will do – and if a piece originally selected for a particular anthology slowly becomes a little too 'out of place' then we have the flexibility to move it – or in this case, them – around.

So it was with *Aran Myracle*'s **Chinese Submarines** and *Alexei Slater*'s **The Taxidermist**, both being brand new Crimeucopians. Originally set for **We'll Be Right Back – After This!**, both eventually became founding pieces for this anthology, and in turn displaced two other pieces which will now be appearing in the next anthology – **Strictly Off The Record**. We cannot guarantee that this kind of domino effect won't happen again in the future, but that's the nature of our dynamic programming.

Those two are also joined by other first time Crimeucopians, starting with *Gerald Elias* and his **Last Night** and *Terry Wijesuriya* takes us to Sri Lanka, with her **Murder at the Aragalaya**.

The Black Glove sees *Issy Jinarmo*'s debut, while humourist *Larry Lefkowitz* gives us the tale of **The Ultimate Serial Killer**, and *Vinnie Hansen* closes out this anthology by telling us all about the **Killer on the Loose**.

Those 7 smoothly rub literary shoulders with a bunch of Crimeucopia old lags and reprobates, such as *Michele Bazen Reed*, who lets us know what it takes to be **Driven Over the Edge**.

Bob Ritchie, also tells of the troubles caused by **Pillowcases**, and *Nikki*

Knight returns with a barrel of **Bad Apples** – a tale split into slices, just like any good pie.

Danger at Death's Door has *Noreen Cedeño* move us into historical waters, while *Wendy Harrison* poses the ever timeless question with her **Tears of a Clown**.

Terrestrial Timeslip shows us just how devious *Andrew Darlington*'s mind can be, and helps ease us into an almost *Weird Tales* triptych in the form of *Madeleine McDonald*'s **Not The Dog**, *Joan Leotta*'s **Ashes, Ashes** and *Howard Vogl* explains the importance of **A Missing Piece**.

Helping to frame the three is *Jesse Aaron*, who gives us one of his Detective Weepy Willy Williamson pieces in the form of **The Gathering Puddle**.

All 17 tell tales that will make you realise there will always be One More Thing To Worry About….

And, for those who might be interested, the 'origin' of this anthology's title comes from an old cassette tape recorded off the coast of Florida, back in 1986. The newsreader closed with:

"And one more thing to worry about – Bubonic Plague. It appears that a West Texas hunter contracted the disease from an infected rabbit he shot and ate…" Back then everything was so much simpler…

As with all of these anthologies, we hope you'll find something that you immediately like, as well as something that takes you out of your comfort zone – and puts you into a completely new one.

In other words, in the spirit of the Murderous Ink Press motto:

You never know what you like until you read it.

Last Night
Gerald Elias

At this point, it's too late for false modesty. You know who I am. The big name draw in Vegas, in Paris, London, New York. The biggest. Platinum all the way, baby. I play the piano. I sing. You name it. If it's been written, I play it in my own inimitable style. I've got a better voice than Tom Jones ever had and I play piano better than Hamlisch ever could. I don't dance. Dancing's for wannabes. I banter with the crowd. The fancy outfits, the techno fireworks, the bevy of scantily clad beauties. It makes for one splashy show.

I've also gained notoriety for leading what's called an "extravagant" lifestyle by polite society. Impolite society might call it "wanton" or "dissolute," which it has on more than one occasion. Mere value judgements, I say. Mostly envy, I suspect. Free from the encumbrances of a wife and kids, it has been reported—with revealing full color photographs in the choicest gossip magazines—that I live life to the fullest. Publicity like that only helps. All in all, no one can beat my marketability on the entertainment circuit. No one. I get about a hundred requests a day to play at fund-raising events for humanitarian causes, because when Mr. and Mrs. Bigpockets see my name on an invitation, Mrs. Bigpockets sends the RSVP pronto and Mr. Bigpockets opens his checkbook. I'm as household a name as Kleenex. I turn down almost every request, not because I don't appreciate the value of the causes or the sincerity of the people behind them but, frankly, because there are only twenty-four hours in a day, and life is just too damn short. You will soon see how ironic a statement that is, because of an offer I did accept. Like they said in the Godfather, it was an offer I couldn't refuse. An offer from the Lysen's Disease Foundation. If only.

A young thing from the LDF by the name of Ástor Moreau called my trusty manager and handler, Lou Savin, who I'd hired years ago to be my unbreachable stonewall to intrusions upon my valuable time. But Lou said the kid's voice was "sweet as honey" and couldn't bring himself to break the bad news in a good way, so he got me on the line with her for me to do his dirty work. Lou was right. Ástor was the princess of sweet-talk, and had an accent to die for that went with it.

The LDF, she told me, was on the cusp of a breakthrough in a vaccine cocktail that would stop the rampaging Lysen's Disease pandemic in its tracks. That caught my attention because my shows in Johannesburg had just been cancelled because of it and I was out six figures, big time. LDF was offering to fly me down to its research facility on the island of Lesser Nolena, "a tiny emerald jewel surrounded by the clear turquois of the Caribbean." The reason? To entertain at a gala midnight dinner where the LDF would celebrate the success of their $500 million campaign to provide the means to mass-produce and distribute the vaccine.

"We can't imagine anyone in the world more than you who would attract the kind of people we've needed to raise this kind of money," she said. She probably thought such flattery would have me eating out of the palm of her hand. And she would be right. So did her offer for me to name my price.

"Continue," I said.

The tests were still in the experimental stage, Ástor went on, but with the pledges they'd already received from this august gathering they were confident it would get them over the hump. Every moment was precious. Between two and three thousand sub-Saharan Africans a day—a day!—were dying an excruciating death from the inside out. Lysen's Disease, named after Harding Lysen, the physician who first diagnosed it in Sierra Leone and then succumbed to it shortly thereafter, is an equal opportunity killer; a virus that strikes young and old, sick or healthy, with such astonishing and lethal virulence that it has universally been nicknamed Shark Flu. Symptoms begin with a mild fever, then dryness of the throat, followed by vomiting, diarrhea, convulsions, internal bleeding, external bleeding through all the orifices including the eyes, and then death. All within three to four days. "And I'm sparing you the nasty parts," Ástor said. The survival rate was zero. Shark Flu was barreling toward North Africa and was threatening to hop the Atlantic to the Caribbean. If it wasn't stopped, it was forecast to reach the shores of North America and Europe within weeks. Nothing to this point, including quarantines and strict international immigration controls, had been able to even slow its progress. The thought that there was an imminent breakthrough was breathtaking.

"We're so close to achieving our goal," Ástor concluded. "At least, we think so," with emphasis on the *we*. "What do you say?"

"Are you French?"

"Why do you ask?"

"Your accent. Your name. And I have an attraction for French women."

She laughed, musical as a right-hand arpeggio.

"No. I am not French. I was born and raised in Trinidad."

"Will you be there?" I asked.

"Where. In Trinidad?" I think she was teasing me. The coy thing.

"I mean in Little Norena, or whatever it's called."

"Of course. It was my idea to invite you."

Around Ástor's little finger I was wrapped. I even declined to accept a fee.

*****

Getting to the more appealing islands in the Caribbean is never a comfortable schlep. Maybe that's what makes them appealing. Fewer tourists. Getting to Lesser Nolena, an easily overlooked dot on the map, was a pain in the rear. And for some reason this whole business was suddenly hush-hush as an FBI investigation. Immediately after saying bye-bye to Ástor, I received a follow-up call from the big man himself, Dr. Liam MacDowell, Nobel laureate and the head researcher of LDF. He thanked me profusely for agreeing to lend my talents, after which he surprised me by insisting I not divulge anything about the event to anyone, even to Lou. I balked at that, but he impressed upon me how delicate a situation this was, with so many people dying every day and not wanting to get anyone's hopes up prematurely. And since, like all the other guests, I could plan to return home the next day, I would hardly be missed. It was probable no one would even know I had been gone.

I asked MacDowell how they expected the bigwigs to come to the island if no one knew about it, which I immediately realized was a dumb question. This was clearly an invitation only event. On the other hand, I would've thought an imminent breakthrough like this should have been advertised on all the front pages, especially since all the news we'd been hearing about Shark Flu was bad. MacDowell politely but firmly demurred, saying that science, not promotion, was his field. He left that to the president of the LDF, Art Henderson. Marketing is definitely not my thing, either, but knowing the little you hear about dueling pharmaceutical companies on the news, I suspected the main reason for secrecy was LDF's desire to keep their billion dollar patent close to the vest. So I agreed to MacDowell's request, and when I phoned Lou I fabricated some malarkey about having to get away for a day for R and R. You know, the strain of the job. That kind of thing. I could picture him raising his eyebrows over the phone, but he wouldn't make a fuss.

I left Miami at about nine-thirty pm in an eight-seat prop-jet for Greater Nolena, a hop, skip, and jump from Florida, but which, the pilot informed me, is as close as one can get by plane to our final destination. When we landed I was pointed in the direction of the marina, all of a ten minute walk from the runway. At the dock I was whisked onto a private yacht named Therapy II, handed a martini, and was splashily introduced (no pun intended) to a couple dozen high roller dinner guests who had been awaiting my arrival. As we skimmed over several miles of dark, open sea to the tiny, newly developed harbor at Lesser Nolena—which until the research facility was built had been inhabited only by parrots and geckos—we exchanged meaningless small talk animated by the import of the event and sounding, I would guess, like parrots. I have no idea what kind of noises a gecko makes.

At the Lesser Nolena dock we were greeted deferentially by LDF staff, who escorted us to barely comfortable accommodations. Clearly constructed in haste for our brief stay, you could still smell the fresh, lime green paint. Our bedrooms were in a plain, one story rectangular building that had more of a feel of a dormitory than a hotel. My room was furnished with a twin bed on a metal Harvard frame, which I hadn't seen since my college days—which maybe explains why I dropped out—a mirror, a portable clothing rack, and a no-frills bathroom. I suspected all the rooms were more or less the same. It certainly wasn't conducive to my fantasies of romancing the fair Ástor. What puzzled me, though, was that most of the guests were extremely busy Fortune 500 execs. If they had known they were going to be treated to such Spartan conditions, they might have chosen not to spend the night, or not have come at all—they could have just sent in their checks—but for the persuasiveness of the Foundation administrators that this was going to be a unique historic event. The LDF also hadn't hesitated to drop my name as the headline attraction, which was okay with me. But I mean, why bother with any of this?

It's no secret I am not unaccustomed to late night activity. My show in Vegas alone doesn't end until the wee hours, and that's when the party gets rolling. So doing a midnight gig did not ruffle my feathers. On the other hand, after being whisked across the Caribbean to Never Never Land and shown my Boy Scout accommodations, I was more than ready for a drink, for which, thankfully, I did not have long to wait. I changed from my travel clothes into a smart, $5,000 Savile Row black tuxedo. Nothing outlandish, like I would wear for the weekend slot addicts in Vegas. But appropriate for a serious occasion such as this one: saving the world. I knew, though, considering the company, that even decked out in my sartorial splendor I would not be a swan among a flock of ducks. I was struck how youthful all the guests seemed—some half my age—both male and female. The world has certainly changed from the days corporate magnates wore three-piece wool suits, carried pocket watches, and sported walrus mustaches. Now they looked like tennis pros and Sports Illustrated swimsuit models, and the high tech billionaires looked like teenagers. Maybe they were.

The order of ceremonies was going to be pretty standard: happy hour, hors d'oeuvres, a welcome from the LDF president, a sit-down dinner on the veranda, my command performance, and then the spiel by Dr. MacDowell, who would talk about their scientific breakthrough and thank us for our participation and support. And after that? The night was young. My kinky imagination took wing.

And so the "evening" proceeded in the manner of well-planned fundraisers, with the momentum gradually building up to the big announcement. Cocktail hour commenced under a starry sky, little waves lapping on the shore mere steps from the wet bar. The bartender and servers were all big guys whose white tuxedos were stretched tight over their biceps. My experienced eye tagged them as bouncers more than waiters, but this whole scenario was already so out of the ordinary I chose not to dwell on that.

There was a gentle tap on my shoulder. I turned to face a man wearing bifocals who seemed about my age—mid-fifties—with a trimmed salt-and-pepper beard, inside of which was a smile that might normally be genuine but which seemed, on this occasion, an attempt to disguise an overriding unease.

"Dr. MacDowell, I presume," I said.

"How did you know?" he asked, the smile brightening momentarily.

"Seen too many sci fi movies on Netflix."

We shook hands and he once again expressed his gratitude for my blah blah blah. The usual spiel. But it was nice. Don't believe what anyone tells you. It never gets old.

MacDowell was clearly preoccupied with the purpose of the evening, so I quickly released him to whatever schmoozing he was obligated to do. One of the servers passed with a silver tray of bubbly. I grabbed two flutes of champagne and asked him to point out Ástor Moreau. Right where the water ended and the sand began I was rewarded with a vision of paradise. Miss Moreau, maybe thirty, maybe less. Bronzed skin the result of serious sunbathing or an intriguing racial mix. Either way, I liked it. Light brown eyes and shoulder-length auburn hair and the profile of a goddess. And did I mention her figure?

"Enjoying the evening, Ástor?"

"Ah! I am so glad you came to our little soirée," she said, holding out her hand. Since I had a flute in each hand, I couldn't shake it, so I handed her a glass, accompanied by my winningest smile, and gave her a peck on the cheek. Both cheeks. We clinked glasses.

"Delighted to be here," I said.

"I've arranged for you to sit next to me at the table of honor."

"I'm honored."

"So then you won't mind being my guinea pig for the evening?" she said, with what appeared to be mock seriousness. Or was it a Mona Lisa smile?

It was a strange way of putting things, "guinea pig," but no stranger than anything else that had taken place on this island. And what is it they say about gift horses? Not that Ástor's mouth wasn't something one could look at for hours on end. Ah, the potential!

"I've been waiting my whole life for an invitation like that," I said, and we both laughed.

With such a compressed itinerary, by the time cocktail hour was over everyone was buddy-buddy, and with the research team conspicuously absent the island vibe felt more Club Med than medical. And that's how it sounded when we were welcomed by the president of the Lysen's Disease Foundation, Art Henderson. He told us all about how well things were going with their fund-raising efforts. What an honor it was to be surrounded by such a distinguished gathering of the rich and famous. In so many words he told us to eat, drink, and be merry. I'm glad he didn't get around to the end part, "for tomorrow we die." That would have put a real damper on the evening.

For dinner, the guests were seated at round tables with white linen tablecloths. Each table seated six, and had a centerpiece of local flowers. Nice touch. Chinese lanterns hung from the veranda's rafters. That was nice, too. At one of end of the veranda was the Steinway piano that had been flown in for the occasion, and thankfully seemed to still be intact. I told them to lose the candelabra. I'm not Liberace. No way.

The menu was highlighted by fresh, perfectly grilled shrimp and swordfish that had arrived from Greater Nolena in the same yacht as the guests. There was a lot of small talk, as if to sidestep discussing the reason we were there. Maybe it was because here we were, being wined and dined in the lap of luxury, just to get us to cough up money to put a stop to the ugliest form of human misery the world had ever known. Maybe it was because the guests felt vulnerable, that even all their money might not be able to save them. Was it excitement in the air? Or was there a hint of desperation?

Every seat on the veranda was taken except the one to my right. That was lucky for me because it enabled me to concentrate on making hay with my partner to my left, Ástor. I had a feeling this was going to be a night to remember. Toward the end of the meal, a musclebound server came up to me and whispered in my ear that it was time for me to perform. I thanked him for the heads-up and excused myself from the other four at my table.

"By the way," I asked Ástor, close to her ear, "who's the person that was supposed to sit next to me?"

"Oh, Liam MacDowell. He's my husband."

One may or may not like my style of music. To each, his own. But no one can ever say that I'm not a professional. I've dealt with more than my share of drunks, deviants, and power outages over the years, so putting Ástor's bombshell out of my mind for the next half hour while I did my thing was all in the line of duty. Not saying it was easy.

My performance of well-known but not too highbrow classics and Andrew Lloyd Webber hits created the desired heart-tugging, feel-good effect. I took requests from the audience for fan favorites from *Les Miz*, *Rent*, *Wicked*, and *Hamilton*, and was able to toss off every one of them as easily as flipping burgers. At the end I put in a good word for "my dear friends" at LDF, who I had met an hour before. By the time I returned to my seat next to Ástor and MacDowell took the podium, I'd primed the gathering to exceed the $500 million goal. One would have thought MacDowell would have been ebullient. He was anything but.

"I would like to thank all of you from the bottom of my heart for coming here tonight," he said, with a tone more funereal than celebratory.

"As you know, Lysen's Disease—Shark Flu—has been the most virulent communicable disease in history. It makes AIDS, Ebola, Zika, or the Black Death seem like a head cold."

A few people chuckled. MacDowell didn't even smile.

"It is a disease," he continued, "which, unless it is stopped, has the theoretical capacity to eradicate the entire population of the world—"

No laughs now.

"Which is why we have been working feverishly to develop a vaccine. Because Lysen's disease is incurable and untreatable, prevention is the only possibility. Let me repeat, we having been working feverishly to develop a vaccine because Lysen's disease is incurable and untreatable. Prevention is the only possibility."

He had the group's attention like a boa constrictor wrapped around a rabbit.

"One of the many challenges to effectively combat this disease is that, unlike any other virus we have ever encountered, Lysen's Disease attacks only humans and no other organism. Therefore, the testing we've done on flies, mice, rats, pigs, and even lower primates has been an exercise in futility. Regardless of the similarity of genetic predisposition, those subjects simply do not contract the disease, so inoculating them with the vaccine neither proves nor disproves anything."

A hand shot up. MacDowell waved it off dismissively.

"What we have tried to do here on Lesser Nolena is understand the nature of the viral organism itself, study how and why it has attached itself only to human tissue, and extrapolate from there, basing our strategy on how viruses we do understand have responded in the past. The serum we have concocted, we strongly believe—I repeat—we strongly believe will be successful in stopping the spread of the virus. But there is only one way to know."

The gathering of the powerful collectively leaned forward in their seats, waiting for the dénouement that would justify the donation of their time and their treasure.

"Ladies and gentlemen, we have brought you here today for two reasons. The first is to thank you for your commitment to humanity, for demonstrating your faith in our efforts by providing the financial means to literally save the world."

"Hear! Hear!" someone called out. Glasses were raised by all.

Out of the corner of my eye, I noticed the waiters in their white tuxedos set a discreet perimeter around the veranda, the kind of thing I'm used to seeing security guards do at the casinos on the Strip when the weirdos get out of hand. What's this all about? I asked myself. This is supposed to be a celebration.

"The second is again to thank you for your commitment to humanity, but for a different reason than you can ever have imagined. Look around you. You have probably noticed how young everyone is. But it is not your youth why you were selected to be on our guest list. Rather, it is because we've determined you have no committed partners or children. We are trying to be as humane as possible."

"What are you getting at, Dr. MacDowell?" someone shouted out. "Is this some kind of game?"

The guy's challenge was making everyone nervous, me included.

"As I've implied by my previous comments, we have had to break every rule in the book. The only way to know if our vaccine will work is to test it on humans. There was no time for double-blind testing. There was no time for peer review, patents, or FDA approval."

"You're going to give us shots?" someone yelled.

"That's unethical," someone else chimed in. "You can't do this, MacDowell!"

The crowd was stirring, but not in a happy way. It looked like things might get ugly, fast.

"We already have, sir." MacDowell was speaking loudly now, as the guests' commotion started to become unruly. One of the men tried to make a dash for it. Where "it" was, was anyone's guess. But he was subdued in short order by one of the heavies, a real pro, and carried away like a sack of potatoes, presumably to his room.

"Ladies and gentlemen, your pre-dinner cocktails contained an oral dose of our vaccine. The delicious fish you enjoyed for dinner was injected with diluted Lysen's virus itself. We pray that we are correct and that tomorrow we will all witness a glorious sunrise over the Caribbean. If not," MacDowell said, raising his glass, "together we leave this world with good food and beautiful music." MacDowell motioned his glass in my direction, and gave me what could be construed as a wan smile. "May God bless you all."

"We're out of here, MacDowell!" someone else demanded. "We're leaving now and you can't stop us." The guy jumped up like a jack-in-the-box and overturned his table, sending the flowers, glassware and everything else shattering onto the floor.

"Stop you? I'm sorry to say, there is no way off the island. There are no boats, no planes, and all communications have been shut down until we have a result. We are all here until we know for certain. Surely you can understand that we can't let anyone go back if there is any chance of carrying this disease. But I assure you, we are confident of a positive result. A result that will save humanity."

Some of the guests were crying, and not just the women. Others sat immobilized, stone-faced as Easter Island statues. As reality set in, the fight seemed to have left everyone. There was either hope or there was hopeless. Whichever, there was nothing more to be done.

"I'm going to my room," someone said. "Wake me up when this nightmare is over."

That ended it. There were a few more mumbles about calling lawyers or "the government," but the insurrection ebbed as meekly as last call at a corner bar.

"Come," Ástor whispered to me.

We slid unnoticed past the numbed guests and stepped off the veranda. Ástor slipped off her shoes and we walked on night-chilled sand toward the water. The dark sea and moonless sky, which had so recently seemed so enchanting, so beckoning, so full of potential, now seemed so empty. We were a speck on a black world and in a matter of hours either there would be a new day, or there would be…nothing.

I looked at Ástor.

"Now I know what you meant by guinea pig," I said.

"I'm sorry. I couldn't tell you. I wasn't allowed."

"He's either a genius or a madman, your husband. Which is it?"

"I wish I knew."

"So what do we do now?" I asked. "Just wait?"

She looked into my eyes and gave me that Mona Lisa smile again.

"What would you recommend? Watching the sun rise?"

Pillowcases
Bob Ritchie

Hannah made the bed, precise in her pulling taut the sheet, in her folding back same, leaving a five-inch band that demarcated the top of the blanket. The quilt, handmade by her grandmother, she stretched to each of the bed's corners, sweeping away the few wrinkles like so many dust bunnies.

She reached for the first of the four pillows. At the corners opposite the opening, knowing fingers searched for and found the corresponding corners of the pillow within. Lifting the whole, she gave a gentle shake, letting gravity do the work of aligning pillow and case. She placed it on the bed, the long sides of the pillow paralleling those of the bed. She repeated the process with the second pillow, the third, the fourth—until all four pillows were flat and perfect and settled comfortably within their pillowcases. Her two she had placed close to the edge of her side of the bed, leaning from her husband's side to do so; it was easier than walking all the way 'round.

She straightened, contemplating her work. A wide gulf separated the two rows. Good. Next step.

Curl of tongue caught in corner of mouth, she transferred the first of her husband's pillows to its place at the top of the bed. As her mother had taught her, she oriented the opening of the case toward the bed's center. "So all of the love will stay on the bed and not fall out, over the edge," she used to say.

She picked up the second pillow and set it on the first, maintaining the perfect contours of both.

She straightened again, and her back cracked, a gunshot that slaughtered the tranquil morning. "Oh!" She giggled at her spine's temerity.

Pillowcases

A beam of sun slipped over the sill of the window that faced her husband's side of the bed. Springing lightly onto the top pillow, it curled up, and went to sleep, making the tiny roses dotting the expanse of white cotton glow. With her palm, she petted a rebellious crease, urging it to relax; nothing should mar the pillow's perfection.

Stepping around to the other side, she repeated the process, minus drowsing sunbeam.

*****

After finishing in the house, Hannah went to the city to visit her sister at the hospital. She stayed overnight and much of the following day but rushed her visit, because being away from home made the network of nerves threading through her body turn to glowing hot copper wire.

*****

It was late when she came home. Late at night, but a day earlier than expected.

The train had been full, and she had had to stand, as not one of the men in her car was gentleman enough to offer her his seat. She was tired. She opened the front door slowly, pulling lightly upward as she did, knowing that if she swung the door too quickly and with its full weight, the bottom hinge would squeak, possibly waking her husband. When she stepped over the threshold, relief at being there, being *home,* flooded her, dampening the internal burning.

Hannah set her purse on the dining-room table and automatically picked up the left-out placemat and put it away. With her having been absent that morning, her husband had made his own breakfast, had cleared away and—she assumed—washed the dishes. But he had forgotten—as usual—to put away the placemat. She smiled, but tension pulled at the corners of her mouth.

In the kitchen, the, yes, cleaned, dishes and small frying pan were stacked neatly in the dish drainer. He had misplaced the plate he had used, putting it at the bottom of the horizontal stack. There were no dinner plates, pots, or pans, so she supposed he had eaten out. It was too late to put away the dishes—what a cacophony! But... She moved the out-of-place plate, quietly, carefully, to the top of the stack, squeezing it between the plastic frame of the rack and the pan. The headlights from a passing car stabbed through the kitchen window, startling her. The faint "tink" that sounded as plate hit pan made her eyes widen, and she froze in place. Too much noise?

No. Nothing. She sighed, relaxing what had become a clutching hold. She turned to hang her keys from the hook on the wall beside the microwave, damping their possible jangling with her cupped palm.

To bed.

She navigated the hall, toward the bedroom, the carpet smothering any potential sounds. She would vacuum tomorrow, she decided. Early, before the afternoon sun warmed the house, but after her husband had gone to work.

Arriving at the bedroom door, Hannah gripped the doorknob and twisted it. Quickly, because the mechanism was damaged: If you turned the knob too slowly, it would get stuck halfway, only becoming unstuck if you forced it open. The grinding of the innards vibrated through her hand, damped by her enclosing fingers and palm.

She entered, the dark more complete than she had expected. Though the bathroom door was open, dark gray against darker black, the nightlight wasn't on. He must have forgotten. She reached her left hand out to the wall, fingers extended, to guide herself through the short vestibule. In the room proper, she frowned, allowing the expression to displace what had been a smile, what had become a thin, near-grimace.

He had made the bed. In the morning, perhaps. The covering spread was all creases and wrinkles.

But where...?

*****

The police found her, perching on the right edge of the bed. The body of her husband was arranged neatly on the left side. Through the window next to the bed flowed clean, late-morning light that haloed the body. The gun that had, presumably, caused the hole centered in his forehead lay on his chest, its horizontal axis oriented along the body's vertical axis.

"He had the openings of the pillowcases facing the wrong way, you see, out instead of in."

Driven Over the Edge
Michele Bazan Reed

As Oscar headed for the bathroom, he cast a wistful eye back at the bed, with its rumpled comforter and the pillow with little fist-shaped indentations. He sighed. Truth was, Oscar didn't have the energy for more than a sigh. He couldn't remember the last time he'd had a good night's sleep.

The irony of it all was now, when he had to get up and go to work, it was finally quiet. Now, when he'd be able to sleep, he couldn't--at least not if he wanted a paycheck. Now, Troy stopped.

It had been going on for months. But last night was the worst. Engine revving. Music--if you could call it that--blaring. Wrenches clanging as they were tossed into the toolbox. And that infernal shop light shining straight into his window until 4 a.m. Troy hung it from the front latch of the hood and the shadeless bulb was angled so it hit Oscar directly in the eye. Turning his head didn't help, it filled the window with light, crisscrossed with lines from the metal cage that enclosed the bulb. And every time Troy bumped into it, the light swung back and forth, back and forth, making little highways of red across the map of Oscar's closed eyelids. Swung like a pendulum. Like a hypnotist's watch, except it didn't put Oscar to sleep, it drilled into his eyeballs until the resulting headache made it feel like he'd never sleep again.

Down in the kitchen, Oscar gulped down a bowl of oatmeal and an orange juice. He poured a cup of coffee with skim milk into his travel mug and packed a Swiss cheese and tomato sandwich on whole wheat, with an apple and a single square of 70% dark chocolate, his little indulgence. Same bagged lunch he took every day. Watching his sodium and calories, trying to stay healthy. Of course, lack of sleep was raising his blood pressure daily. Last visit, the doctor upped his meds and told him to avoid stress. *Ha! Fat chance.*

As put his trusty Prius into reverse and backed out of the driveway, Oscar glanced over at Troy's place. He shook his head. Transmission fluid sat in a battered turkey roaster, glowing red like blood in the dawn light. The forecast called for a thunderstorm. Rain would fill the roaster to overflowing and that poison would be washed into the soil. *Now he's not satisfied with just killing me,* Oscar thought. *He wants to murder Mother Earth, too.* It made him sad and angry in equal parts, and he tuned the radio to National Public Radio, hoping to get his mind off his problems.

The first story was about petroleum products and the harm they were doing to the environment, which only made Oscar sadder over the turkey roaster. The next went into great detail about the effects upon the body--and mind--of not getting adequate sleep. The researcher droned on: memory loss, weight gain, risk of heart disease, poor concentration, on and on. *I don't need this,* thought Oscar. *I could be reporting it.*

A car horn woke Oscar from his reverie, and he swerved back into his own lane just in time to avoid a head-on collision with a red pickup truck, as the angry driver gave him the finger. Hands shaking, Oscar rolled down the window, breathing in the brisk air, and turned to a classical music station, hoping the Wagnerian version of heavy metal would help him make it to work without crashing.

At the office, things went from bad to worse. In the breakroom, Oscar spilled coffee on his pants, his hands were shaking so. He misquoted a figure to his boss, transposing the numbers and causing the man to order two truckloads more of widgets than the company could use in a quarter. At 3 p.m., he fell asleep in a meeting and, when called upon to give his report, he stumbled to his feet and looked blankly around the room, until recovering and reading in a monotone from the paper in front of him. That earned a call down to HR, where he had to spend half an hour having rules read to him. (*Two such incidents and a report goes in your file. Three infractions and you'll be on probation. And oh, by the way, shall I set you up for counseling for alcohol? Hmmm, or maybe drugs?*)

After reassuring the HR lady that he was, in fact, merely tired from a sleepless night, Oscar returned, red-faced, to his unit. Keeping his head down helped avoid the stares of his coworkers, but nothing could keep out the whispers. "No, really, sleeping!" "Losing it." "What a shame. It won't be long now." He packed his briefcase and headed home.

The long ride home helped calm him a little. As he turned the corner to his road and felt the bumpy country paving jostle his seat, he smelled the hay in the fields to either side, and the warm aroma of the neighbor's cows as they made their way to the barn for the evening milking. Approaching his home, he heard the song of peepers in the pond, a music that never failed to lull him to sleep--until it was drowned out by the roar of Troy's souped-up Charger.

For a decade now, he'd relished his little slice of paradise. "Oscar's Park," he called it. He breathed deeply of the lilacs blooming outside the kitchen window in spring and the fallen leaves every autumn. He watched deer and rabbits forage in the fields to the north, and thrilled to the riot of avian color --red cardinals, blue jays, orange orioles, and when the rhododendrons were in bloom, the crazy quilt of iridescent feathers that made up his little hummingbird. Along with the peepers' song, he slept to the yips of coyotes and hoots of owls. His alarm clock was a woodpecker, drilling for bugs in the old maple outside his window. *All that stolen ... by him,* he thought, his good mood vanishing as soon as he saw Troy and his friends starting to gather around the Charger. They'd already broken into a 30-pack of Busch Light, and he could hear the first beer cans clanging against the sides of the galvanized trash bin Troy kept around for empties. The rabbits hid from the noise, and the deer, spooked, galloped away when the engines roared. *No peeper refrain or coyote chorus tonight,* Oscar thought. *Paradise lost. All in the service of the automotive gods.*

Once inside, he bolted the door, something he'd never done till Troy moved in. He made a quick supper of fish sticks in the air fryer, with some healthy broccoli florets as contrast. He ate in front of the TV on a little tray, hoping to get a whole episode of *Mystery Theatre* in before the cacophony started outside. You had to catch every word, or you'd be clueless.

The rumpled, mustachioed detective was just calling the suspects together in the drawing room of the Art Deco mansion that was the setting for this week's episode, getting ready to reveal the killer, when it started up: the roar of engines as Troy and his friends revved up for an evening of racing, interspersed with clanging tools and the beat of that infernal music. He switched off the television, glad the show was on streaming, though when he'd get a chance to finish it was beyond him. He heard two cars head north on the road, the engines building to a whine. Suddenly brakes screeched and he heard a thump. He hoped they hadn't hit one of the rabbits or the fat raccoon that lumbered across the road after dark to raid the dumpster at the electrician's warehouse.

As he took his plate to the kitchen to wash up, the acrid aroma of exhaust had managed to seep into the cracks around the windows and overcome even the fishy smell that usually dominated on fish stick night.

With another sigh, Oscar headed upstairs to brush his teeth and settle into bed with a book. He hoped he could concentrate long enough to read a chapter before things got even noisier.

No such luck. The music started up as soon as Oscar's head hit the pillow. He didn't know what genre it was – Heavy metal? Punk? Rockabilly? It was all noise to him. Loud, loud, LOUD noise.

Oscar tried the deep breathing exercises he'd seen online. Breathe in, hold for five seconds, breathe out. Repeat. They were supposed to calm your mind, allow you to sleep. If anything, he felt worse, the headache started by the music got stronger with holding his breath. Now his temples pounded in time with the racket coming out of Troy's stereo.

The drums. The bass. The screeching. And those lyrics. Not that Oscar could make out actual, coherent lyrics, but certain shrieked words entered his mind unbidden and repeated: hate, death, kill. *What kind of people listened to this music?* he wondered. As the throbbing bass and the throbbing in his head started to sync, Oscar pounded the pillow. *No... no... NO.*

Over the din of the music, Oscar sensed a new sound. It was like

Troy's Charger was multiplying. At first it was two engines revving, then, three. Soon there were half a dozen or more, each with its own distinct frequency adding to the dissonance coming from Troy's drive. His friends were there in force. *Great,* thought, Oscar. *A gear-head convention.* More beer cans ricocheted off the sides of the metal trash bin, more car doors slammed, more tools clanged as they were tossed into the communal toolbox.

Oscar tried his best not to look at the clock, but finally he gave in, and raised one heavy eyelid just enough to see the greenish numbers as they clicked over to 3 a.m. The devil's hour.

Oscar padded to the bathroom and turned on the overhead fan, drowning out a bit of the noise from outside. He sat on the toilet with his head in his hands and moaned. *Why me, Lord? Why me?* As he swayed back and forth, his little sobs gave way to silence, and his eyelids drooped.

Oscar didn't know how long he'd dozed off, but he lurched to one side, catching himself on the sink before he hit the tile floor. Shaking his head, Oscar poured a paper cup of water and downed it in one swallow. Then he shuffled back to his room and pulled the covers up over his head.

The party was still going strong across the street. As more beer cans were tossed, the voices got louder. Words started to penetrate Oscar's consciousness. "Car show up the mountain." "Better tune 'em up for the race!" "Hundreds in prizes!" This was the final straw. Oscar had more of this to look forward to as Troy and his friends readied their hot rods for the big show and race. His last thoughts as he slipped into fitful sleep were of the beer cans, tools and bass chords that would multiply in the run up to the race.

*****

Oscar woke up to sun streaming through the window. After a moment of panic--he couldn't afford to be late after yesterday's debacle at work--he realized it was Saturday. First Saturday of October, time for his regularly scheduled oil change. He smoothed the covers over his bed, wishing he could climb back in and take advantage of the peace and calm that daytime brought, maybe grab a catnap or two. But an appointment's an appointment, and besides, he couldn't risk voiding his warranty over a missed oil change.

Down at the dealership, the techs greeted Oscar with respect. Now, these were car guys he could appreciate. Neatly dressed, polite, competent. The music that streamed on the PA system was peaceful and melodic, with nary a foul lyric to be heard. Tools were organized by size and even the work bays were tidy. No turkey roasters here! Why, the service manager, Mike, even told him the waste oil was re-used in a special system that heated the shop, helping the environment and saving the dealership money that would have been spent on disposal. Oscar approved.

He dropped off his keys and sat in the waiting room, enjoying the peace and quiet, and finally getting to finish the chapter in the murder mystery that he hadn't been able to read with the noise from Troy's driveway. All too soon he heard his name being paged.

Oscar went up to the service desk and took his place in line, to pay his bill and retrieve his keys. It was busy for a Saturday, and the techs were chattering among themselves.

"Can you believe this guy?" he heard one tech say. "He brought his car in for brake work, and I find THIS connecting a break in the line!" He held up a piece of rubber tubing, just a few inches long.

"Whoo!" said another. "If he applied any pressure on the brake line, that little bit of rubber would have popped, causing his brakes to fail. That idiot could've died in a car crash!" All the techs shook their heads, and so did Oscar. He didn't know much about brakes, but what the guys said made sense. He couldn't imagine dying, just to save a few dollars on proper automotive maintenance. Idiot, indeed.

On the way home, Oscar couldn't get his mind off the little piece of rubber and what the guys at the shop said about the brake line. How a little piece of rubber could cause such a catastrophic failure of a major safety system. It boggled the imagination.

As he pulled into his driveway, he gritted his teeth at the colored pieces of paper blowing around. Someone was littering, and a couple of sheets had lodged themselves under the wheels of his garbage can. Picking them up, he thought, *Of course, it's Troy's litter.* The flyers gave the dates for the car show, in two days' time. Oscar was so elated at the thought of Troy being gone for a couple of days, he brought one of the flyers in, and put it on his refrigerator to remind him of his upcoming vacation from noise.

That night was the worst ever. Troy and his buddies were working overtime to get their cars ready for the show and race. Fueled by Busch Light, the clanging and banging increased in volume. More shop lights illuminated his bedroom. One of the guys even brought one of those new-fangled LED lights. The white light streamed through Oscar's window, illuminating his room like an operating theatre . . . or morgue.

He tossed and turned. He tried earplugs, an eye mask, his white-noise machine--nothing helped. Pulling the pillow over his head, he muttered into the mattress, "Is this really happening?"

*****

The next morning, Oscar wandered around the kitchen in a daze. Sunday morning was for relaxing with a cup of coffee and *The Times*, but Oscar was too groggy to retain a word of what he read. Slamming his cup down onto the end table in frustration, he splashed coffee onto the cuff of his favorite robe. Muttering about this being Troy's fault, too, he started to root around in the junk drawer, looking for the stain-removal stick he always kept there. His fingers touched something rubbery, and he pulled out an old balloon, left over from a birthday party at work, the month it was his turn to provide the celebration for a colleague's special day. He looked down on the deflated piece of rubber, the bulbous tip, and the long, skinny end you pumped air into. A tube of rubber. Like the tube the guys at the shop found on the brake line.

Back in his chair, trying to finish his coffee and the lead editorial, he couldn't concentrate on the columnist's words. He kept hearing the tech say, "This idiot could've died in a car crash." *Car crash. Pressure on the brakes. Like braking on a curve on a twisty mountain road. In the middle of a ... race.*

Once thought, Oscar couldn't unthink it. In the shower, he pictured a rainy day, mountain roads slick with moisture. *A hot rod hydroplaning. The driver presses the brake pedal. Brakes fail. Car crashes into a tree.*

Tying his shoes, the limp shoelace looked like a twisty road. Maybe on a mountain top. *Approaching a curve too quickly, the driver stomps the brake pedal. Failure. Car goes over the side of the mountain.*

Brushing his teeth, Oscar looked down at the foamy toothpaste in the sink. Like fluffy snow. *An early snowfall on a mountaintop. Car brakes to avoid a snowbank. Crash.*

A plan started to form. Oscar went back to the junk drawer and took inventory. Twist ties from old bread packages? Nope, wouldn't hold. Super glue? Might hold too well. Zip ties? Perfect.

*****

That night, Oscar went to bed fully dressed in black pants and a dark turtleneck. On his nightstand was a black beanie he dug out the glove and scarf box on the top shelf of the closet. He set his alarm for 4 a.m. Troy's crew would be gone by then, and his neighbor sleeping off a massive drunk. He still wasn't sure how he was going to cut the brake lines, but he knew something would come to him, as he sank into bed and waited.

When the alarm rang, Oscar hopped up, thankful for once for a sleepless night. All his senses were alert. He pulled on the beanie and grabbed a tiny flashlight off his nightstand, cupping his hand over it to point the light only where needed. As he opened the outside door from the garage, he noticed the pruning shears he kept on a shelf by the door, along with the gardening gloves from last spring's pruning. Perfect.

Feeling a bit like the cat burglar from the last episode *of Mystery Theatre,* Oscar crept silently out his driveway and crossed the road to Troy's. He wore rubber-soled shoes to be silent, but he needn't have bothered. He could hear Troy snoring from the drive. *Thank you, Busch Light.*

Lying on his back his pushed himself under the car with his heels, feeling for the brake line as he went. One precise cut with his pruning shears, then he fitted the balloon segment over both ends of the line and secured it with the zip ties. Satisfied with his handwork, he scooched out from under the car and crept away, keeping his flashlight angled far from Troy's window.

Back in his bedroom, he glanced at the clock. It had taken only 20 minutes. A decent investment for a lifetime of good sleep. Satisfied, he settled into bed, to grab a snooze before the workday alarm.

*****

Oscar put his Swiss cheese sandwich lunch in the breakroom fridge, and pulled his chair up to his desk, but he couldn't concentrate on work. Every few minutes he kept checking the local news feed. A couple of times, he had to minimize the window, when a nosy colleague eyed his screen suspiciously.

He paid special attention at the daily meeting, to redeem himself from Friday's mishap, and took care to greet colleagues as if nothing had happened. He was the picture of confidence. Inside he was writhing with worry. Did his little fix work? Would he finally get peace?

The news came through his feed at 2:37 p.m. "Tragic Crash at Car Race," the headline read. "One dead in a crash on a treacherous mountain curve. Name withheld pending notification of next of kin."

*****

That night, Oscar enjoyed a peaceful dinner, seated in front of the TV. For the first time in months, he watched *Mystery Theatre* all the way to the end, even guessing the culprit before the big reveal. He brushed his teeth and took special care turning back the covers. He tossed the eye shade and earplugs, certain he wouldn't need them again, and slipped between the sheets with a favorite book.

Closing the book after the final page, he turned onto his side and felt the cool pillowcase against his cheek. He turned off the nightstand light and relished the peaceful darkness of his room. Closing his eyes, he smiled.

As he drifted off, in that moment between consciousness and sleep, he heard it. *Vroom. Vroom.* Headlights filled his room, the air smelled of exhaust and his head pounded with the sounds from a car radio.

Murder at the Aragalaya
Terry Wijesuriya

It was sunny and hot as heck. I could feel my sweat being burnt up by the sun as soon as I sweated it out. I imagined my body losing the 60 or whatever percentage of water, bit by bit. Prashani took her water bottle out of her bag and was about to take a swig when she saw me, looked guilty and put the bottle away.

"Drink it, stupid. I don't mind, honestly," I said, glad she couldn't see how my mouth was watering at the thought of that lukewarm plastic bottle of water.

"Such a rude creature," Jaliya said, coming up to us through the crowd. "This good girl is fasting and you are drinking water in front of her. Awful friend."

Prashani put her bottle away unopened. "Don't let him bug you," I said. "I really don't mind if y'all drink in front of me."

She shrugged and we started off towards the Presidential Secretariat.

"So what do you think of the village?" Jaliya asked, smirking behind his surgical mask.

"It's... kind of cool. I love how everyone has just turned up and is sort of united," Prashani said, dodging a child holding a poster saying *No milk for me today.*

"I hope they pay attention to these protests. No point if they're just going to stay hiding wherever." I added. We were getting closer to the call-and-response people on the barricades outside the Presidential Secretariat, and I had to shout to be heard.

Jaliya said something, but I only heard the phrase 'bourgeois protest'. "What did you say?" I shouted up at him. Jaliya is about a head taller than Prashani, who is an inch taller than me. He also mumbles a lot. Even in normal surroundings we find it hard to hear him sometimes, and this place was noisier than a primary school during interval.

He bent slightly and roared in my ear. "This is a BOURGEOIS protest," he said.

I winced "Ouch! Must you shout like that?"

"What did he say," Prashani asked.

Before I could answer her, we were sort of swallowed up into the crowd at the barricades. I became wedged between this old aunty whose head came to my shoulder and a cute guy with a V-for-Vendetta mask hanging around his neck. Prashani had disappeared from sight and I could only just see Jaliya a few feet away.

"This government has gone on for too long! Stealing and robbing and lying!" the guy with the megaphone shouted. People cheered. I did not cheer because I always feel a bit stupid cheering unless I am in an unselfconscious mood (which is hardly ever).

People were shoving a bit now, and I started feeling dizzy. That was probably also because of the fasting and the hot sun, so I started making my way towards the nearest uncrowded piece of pavement, which was near a small marquee. Prashani materialized at my elbow. "You ok?" she asked.

"Need to sit in the shade," I said. She went in front of me, shoving people out of the way. I am too shy to do that but Prashani can do it without feeling any awkwardness. She also has a way of shoving people out of the way that leaves said people still friendly and willing to be helpful. I followed in her wake, and the crowd closed up behind me like water.

We reached the pavement and the marquee. "Can you wait alone?" Prashani asked me, retying her ponytail.

"I'm fine, the sun was just a bit hot. I'll sit here for a while." I plonked myself down on the edge of the pavement, in the shade.

"Call me if you feel dizzy ok? I'll go back into the crowd for a bit, I want to hear what that man was saying." She disappeared back into the crowd.

I leaned against the pole at the corner of the marquee. There were several other marquees stretching along the bridge over the Beira Lake, and I was in the cornermost one, closest to the barricades. There was a lady with a baby in the same marquee, and she grinned at me. We chatted a bit, she complained about the current situation.

I felt awkward. From what she said, she was a daily wage earner. I felt bad for complaining about the temporary discomfort I was facing. I stored the conversation up to rebut Jaliya's claim that this was a bourgeois protest. A couple of young boys, maybe teenagers, went past and almost tripped over my legs, so I decided to move towards the back of the marquee. The lady and the baby went out to get something to eat from the free food stalls.

I sat alone against the railings overlooking the Beira. If I looked to my right and slightly behind I could see the rows of cops, all looking awkward and wearing helmets and holding truncheons. On my left was a sort of canvas wall of the next marquee. There was about two inches between the bottom of the wall and the pavement. I was idly looking under the wall when I noticed two sandals. There were feet in them.

Awkward, I thought. Some man had fallen asleep in the next marquee. I started looking at the crowd at the barricades to try and spot Prashani and Jaliya. Something was nagging at my brain, but I couldn't figure out what it was. I zoned out and was idly staring around (probably looking like a waste of tax-payers' money rather than a keen young university student) when it struck me. The feet of the sleeping man were upside down. The man must be sleeping flat on his stomach, but what a weird way to sleep! I imagined sleeping in that position. It was rather funny.

I was feeling fine now, so I stood up and stepped out of the marquee. I didn't feel like reentering the huge crowd so I walked a few steps away just to take a glance at the next marquee and confirm that the sandalled man was sleeping on his stomach. To my disappointment the marquee had a sort of awning that had been dropped down in front to form another wall.

I turned back and scanned the crowd for my friends. Jaliya's head bobbed into view at the far end of the crowd. I thought I saw Prashani's bright blue bag but I couldn't be sure. I went on tiptoe to see if it was her.

"Are you ok?" someone asked, from behind me.

I spun around and almost lost my balance. The person reached out to catch me and then stopped at the last moment.

"Sorry, haram ne," he said, apologetically. I laughed awkwardly. It was Jaliya's cool older brother, Thisura. "You're waiting here alone?" he asked, looking around.

"No no," I said, hastily. "Jaliya and Prashani are somewhere in the crowd. I just came to wait in the shade."

"Ah ok," he said. "Fasting ne?"

"Yeah," I said.

He waited awkwardly for a bit. I had nothing to say so I too waited awkwardly.

"Ok then I'll be going. Coming for the discussion at six?" he asked.

"Ah no, I have to go home to break fast," I said.

"Ah right. You can have ifthar here though, they have organized something," he said, gesturing vaguely towards the other tents.

"Yeah, but my family normally breaks fast together and then we pray," I explained.

"Ah right right," he said. "Bye then." He waved awkwardly and went into the crowd.

I went back into the corner marquee to avoid having to talk awkwardly to more people. I sat down.

Something was wrong. The sandalled feet hadn't moved at all. I'd noticed that they were lined up with the crack in the paving slabs, and they were still there. I suddenly felt a heavy feeling in my stomach, the same heavy feeling I felt when my mother shouted for help when she found our cat dying in the garden.

I crouched down and squinted under the canvas wall. It was dark and gloomy inside, and it took some time for my eyes to adjust. As soon as I realized what I was seeing I closed my eyes and sat up. There had been blood all over the man's head. His limbs had been spread awkwardly, as if he had fallen bonelessly to the ground. I thought I was going to pass out, but managed to put my head between my knees and calm down. As soon as I could, I stood up and got out of the marquee.

I wanted to see Jaliya or Prashani, or Thisura or anyone I knew so I could tell them but they weren't in sight. I saw an older man who looked capable so I managed to get to him, and I told him what I thought. He went over to the tent and quietly looked inside. I was shaking too hard to stand so I sat where I was, on the side of the road itself. The man came out, looking a bit sick, and he quickly went and spoke to a few other people. The crowd heard something and started looking over at the tent, but no one was really moving towards it. By the time the St John's ambulance had come, people were starting to come over to see, but some other people sort of blocked them so the ambulance could get close.

I tried to stand but I was still too shaky. I realized I was crying.

"Are you hurt?" Prashani dropped to her knees next to me.

"No, no," I managed to say. I was sobbing now.

"What's wrong?" Jaliya asked, opening an umbrella to hold over me.

"There's a dead man in there. Head smashed." I said, jerkily.

Prashani gasped.

"A dead man?" Jaliya asked, turning around to stare.

"I saw him," I said, and cried. Prashani hugged me tightly until I had stopped sobbing and calmed down a bit.

Once I was able to speak properly, Prashani poured some water from her bottle onto my hands and I washed my face. "Will I have to give a statement or something to the police?" I asked Jaliya.

"I think so ne. You were the first to see the body."

The man I'd originally spoken to came over.

"Are you ok?" he asked.

"Yes, thank you, uncle," I replied.

"If you want, I can tell the police that I found him first," he said. "You didn't see the body properly even so it won't be a problem."

"Is that ok, uncle?" I asked, greatly relieved.

"Yes. I will tell them that someone asked me to look in the tent, then if they need to find out more maybe they can get in touch with you." he told me. I gave him my phone number to give the police if they asked, and then the others walked me to the bus stand. Prashani and I caught a bus and she dropped me off at my bus stand, which is right next to my house.

*****

The next day I was feeling much better. My mother was not anxious for me to go out again after such a traumatic day, and to be honest I was lazy so I stayed in bed. Prashani had been in the library doing some work, and she texted me to ask if I was ok. We were chatting about geese when Jaliya suddenly called me.

"Why are you calling?" I asked, confused. We normally only texted.

"Something's gone wrong at the aragalaya," he said, sounding tense. There was background noise as if he was in a bus.

"What?"

"Someone has seen Thisura near the tent where the dead man was found and they think he's connected somehow."

"Oh shoot," I said, "will they arrest him?"

"That's the problem," Jaliya said. "It's not the police. The protestors are saying that this is an internal affair that they will sort out on their own."

I was silent. "What do they mean?" I said at last.

"They came and said something to him yesterday at that discussion. Then we were sleeping in our tent and early morning they came and dragged him out." Jaliya's voice was close to breaking. "I don't know where he is now."

"It's ten o'clock," I said, stupidly, looking at the clock on the wall.

"I was finding his friends and asking them if they knew anything," Jaliya explained. "Then I didn't have signal so I had to wait to call."

"Did you tell your parents?" I asked. I put the call on loudspeaker and started pulling clothes out of the cupboard.

"No, I don't want to worry them until I know what has happened," he said. I pulled my home trousers off and put my going out ones on.

"Don't worry ok? I'll call Prashani and we'll come there." I told him, pulling a crumpled shirt over my head.

"There might not be signal. Wait near Banda for me when you get here." he said.

"Don't worry, Jaliya. We'll sort this out ok?" I said, but the phone vibrated as Jaliya hung up.

*****

Bandaranaike's statue loomed over Prashani and I as we waited near it. We had a nice view of the campsite part of the aragalaya, and we were squinting around in the sun for a glimpse of Jaliya. The sea was calm and glittering in the late morning sun, and it seemed like too good a day for political and economic crises- and, of course, Thisura being basically kidnapped.

"Is that him," Prashani asked, pointing across the road.

Jaliya was too far away for us to recognize him, but no one else had that odd way of walking. The crowds were thin here, so we started walking towards him.

"What's happened?" Prashani called, when we got close enough.

Jaliya doesn't normally show emotion, but he seemed relieved to see us. "Hansini- Aiyya's friend- said she thinks they have started a sort of informal court. He might be there."

"Who is this 'they'?" Prashani asked.

"Where is this court?" I asked at the same time.

"The protestors who have been camped out here every day," Jaliya explained. "I don't know where the court is. But until now they have been practicing an 'eye for an eye' type of justice."

"Wow, that's… interesting," Prashani said, getting that sociological gleam in her eye.

"They're going to do it to Thisura," Jaliya reminded her, coldly.

"Oh shoot, I forgot. We need to go and talk with them," she said, looking guilty.

"Hansini has gone to see," Jaliya said. "She knows a lot of people here so she should be able to find out where it is."

Jaliya's phone rang. "Hansini?" he said.

"Where? Ah, near that… ok ok. And who is there?" He listened for a bit. "Ah. Ok. We're coming," he said.

He began walking as he ended the call, waving at us to follow. He was heading for the area along the Beira where the porta potties were.

"They have it somewhere there. It's kind of away from the areas where the police and all are. Jerry is there, Hansini said. Let's go see what we can do." He was striding away, so that Prashani and I had to hurry to keep up.

We got to the area Jaliya said Hansini had told him. There were two tenty things that were more permanent than the canvas ones we'd left behind. These had takaran roofs and black cloth tied down around the sides so we couldn't see in.

"Jerry must be inside?" Prashani asked, quietly. There was not much noise here, we'd left the people chanting slogans behind and the takaran roofed-tents seemed ominously silent.

My palms were sweaty, and my heart was beating too fast. I was certain that something bad would happen if we went into that awful tent. Jaliya's face above his mask was also drawn, and his eyes darted all around. Prashani alone seemed unaffected by the fear. She adjusted her mask and drew slightly ahead of us as we approached the tent.

We reached the tent. Prashani lifted the corner of the black material nearest to us. I closed my eyes as we moved into the twilit gloom, not because I was scared but so that my eyes would adjust easily to the darkness. It kind of worked except by not being able to see I trod on the back of Jaliya's shoe and we both stumbled a bit.

There were a whole lot of people, dressed in black, standing in a sort of circle and most of them turned to look at us. To my relief most of them turned away again. I saw a guy with a beard give us a look and then he started sidling over to us. This freaked me out and I crowded as close to the other two as possible.

"What's happening?" Prashani asked the nearest person. It was a boy of about our age, wearing a black headband over his long hair. He turned slightly and frowned. "Trial of a murderer," he said, shortly, and turned back.

"This man was found close to the place where a man was killed." A man with an awful scary voice suddenly said over the low mumble of talk in the place. Everyone else fell silent.

"Let's take a vote on who finds him guilty," a youth with a high-pitched voice said. I suddenly realized, looking around the crowd, that Prashani and I were the only two girls. Instantly my feeling of unsafety grew worse.

"Guilty," said a voice nearby. Then "guilty" came another voice, from further away. The place was filled with people muttering "guilty". The crowd shifted slightly and I gasped. Thisura was kneeling in the middle, his shirt half torn and wet with blood. He seemed dazed. His hands had been tied behind his back with some rag.

The man who seemed in charge took a step forward. "Let's see." he said.

"Not guilty," a voice said, crisply. It was the sidling guy with the beard. Everyone swiveled around to look at him.

"What do you mean, not guilty?" the man asked.

"Innocent until proved guilty," the bearded one said.

"It's Jerry!" Prashani breathed in my ear.

"He has been found guilty by this court." the man said, in a final tone. "He must be punished according to the crime he has committed."

"Of course he must be punished," Jerry said, easily. "But not until he has been proved guilty. We've seen enough miscarriage and deliberate thwarting of justice by the government. We want to build a new society here, not continue what is foul and rotting in the old one. We need to make sure that we follow the most just route."

There was an angry muttering. I read a lot of Westerns, and I frequently come across lynch mobs, but I never understood the raw anger and fear you feel when you're actually faced with one.

"The people have spoken," the man said, indicating the crowd.

"This lot isn't representative of the whole of the people," Jerry said.

The man frowned. He turned. "If there's anyone here who agrees with this man let them speak."

Prashani shoved me towards the right. I was taken unawares and almost stumbled. When I turned to look at her she gestured to me to move further away, and then she slid off in the opposite direction. I had no clue what she wanted me to do but I moved off.

"I agree with what this man says," Prashani said, now quite some distance away.

"I agree with what he says," Jaliya said, from our original position.

Finally I understood the plan. "I agree too," I said, from my new post. "And restorative justice would work better than Mosaic law or the western model." I could have gone on but Jerry was looking at me in a perplexed way so I shut up. We could go into models of justice after they had had a proper trial.

There was a shifting in the crowd. "I agree," a man said.

"We need to be better than the crows," another man spoke up. "Let's find proof first and then move on to punishment."

"Ok," the man in charge said. "We will meet again here this evening at six. Court is adjourned."

We started making our way out. Prashani grabbed me by the elbow. "Wait," she hissed. I glanced round. Jaliya was moving through the crowd to Thisura, and the man in charge was speaking to Jerry in an urgent way.

We joined Jaliya. Thisura seemed in a bad way, he had some head wound as far as I could see, and blood had dried down the side of his face. He was dazed, and Jaliya knelt behind him and untied his hands.

"No no, no removing the prisoner from the premises," the youth with the high-pitched voice said. He was frowning at us, and his mouth seemed permanently fixed in a scornful look.

"We will clean him up and then leave him," Prashani said, calmly. "We are building this new society on compassion and kindness, not on the inhumanity and brutality that we are protesting against."

The youth was about to say something else when the man in charge came over.

"Let them do it," he said. "But the prisoner must remain here until the court is over tomorrow."

Jerry also came over.

"Guys, this is Roshan," he said, indicating the man in charge. "He wants us to act as defence."

"Why aren't the police getting involved," I asked, timidly.

"The police are corrupt," Roshan said, looking serious and more than a little fanatical. "They have repeatedly proven themselves to be the lapdogs of authority. They are delegitimized in the minds of the people and so this case that concerns the people is no concern of theirs. The man who died is a poor man, there is no incentive for them to find the murderer. It's up to us."

Prashani was almost vibrating with enthusiasm. She was listening very carefully, and I was sure she would remember this entire conversation and write it down later to use in some sociological research. "But why was this man beaten?" she asked, indicating Thisura. Jaliya had removed his bonds and was speaking to him quietly and giving him water.

"We thought he was the murderer," the man said. "If he isn't, then he should have realized why we thought so."

"What the" I began, but Jerry glared at me. I shut up.

*****

"So we've got to mount a defence," Jerry said, once Roshan and the high-voiced youth had left. Thisura was sitting on a mat on the ground and eating a maalu paan that Prashani had rushed off to get. Jaliya was bandaging his head, with a gentleness that seemed surprising.

"Good thing you're here," Prashani said, glancing up at Jerry. She was kneeling next to Jaliya, handing him supplies from a first aid kit she had procured on her maalu paan-scavenging journey. I never knew how exactly she got things we needed, I think most of the time people just gave them to her because of her weirdly magnetic charm. Anyway, she had gotten the kit from somewhere and Jaliya was putting it to good use.

"Why is it a good thing," I started asking.

"Jerry's a lawyer," Prashani explained.

Jerry looked at her thoughtfully. "Yes, but this is a completely different sort of thing. I don't know what the sort of protocol will be."

"Maybe you should plead insanity," Prashani began, her eyes gleaming.

"Hoi!" said Thisura, sounding annoyed.

"Stop shouting," Jaliya said, pinning the bandage around his head. He stood up.

"Wouldn't it make more sense if we could find out who the actual murderer was?" he asked.

Jerry nodded slowly. "That would make sense- if we had the foggiest idea of what exactly happened!"

Prashani and Jaliya turned to look at me.

"Unfortunately," Jerry said, "the person who found the body is a political type. Member of that party, you know. I don't think he will tell us straight what exactly happened. He'll have his own reasons for wanting it to seem like someone or other had killed the man..." he trailed off as he noticed the other two staring at me. He turned.

I felt very awkward, as if I were bragging in public or something. "Uh, actually," I began. "It was me. I found the body."

*****

The tent was getting too claustrophobic for us, so we moved our discussion to the shade of a couple of trees a little away from the tents. Jerry had to hunt up the high-voiced youth to let him know we were taking Thisura out. We felt annoyed and expressed our annoyance that we had to ask anyone for permission, but Jerry wisely pointed out that since we were going to antagonize people anyway it was probably best to avoid doing so until the last moment. We all sat under the trees. Thisura had changed to a t-shirt Jaliya brought from their tent, and he was still looking a bit woozy.

"Ok," Jerry began, squatting on his haunches and using a stick to doodle in the sand. "The way I see it, we have several options for the murderer. Number one, Thisura did it for some random reason."

Thisura frowned. "I don't even know who was killed!" he said.

"Oh, he has a point," I said. "Who *was* the victim?"

"A 'villager' named Lakshan," Jaliya said.

Prashani scowled. "Villager?" she asked.

"That's what the permanent residents of the protest village call themselves," Jaliya explained.

"Oh," I said. "So are you and Thisura also villagers?"

"No, cos we only spent two nights here. The other guys have been here since last month, and they've got this weird hierarchy going on."

Jerry broke in impatiently. "Well, anyway, this Lakshan was apparently a bit of a chandiya. Had some dodgy links to the underworld and stuff. Which leads us to option number two- it was some sort of underworld killing, unrelated to the protest."

"Hmm," Prashani said, sounding unconvinced.

"Option three is that it was a politically motivated killing. Our friends in government might have arranged for a villager to be killed to sort of demonstrate how the protests are actually violent."

We all nodded. This sounded like the most convincing argument.

"Option four- it's a personal matter, completely unconnected to the protest and political stuff."

"But what if it is connected to the protest? I mean like a personal matter but connected in some way?" I asked.

"Like how?" Jerry asked.

"Well, for instance, if he had broken some village law? I'm not sure about that stuff but it seems likely that they would react badly to that sort of thing," I said, gesturing towards Thisura's bandaged head.

Jerry nodded thoughtfully. "That could be," he admitted.

"It's also very convenient for the villagers to have an 'outsider' here to blame," Prashani said.

"It's not just that," Jaliya began. Jerry suddenly shook his head once, vehemently, and Jaliya had barely closed his mouth again when Roshan appeared behind him.

"Have you seen Mahen?" he asked Jerry. I had no idea who Mahen was. Jerry shook his head, and Roshan looked perplexed and moved away again.

"Who's Mahen?" I asked, inquisitively.

"Boy with the squeaky voice," Jerry said. He turned back to his scribbles on the ground.

"How should we begin this?" he asked.

"Well, we've got a nice list of motives. How about opportunity?" Jaliya asked. We all stared at each other.

"Literally everyone had the opportunity," Thisura groaned. "Noone was paying special attention to that marquee."

"And there was a massive crowd, too," Prashani said.

Jerry sighed. "Ok then. What else?"

"Suspects," I said. "Murder weapons?"

"You're the one who saw the body," Jaliya said, unfeelingly. "What did it look like?"

I was already regretting bringing up the question of weapons. Jerry seemed to notice that I looked a bit green. His voice was gentler than usual when he said "Take your time, don't force yourself to think about it."

"Please force yourself to think about it," Thisura pleaded.

"I didn't see much," I told them. "It was dark. It just looked wrong, like his head had been smashed. There was blood everywhere."

Jerry made a face. "Sorry you had to see it. Was there anything else unusual about it?"

I thought hard. "He was lying on his face," I volunteered, finally.

"Ah," said Jerry, scratching at the ground with his stick. "And was the back of his head wounded, or had he been moved after he fell?"

"I don't know," I said, "I freaked out as soon as I realized he was dead. But I did get a clear- too clear- look at the injury, so I guess he must have fallen down like that."

"Interesting," Jerry said.

A phone rang, and Thisura dug his out of his pocket. The screen was cracked badly, and it looked pretty bashed up. He answered.

His face went through several emotions as he replied in monosyllables. Finally he hung up and turned to us.

"The media has gotten hold of the story and Sri Lanka is headlines across the world," he said, glumly.

"Of course, they're just waiting for something awful to happen so it can live up to their preconceived ideas of a third-world country," Prashani said, bitterly. "Two months of peaceful protest and we didn't even get a mention- and as soon as one murder happens we're all over the news."

Jerry shrugged philosophically. "I don't know how you manage to get all the news, Thisura," he said. "Maybe you are working for Intelligence after all."

We laughed a bit, but Jaliya looked worried. "Don't make jokes like that now," he hissed. "These jokers might take it seriously."

"This is public domain news," Thisura grinned. "I'll let you know when my informants give me hot hot secret stuff."

"What happened to your phone?" I asked.

"They beat me up a bit," Thisura said. "Phone also got bashed up."

"That's why you should have a Nokia button phone like me," Jerry said, laughing.

"Guys, I don't know how we're going to actually find out who the real murderer is," Prashani broke in.

We sobered up a bit.

"Do we have a way to get Thisura off if we can't prove who actually did it?" I asked.

Jerry looked serious. "I can't think of a way," he confessed.

"What will they do to him if we can't?" Prashani asked.

Thisura looked a bit green around the gills.

"Well, when they caught a thief last week they beat him quite badly and then made him work as slave labour in the kitchens," Jaliya said, helpfully.

"I'd think they'd go further for murder," Jerry said, thoughtfully.

Thisura gulped. "How much further?" he asked.

We looked at him in silence for a while.

"Ok, let's get to work and catch this murderer," Jerry said, finally. We avoided eye contact with Thisura and stood up.

"You'd better get back to the tent," Jerry said. He and Jaliya walked Thisura back to the tent, promising him to return at lunchtime with food.

Prashani and I stood where we were. "Did you see anyone looking suspicious around the marquee?" she asked me.

"Not really- but we don't know when he was killed! It could have happened the night before, even. I was next to the marquee just for an hour or so."

"They had used the marquee at nine am," Prashani said. "I heard some dude saying they'd made their posters there before the big crowd came at noon."

"So between nine and 12.30," I said. "The man was dead, I think, when I went into the marquee next to him."

Prashani sighed. "And how many thousands of people must have passed during that time."

"And just because someone was passing that way doesn't mean they're responsible. Hell, I met Thisura there. I saw that boy Mahen also, and I also saw that journalist lady. That doesn't mean any of them did it." I was frustrated.

"Maybe if we can prove that Thisura had never met Lakshan?" Prashani wondered.

"No go," I said. "They'll only suspect him of being a government spy trying to cause a fuss."

Prashani's eyes gleamed. "If we can prove that he has no links to the government?"

"How on earth would we do that?" I snapped. Prashani's imagination is too far ahead of reality sometimes.

"I don't know… yet. I'm sure we'll be able to do something."

"But it's already 2 pm, and that leaves us with like four hours in which to sort everything out and get Thisura off."

We had been engrossed in our conversation and so it took Jaliya, Jerry and Thisura running towards us for us to notice anything. I looked up and all around the protest site, and noticed that other people also seemed disturbed.

"What's happened?" Prashani asked Thisura. He had his phone out and was squinting at the cracked screen.

"Government thugs are beating up the protestors in front of Temple Trees," he said, tersely, typing something.

"Heading this way. Police aren't reacting." Jaliya said, looking across the site towards where people were beginning to organize themselves. They were throwing boards and bits of furniture across the road, forming a sort of barricade.

"You girls should leave," Jerry said.

"Not on your life! Besides, it's probably safer to stay put here than try and get out, they might have cordoned off the area." Prashani said, indignantly. I was secretly relieved no one asked me what I wanted to do, I badly wanted to be far away from any violence but at the same time didn't want to be a coward.

Jerry seemed furious. "Listen. Those bastards aren't going to be nice. You might be risking your fool neck if you stay around. They might decide to fire with live ammunition- who knows? I can't be responsible for you getting killed here."

Prashani was angry too. "Who the hell said you were responsible? I will stay if I want to, and if I die my blood is on *their* hands, not yours. You shut up and take your sexism somewhere else."

"What if the girls promise to move to the parking lot of OGF if things get too violent?" Jaliya said, interrupting.

"Not only us, all of you too," I put in.

Prashani glared at me. "No surrender!" she shouted.

"Calm the hell down," I hissed.

"Fine." Jerry said. "Now let's go!"

We ran to join the main group of protestors, who had formed a human barrier across the road and stood waiting expectantly as the shouts and noises of the thugs grew closer. I was shivering uncontrollably, but no one noticed. I remembered all the foolish death or glory things I'd ever read and longed for an inglorious safe day in bed. My phone rang, it was my mother- probably panicking and wondering where I was. I cut the call and sent her a message saying I was fine and had no signal.

"Put your phone away," a squeaky voice said in my ear. I looked around. It was Mahen. He scowled at me.

"Join arms!" someone bellowed. "They're coming!"

I had no choice but to link arms with Mahen on one side and Prashani on the other.

I had just registered the main wave of thugs hitting the front of the knot of protestors when I looked to the side and saw the library tent smouldering.

"They're burning the library!" I screamed.

Jaliya, Prashani and I broke the chain and sprinted towards the library, where other protestors were frantically passing books out.

Others were trying to put the flames out, and we soon succeeded. Looking around, I saw other tents burning, and men with iron bars breaking down yet more. I was now more angry than scared. I looked back towards the road. Thisura and Jerry were in the middle of a fight, and as I watched, Thisura stumbled and fell. A man started kicking him hard, but Jerry soon shoved him off. Jaliya rushed back to their help. Mahen was acting weirdly, standing around instead of either helping or running. I supposed I was the same, though.

The area where we stood was comparatively calm, and someone rushed by us, with their arms full of first aid supplies. We ran alongside and were soon given things to do. The next hour or so passed in a daze, and I saw probably more injuries in that one hour than I ever saw in my twenty-four years. Prashani and I got separated pretty soon. Once we finished the bandages that were available, I managed to get a moment to take stock of the situation. There were injured people everywhere, and I caught someone shouting something about the Beira- I wasn't sure what.

The ambulances were coming to take the wounded away, so I left the other first aid people and began walking back towards the court tent to try and spot any of the others.

Prashani caught up with me. She had blood all down her shirt and I panicked before she quickly told me that it wasn't hers.

We sat in the same clump of trees we'd been sitting in just a short while ago, and I called Jaliya to see where he was.

He, Thisura and Jerry joined us soon enough. Thisura was bleeding again, and I retied his bandage as we all rested and calmed down a bit. Now that the worst was over, I felt pretty satisfied with myself- until I pulled out my phone and saw fifteen missed calls from everyone in my family.

I hurriedly called my mother and acted as if I had not just been in the middle of an actual riot, and when she began shouting about coming home immediately I shouted back "There's....signal… call…later" and cut the call. I'd probably pay later but I had to stay to see the trial through.

I turned back to the others. They'd been joined by a group of the people who'd been at the 'trial' earlier.

"Roshan was beaten up, he's in the hospital," one of them told Jerry, coldly. I looked around, Mahen was nowhere to be seen either.

"They had no way of knowing that Roshan is one of the organizers," the man who had spoken earlier said.

"Why do you think they did?" Jerry asked, puzzled.

"They ignored the rest of us. Targeted the leaders. Most of them are in hospital now. That means only one thing," the man said.

"They've got a spy on the inside." Another man said, in a flat voice.

There was silence for a bit. I had no idea what this group was normally like, so I couldn't have figured out who the spy was in any case. Jerry had a tiny crease in his forehead, like the start of a frown. The man stared at Jerry. The moment was getting quite intense.

Then he broke the silence. "Let's have the trial. Defend this man."

The others formed a ring around us.

"Thisura didn't know the man," Jerry said. "Why would he have killed him?"

"Because he is the spy! He is the one who sold us out." The man growled, and the crowd growled again. I had a strong sense of déjà vu.

"Talk sense," Jerry said, scornfully. "If he was the spy, would he have come here? And would he have been beaten up like this?" As he said that, he pulled Thisura's t-shirt up and showed an awful bruise across his ribs, from where the thug had kicked him.

"To deflect suspicion," the man said, but he sounded as if even he didn't believe it.

"I think we should look for the spy among those who are not here," Jerry went on.

"They are all in hospital," the man said.

"I'm sure there are more who have left," Jerry persisted. "And anyway, we won't know who it is until we wait and see who never returns to the aragalaya."

"This man murdered Lakshan and needs to pay," the man insisted.

Jerry sighed impatiently. "You cannot punish a man without proof! He is innocent until you can prove him guilty."

I looked around at the circle of men. Noone seemed that interested in punishing Thisura. All of them had been knocked around in some way, and seemed exhausted.

"Do we need more violence?" I asked. They all looked at me.

"You know this man now," I said, indicating Thisura. "If you ever get proof that he killed Lakshan, then he must face the consequences. But until then, can't we just assume him innocent and let him go? We're all tired. We can't spend the day resisting the government and then the night resisting each other."

"So what do you propose we do?" the man asked, rudely.

"Find out who did it, and hand them over to the police," I said. "Let this fellow go unless there is proof he did it. And let's finish this trial off."

Everyone was tired. Some at the back had melted off, to find something to eat or maybe to retire to their tents.

"Let's do that," the man said, finally. "We can always find him again." He stared hard once more at Jerry, and then stalked off into the dark.

Most of the circle followed, but one man hung back.

We breathed a collective sigh of relief.

Jaliya smacked Thisura on the back, a bit too hard for his bruised body. Thisura yelped.

"Let's go home," Prashani said. "I want to sleep for a week."

"We're going home too," Jaliya said. "Just as soon as I find out whether our tent is still standing and our things are retrievable."

The man who was hanging around came up to us. He spoke to Jerry.

"You know, what you said about the spy being from those who aren't here now?" he asked.

"Yeah?" said Jerry.

"Mahen isn't here. He isn't in the hospital. And I've a feeling we won't be seeing him around here again."

Leaving us with our mouths open, he went off towards the food tent.

Chinese Submarines
Aran Myracle

It's hard not to think of that night in Iraq. In many ways it has become a sort of perverse self-indulgence. Something with which to castigate myself. Now more than ever, I need the self-loathing.

If I'm going to do this successfully I need to hate myself enough to follow through. It's alien to override the instinct to live but this isn't my first time and I've learned a few tricks.

My mantra keeps me focused on the goal.

"It's my fault. It's my fault. It's my fault."

The magazine is half-loaded, even though I only need one round. A nearly-empty magazine doesn't feed as well. I don't want any stoppages or jams messing with my resolve at the last minute.

The gun oil smells sweet. I love its scent. I also love the aroma of gunpowder, too. But I won't be smelling that today.

My hands are shaking. My sweaty palm prints cover the rifle's plastic grips. Fuck, I should check the angle again. It should be easy enough to remember, but…

I pull out my phone. There are websites with detailed instructions and I have them bookmarked. Efficiency at the tap of a finger. I balance the rifle across my knees as I read. After confirming for the Nth time what I already knew, I switch back to the open document on my phone.

It doesn't say much:

"I read a news story awhile back about a Chinese submarine that became snagged in fishermen's nets

"It dragged the boat under and the people on board the fishing boat were killed.

"I now know I'm the sub, and salvation means I have to cut loose the nets.

"I'm cutting you loose."

Even this note is a way of strengthening my resolve. A ritualized public declaration of why I need to engineer this my way.

Enough stalling.

I poke the dowel through the trigger guard. I worry for a moment about chipping my teeth on the barrel before realizing what a pointless concern that is.

I wrap my lips around the barrel. Feel the tang of cold metal in my mouth. Lift my feet to push down on the dowel and fire the rifle round into my brain.

*****

Nothingness. Darkness. Nothingness.

*****

My head hurts. I mean really fucking hurts. The light hurts my eyes and I slam them shut again without seeing anything. I hear a whispering voice to my left. Keith's. I try to turn my head toward his voice but pain hammers my brain like a sledgehammer.

"Dad are you awake? It's Keith. I… I love you dad."

Slowly the confusion fades. I failed. I'm not supposed to be here. This isn't what's supposed to happen. I'm supposed to be dead.

My voice croaks as I reassure Keith that I'm ok. I hear myself speaking and I'm horrified. I'm stuttering. Badly. I'm able to force out a choppy, "I'm OK. I-I-I…love you too," before giving up.

My body feels heavy and I'm aware of myself growing immensely tired. Eyes already closed, my attention softens as I sink back into sleep.

I awake an hour later to a nurse's insistent voice.

"Mr Myracle, I need you to wake up. We need to do a quick exam and then you can go right back to sleep, ok?"

I look slowly around, moving my head as little as possible. But even staying still, the pounding in my head is nearly blinding.

The nurse gently touches my face. "Does this feel the same on both sides?" It does.

"Stick out your tongue"

I do.

"Hold out both hands like you're carrying a pizza box."

Through half closed eyes I see her hold her hands out in front of her, palms up.

I lift my hands to hold the imaginary pizza box.

Correction.

I lift my right hand. My left lies limply next to me on the bed. Panic as I realize I can't move anything on my left side.

I can't move. I CAN NOT FUCKING MOVE!

The nurse is telling me to calm down. Another nurse enters. I'm dimly aware of them moving through my fog of fear and pain – until my peripheral vision starts to darken and the room tilts precariously. I'm right at the point of going over the edge into passing out when I realize I've been sedated.

*****

Days pass in a blur of doctors and tests and therapists, each reassuring me I'll regain much more functionality after some physical and occupational therapy.

When that'll be exactly they can't say, just 'keep up the good work,' they chirp.

I want to punch their smiling faces with my good arm.

I ponder how much of their reassuring is medical and how much is designed to prevent another suicide attempt. I've regained some ability to move my left fingers so perhaps they aren't totally full of shit.

The only cool part of this whole ordeal is the bullet fragments still lodged in my brain, too deep to operate. I like the image of setting off metal detectors.

I'm lucky, they say. I should have died. I should be a vegetable. My kid should be fatherless.

What a chilling phrase to think on as time goes on. He would have been without his father.

Why did that not occur to me before? It's so stupidly obvious— I nearly made my son bury a second parent.

When I enter therapy at the rehab facility this is the first thing I talk about. Why did I not think about my son being orphaned beforehand? I'm desperate to know what could make me so short-sighted that I hadn't factored my son into the decision to kill myself.

*****

The time comes to leave the rehab facility. I'm mostly independent: I can walk and perform my ADLs – shit, shower and shave – without too many problems. I still need mobility aids to move well, and also a smartphone so as to function well with the memory loss, but I'm ready to be released, like a too-small fish off the hook.

So we head home, Peggy driving. It's an hour's drive and I get carsick for the first time in my life. Vomiting aggravates my headache and ultimately I switch places with Keith so I can stretch out on the backseat, clammy and in pain, numb to the rest of the journey home.

I see it as we pull-up but it's still a few days before I feel steady enough to go out to it.

*****

The shed is padlocked. The neighbor across the street, Jim, heard the gunshot and called 911. Later, the same neighbor padlocked the shed. Leaning heavily on my cane I wait for Keith to scroll through his text messages with Jim for the combination to the lock.

As soon as the lock is open I tell Keith to go back in the house. I don't know if he's already seen it, but if so he doesn't need to see it again. And if not then he needs to never see it. He looks reluctant to leave but I assure him his stepmom has already sold all the guns. I'm safe.

I remind myself for the hundredth time to talk to Keith about his experience, and I tap it jerkily into my new smart phone. We've avoided the subject so far. Everything has been about me and he's been swept under the rug. And how can I ever inoculate him against this suicide risk if we don't talk about it?

*****

I'm surprised how little blood there is on the floor of the shed given that it was a penetrating head wound. Most of the mess was absorbed by the towels I laid out for that purpose, I suppose.

I try to imagine how Keith would feel if he'd come running in and found me like that. I cannot, and my heart breaks repeatedly for the cruelty I've already put him through.

And what I hope I never put him through again.

The fear in his eyes is my motivation daily. The fear in his eyes, more than my stutter slurred speech, the dragging foot, the memory loss, the unpredictable mood swings and fatigue that set in on their own inscrutable schedule, the incontinence… It's all been terrible but the fear in my son's eyes pushes me through therapies and groups and appointments at the Veteran's Hospital and I will do anything to take the look of anguish and uncertainty from him.

"It's my fault."

That mantra still rings in my ears.

And the only way I can see to fix it is not to be at fault for more orphaned children — least of all my own.

The Taxidermist
Alexei J. Slater

Kimberly Raffle was a beautiful young woman who happened to spend most of her time skinning animal hides, elbows deep in entrails and inserting glass eyes. I was immediately smitten. The past week introduced me not only to her but to a world I hadn't known existed of pygmy three-toed sloths, Chinese giant salamanders, Rondo dwarf galagos, Mediterranean monk seals, Peruvian spider monkeys, Chacoan peccaries and hooded grebes to name just a few.

Allow me to start back at the beginning. My name's Wesley P. McGraw. Aside from my mother, clients, friends and my assistant Dina call me Wes for short. Sometimes I use my middle name Peter, which I'll explain later. I'm a private detective whose last major assignment was to track down a Cebu flowerpecker, a spoon-billed sandpiper and a white-winged flufftail. Each one would land me fifty thousand dollars. All three meant I could take a couple of years off.

As a bonus, if I happened to land a white-rumped vulture, a Seychelles sheath-tailed bat or a Philippine eagle, I would be rewarded handsomely with twenty five thousand a piece. I expect like you, I had never heard of these creatures until a week ago when I was approached by my client – known to me simply as Mr Dee – via his middleman, Mr Carroll Benning. And like you, I hadn't heard of a man with that name either. Who knew if it was his real name anyway? I was certain Mr Dee was an alias.

Anyhow, my adverts in the diner and barbershop windows of Little Italy obviously found their way to Benning. Either that or I was recommended, though I never ask new clients how they came to me. Benning was a chain smoking prematurely balding Eastern European in his thirties who wore a hideous cream coloured suit.

'McGraw?' he snapped, as I was going down the rickety stairs for a coffee in the diner across the street.

I looked him up and down and nodded.

'I have job for you,' he said, like a KGB operative.

I nodded and we headed upstairs to my office. My late father was brought up to hate the East during the Cold War but I take any job I can get. I felt his eyes on my back and sensed he was probably underwhelmed by the cheap furniture and plain décor. My assistant Dina was on a week's honeymoon in the Tropics. I usually left her to take care of these things. I beckoned this odd looking, weird sounding stranger to take a seat. He lit up without checking my smoking policy and exhaled a big cloud in my direction. Under the light I observed his oily face, saw the subtle scar on his right cheek, the slight pot-marked complexion and waited.

'Military or cop?' he asked accusatorily before taking another lungful of smoke.

'NYPD. Only lasted five years. This is better for my health,' I said, as he coughed and exhaled.

'Listen Wesley McGraw.'

'Wes,' I said.

'Okay. Wes. You deal only with me. Understand?'

I shrugged, impatiently wondering what his deal was.

'Very good for you. Lots of money,' he said, rubbing his forefinger under his thumb, 'if you please my boss.'

'Who's your boss?' I asked.

'He is Mr Dee. But you deal only with me. Carroll Benning.'

Over the next ten minutes, this odd man whom I guessed was Czech or Slovak, told me that his boss was a collector of rare and beautiful creatures. Fish, reptiles, spiders, insects and so on. I immediately pictured a Bond villain mischievously stroking a white cat. There were a number of rare birds he wanted and his usual sources were not working. He would pay handsomely on delivery. I would receive a non-refundable thousand dollars a day plus expenses. If I had to take any flights of over a thousand dollars I was to call Carroll to approve the costs. He then proceeded to take out his little notebook and read these strange names beginning with the Cebu flowerpecker. At first I thought it was a joke but he was deadly serious throughout.

I kept a poker face and tried to tell him I usually dealt with marital infidelities, lost children, stolen heirlooms and alike but he told me Mr Dee was all out of ideas and what he was prepared to pay per specimen. If I located all three alive there was a bonus fifty thousand in it. The other birds, the white-rumped vulture, the Seychelles sheath-tailed bat and the Philippine eagle were worth another twenty five thousand each. He wrote down a number that he insisted I was to call every week with updates on my progress. Whilst there was no exact time window, he hinted there was an additional bonus for quick delivery. As a parting note, he told me that the fees were only for the birds delivered alive and although they would still accept a dead specimen, the fee would reduce to a quarter.

I knew nothing about the exotic or rare bird world. Something told me it was a bad idea to get involved, that Mr Dee was some foreign dictator, if not Putin himself. The money though, I admit, pulled me in. I was making around fifteen hundred dollars a couple of times a week taking illicit pictures of some guy's wife screwing her therapist and re-interviewing shady witnesses on cold cases for bereaved mothers the cops had long forgotten about. I'd been thinking for a while that the agency was a dead man walking, that I should go into private security or go work for some corporation for a steady pay-check. Though I had no idea where to begin, when Carroll had finished his little speech, I nodded, accepted his scrap of paper and offered no objection before he had descended the stairs and headed out into the noisy street with a slight limp on his left side. I followed five minutes later to grab that overdue coffee as I pondered what I had gotten myself into.

*****

Back in my office there was a letter and a parcel waiting. There was no Dina to deal with the office administration. I threw them on my desk as I began Googling each of the three main birds Carroll had mentioned, beginning with the Cebu flowerpecker. Initial research told me there were barely a hundred remaining on the planet and that its population had been decimated by catastrophic deforestation. It was described as critically endangered. This was the first sign of trouble.

The other birds were also rare and endangered. This was when any normal person would have walked away. Even I knew endangered animals was a risky business of illegalities and moral tightropes. I was struck though by the bird's beauty. Its array of colours were reminiscent of Native American war paint. It had a black feathered back which contained a red patch almost in a triangle, with a white underside and another thinner red stripe along its belly as if it were ready for battle.

I sat back wondering where to start, then thought more about Mr Dee and what he wanted with such creatures. Whilst I meditated on my next moves, I opened the envelope on my desk. It was a paternity test I had managed to squeeze out of a clinic for a client chasing a bigger alimony from her attorney husband over his marital infidelities. She was paying me peanuts. Maybe I could bump her up another five hundred dollars.

Next, I opened the package. It was a framed picture from my mother of myself aged ten with my late father at the zoo. It was unexpected. I was touched. I knew she was tidying up her place. Maybe she found it in an old box. I filed the paternity test in my drawer and stood the picture on my desk. I studied my father's expression. He was never one for showing emotion but he looked happy. Then it struck me. Central Park Zoo was a good place as any to start.

*****

I hadn't been to the zoo in years and spent fifteen minutes browsing the enclosures until I found a grizzly bear named Joe. I watched him waddle around until I got bored and visited the flapping sealions. There were a few young couples, moms with babies and some serious looking middle aged men. I followed one such man around a corner and found myself in the bird sanctuary. I scrutinized the wall charts and saw a host of exotic looking birds which resembled those walking and flapping around in the adjacent cages. I realized as I went down the list that I couldn't possibly have attempted to remove one of the specimens from the zoo and that hadn't occurred to me until that moment confronted by them. It was more likely that a zookeeper might have more useful information.

According to the zoo wall, there was at least one African Pygmy Goose somewhere behind me. There was also something known as a Bali Mynah, a Blue-gray Tanager, an Emerald Starling, a Crested Coua, a Scarlet Ibis and one Kookaburra of which even I had heard. There was the brilliantly named Blue-crowned Motmot, six Pied Avocets, a bizarrely named Speckled Mousebird, a pair of Sunbitterns, many Superb Starlings, four Troupials and an almighty ten Taveta Golden Weavers. As I noticed a young man who seemed to be feeding one of the aforementioned birds, it struck me that this was just one zoo, though admittedly a grand one, and it housed all these bird species. Could Mr Dee not have settled for one of these?

I stood with one of the serious looking middle aged men for five minutes interrupted only by intermingled bird calls of all varieties. He stood perfectly still and watched something through binoculars as I waited patiently for the young man to exit the bird enclosure.

'Hey buddy, can I ask you a..?' I said as friendly as I could as he turned to me with a handful of some bird feed and waved for me to follow him. After he put the remaining bird feed into a bucket he looked back at me, waiting. He must have been about twenty years old. It was hard to tell in that moment if this was the job he chose or if it were a punishment from a judge for some misdemeanour.

'Beautiful birds back there,' I said, buying time as I quickly brought out my little pocketbook. 'I was wondering, I know you have a lot of beauties, but I was looking to see a Cebu flowerpecker, and errr, even a spoon-billed sandpiper or a white-winged flufftail. You know where I could find those?'

He looked at me with a vacant expression.

'Where you from, mister?' he asked, as if I was sent by the court to check up on him.

'Oh, I just, you know, I love birds,' I said unconvincingly, 'and never saw those ones.'

He narrowed his eyes. I knew he was thinking that I was standing in Central Park Zoo, barely thirty years old in a worn out suit and most certainly was not any kind of ornithologist like those older men perched around the enclosure.

'Go up there,' he said, pointing, 'on your left, there's a lady called Sandy in the office, she knows about them bird questions.'

I nodded thanks but he'd already turned back towards the vast collection of bird feeds.

*****

I found the little office the cynical young man had described. A friendly woman of about fifty greeted me with a huge smile.

'Sandy?'

She nodded, perhaps thrilled that she had a human with whom to deal to break up the bird monotony.

'Hey Sandy, I was admiring the beautiful birds you have here, absolutely magnificent.'

Sandy smiled again as if she had individually hatched each of them.

'They are just beautiful, aren't they?' said Sandy, flicking her dyed blonde hair which was clearly black at the roots.

'Oh yeah,' I said trying to recall one of the breeds they had there. 'Those Superb Starlings,' I said relieved, 'absolutely...superb.'

This seemed to make Sandy's day and she beamed delight.

I opened my pocketbook again. 'You know, I'm kinda interested in birds and I noticed you didn't have any flowerpeckers, Cebu flowerpeckers, you know those right?' I said casually, as if there were any doubt Sandy was familiar with them.

She nodded eagerly and I surmised this bird talk was like foreplay to her.

'Also, a couple other breeds I love, the spoon-billed sandpiper and white-winged flufftail, I noticed there weren't any of those either?'

Sandy stood up and came to the door. She was overcome.

'Oh, a true bird lover. Those three breeds are very rare...' she said waiting for me to give a name.

'Peter,' I said, as I generally used my middle name on snooping assignments.

'Peter, there are sadly so few of those birds in existence. The Cebu's in Asia. The spoon-billed sandpiper's Asia too, they breed in Russia. What was the third?'

'The white-winged flufftail,' I said like a young David Attenborough.

'Ah yes,' said Sandy gravely, 'found in Africa, but very rare. Really tragic.'

I felt the heat of the day suddenly hit me and was sure my underarms were sweaty but Sandy was undeterred and I was compelled to push the issue.

'I guess it's impossible to find them in the US?'

Sandy stared at me intently. I sensed she was suddenly unsure of my real motive.

'Just a bird lover are you?' she said.

'Well, okay you got me,' I said, thinking quickly, 'my mom bless her, she's old now but was a keen ornithologist and never saw those breeds. I was desperate to find them for her to see before...'

Sandy's expression changed again. She lent her head and silently mouthed *awww*.

'I shouldn't be saying this but there are ways,' she whispered. 'It's a bad area you know Peter, lots of bad people out there, dealing in rare birds and other animals. You stay clear of all that. But I know a nice lady who might be able to help. Let me see if I have her card somewhere,' said Sandy, going back to her messy desk and shuffling through her drawers for an eternity. She finally brought over a card.

'Give her a call, maybe she has an idea, but don't let anyone here know I suggested it,' she said quietly and hurried back to her desk.

I studied the card on my way out the zoo to the sound of a distant bear or leopard's half-hearted growl. It read Kimberly Raffle – Taxidermist with an area code that looked like Brooklyn.

*****

Back at the office, I negotiated another five hundred bucks out of that vindictive divorcee for her former husband's positive paternity test for a boy he'd fathered with the housekeeper. I figured even if I made no hay with these rare birds, I'd stay on the case for at least a week, or even ten days before Carroll would get suspicious with my lack of inroads and I'd take home ten thousand dollars plus this five hundred and it would be a great week.

I looked at the picture of my father again and I was sure he wouldn't approve of my current line of work. I studied the card Sandy at the zoo had given me. As far as I knew, taxidermists were those strange men who stuffed and mounted wild animals shot for sport for other strange men to boast about to their strange friends for years afterwards. I pictured deer heads on walls above grand fireplaces and wild boars on never ending staircases of rich old Republicans from the NRA. I was sure some also did lions posed as if they were about to tear you apart.

This made it somewhat surprising that Sandy had described this taxidermist as a nice young lady. Why would she be mixed up in all that? I Googled Kimberly Raffle. She had a sparse website that said, 'by appointment only' and a few images of small birds, presumably stuffed, perched on a stool. Perhaps she was a bird specialist. There was a number and I called for an appointment. I bluffed that I was a private collector looking to commission and wanted to see some samples. That was around a Wednesday lunchtime. She could see me Friday morning.

Having secured the meeting with Kimberly Raffle, I spent some time reading up on taxidermists. It was like a whole weird universe I hadn't known existed. There were some strange people out there including some old guy called Dr E.A. Billy Hankins who ran a place called the World Museum of Natural History at La Sierra University in Riverside California. He had started this strange hobby when he was five years old, skinning, drying, stuffing and mounting small creatures. It sounded more like the early biography of a serial killer than a college professor. Now his museum was an institution. He'd been an army doctor in Thailand and shipped dozens of dead animals back to the US and had perfected a freeze drying technique. I felt as I was reading all this that any information I could garner would also help my approach with Kimberly Raffle, to display a certain knowledge of the taxidermy world for authenticity.

There was another taxidermist in England who'd been sent to prison for trading in endangered species. This caught my attention. The man had illegally transported rhino horns, bought and sold sperm whale teeth, dealt in tiger and dolphin skulls and attempted to sell a snowy owl without a permit. A police house search led to more illicit materials. Stuffed tiger cubs, rhino horns in a freezer, rhino heads and several elephant tusks. Call me naïve, but of all the black markets out there dealing in drugs, weapons, human organs, I just never considered this one until now.

I found another taxidermist in Miami who created hideous hybrid creatures as artworks that he sold for thousands of dollars. He attached beetle wings to rhino busts and numerous other nature defying abominations and in the process illegally trafficked endangered wildlife across the world. He was prosecuted for importing snakes, birds and orangutangs from all over Southeast Asia but claimed 'I am not a criminal, I am an artist.' I stopped again to think what the hell I was getting myself into as a grotesque image of a goat body with two swan heads stared back at me. I shook it off and continued searching.

There were yet more one-man-bands in Texas, Georgia, even Australia, who'd decided early in life that instead of becoming dentists or car mechanics, they wanted to skin and stuff a whole host of domestic pets and creatures shot down on hunts. There were pictures and interviews with these middle aged men in their workshops with animal busts on the walls behind them discussing their various methods honed over decades. I thought of Kimberly Raffle again. Was it possible she too spent her day doing this sick work?

Just as I was thinking about Kimberly Raffle, she called. There'd been an afternoon cancellation. Could I make it there by four? I agreed, checked the status of my other open cases, grabbed a baloney sandwich downstairs and whistled for a cab to Brooklyn. On the half hour journey, I rehearsed my story to myself. I was a private collector. A wealthy broker. My regular taxidermist in Switzerland had died suddenly. I collected rare birds. Money was not an issue.

*****

When I arrived, I couldn't find the entrance. I heard a voice, 'Down here.'

There was a small alley she hadn't mentioned on either call.

'Mind your head,' she said. I crouched under the low entrance way and the smell of formaldehyde hit me.

Inside on the white walls were carefully spaced small-framed photos of birds. I assumed they were all past projects and each bird now resided in some distant home. There was no sign of Kimberly so I took the opportunity to check my cellphone on which I'd saved images of the Cebu flowerpecker and the rest. By now that bird's unique feathered colour scheme was imprinted on my mind and I knew it was not one of the stunning wall images. I quickly moved on to the spoon billed sandpiper, a grouchy looking creature reminiscent of a dozen common park birds but with an odd beak to my untrained eye. I waltzed past the images for a likeness when Kimberly Raffle was suddenly watching me. I awkwardly put away my cellphone and stuck out a hand.

'Greyhound entrails,' she said, grinning at her glistening hands. 'Peter?'

I smiled and nodded uneasily. Despite having the insides of someone's deceased dog on her dainty fingers, I felt an instant attraction. Even so, the first words out of my mouth were, 'I thought you specialised in birds?'

Kimberly smiled.

'Dogs pay the bills. And the occasional deer or rabbit.'

I nodded. It certainly wasn't a conventional route in life but the strangeness of it captivated me. As I proceeded, I tried to hold off thoughts of that oddity Carroll having led me to here to Kimberly.

'I was just admiring your pictures,' I said. I vaguely made out one or two birds that resembled some at the zoo earlier in the day.

'I like to take a picture before I send them out to their new lives,' she said, looking up at the walls.

I found myself staring at Kimberly's long dark hair a moment too long as she looked up and immediately away as she wiped her hands on her brown apron.

'You mentioned on the phone that you're a private collector? You have something you want to commission, is that right?'

I nodded, wondering if I had the heart to immerse this lovely human specimen in the unscrupulous affairs of Carroll Benning and Mr Dee. I wanted to buy time to ponder this dilemma and also to spend some more minutes in her delectable company before she returned to skinning the next dead dog.

'Yes, absolutely, but I was wondering if I could see some of your work, if you have birds that haven't yet flown the nest?'

Kimberly smiled politely as I internally kicked myself for such an awful avian metaphor. I'd also looked up birds on Wikipedia in the taxi over and learned the word avian.

'Sure, yea, I have a finch that's not been collected yet and actually a beautiful little warbler I named Barnie that's still in the studio. Follow me,' she said and walked off in her flat blacks to another room where I distinctly recognised Dionne Warwick's Walk on By playing quietly.

'It's a lovely space, Kimberly,' I said as we entered the new room.

'Kim, call me Kim,' she said looking back with a new confidence as if we'd now entered her true domain. She quickly rinsed her hands in a sink in the corner.

I recalled the images I'd seen online of those redneck types with deer heads and antlers in every corner of their workshops. This room was quite different, even serene, apart from the taut brown coat of a dog stretched over a small ironing board. I couldn't help but stare.

'Oh, don't mind that, it's just a girl's pet that died in a hit and run. Her dad wanted me to do him up like new for her birthday. It's good money,' she said moving to the end of a worktop where a miniscule bird lay motionless. 'Come on over,' she said, beckoning me.

I moved over as I looked around the room. There were a few animal books on a shelf and various implements, scissors, cutters, scalpels, hammers, pins, glues and other things I didn't recognise. Even so, the room remained strangely feminine and I was under this taxidermist's spell instinctively imagining her working alone on the tiny birds for hours.

'This is the warbler,' she said, putting on a sidelight.

I looked down at the tiny yellow feathered thing. A few grey feathers were intermingled on the wings. It was so small and cute it immediately struck me the detail and the care which she must have invested in this piece, and likewise all those on the walls in the entry hall.

'There are quite a few warblers, some are on the white, blue and black end of the spectrum. I always like the yellow ones. The colour's so vivid,' she said.

I stared down at it wondering how long it took and who in their right mind would pay for such a thing.

'Beautiful,' I said.

'Here's me telling the collector about warblers, I'm sure you know more than I do!'

I smiled awkwardly again thinking that I knew the pigeons of Little Italy that crapped all over my office window and could probably spot an owl and a Robin in a crowd, and maybe an eagle. Meanwhile, Kimberly brought out a small wooden box and carefully removed a finch and placed him down next to the warbler. I moved closer as if I were inspecting the handiwork.

'Let me lift him up, you can get a better view,' said Kimberly, picking up the tiny bird. I kept staring at the thing and nodding and smiled occasionally at Kimberly whose sparkling green eyes were clear to me for the first time. I was glad at that moment that Carroll had come to me with his bizarre proposition just so I had the good fortune of meeting Kimberly.

'Excellent,' I said, nodding like the judge of an art talent contest until Kimberly placed the finch back in his box. I turned away again to quickly examine my pocketbook of assorted rare bird names.

'So, you've seen my work Peter,' she said, turning back to me. 'I guess now it comes down to what birds you're after? I don't need to tell you about the whole process of ethically sourcing birds for taxidermy but you know, it can take some time.'

I involuntarily rolled my tongue around my mouth suddenly feeling queasy. I didn't want to blow it all by scaring Kimberly away too soon. I guess that's where the phrase tongue-tied originated.

'Before we get to that, I'm always interested in the craftsperson behind the work,' I said, trying to stall, 'tell me, how did you get into taxidermy?' My eyes lingered on her coffee mug illustrated with colourful tropical birds.

Kimberly smiled coyly as if she'd never been asked this by a client. I breathed a sigh of relief as it might have bought me more precious minutes to decide whether or not to divulge my true intent. Kimberly looked at the white wall clock that had images of tiny black chicks dotted around it. I could sense she wanted to tell me more about her career and her work but she had other commitments.

'That's so nice of you to ask, I'd love to tell you about it, it's just I have this greyhound due early next week and a couple of scarlet tanagers arrive tomorrow for a regular client in the Catskills.'

I'd noticed no ring on her freshly washed entrail-free fingers and I knew I'd regret it forever if I didn't ask the next question.

'How about we grab a drink when you're finished? I've not been in Brooklyn for a while, I can catch up with an old friend for a few hours,' I said, about to take out my card before remembering I wasn't about to tell Kimberly I was a private eye just yet.

She was caught off guard so I felt compelled to give one last push to birth that evening date.

'I love your bird work, I honestly didn't think I'd find another Pierre-Sebastian anywhere, but now...' and I left the reference to my fictional dead Swiss taxidermist to hover in the air.

'Okay, sure, it would be nice to talk to a fellow enthusiast and it seems you're not just about the birds, so it would be nice to tell you more about my journey,' said Kimberly, talking herself into it. 'There's a little bar on the corner, see you there at seven? And you can tell me about your mysterious commission huh?'

*****

I wasted a few hours in Brooklyn reading up on endangered animals on my cellphone. I realized that a lot of these creatures only sounded exotic because of their prefixes. Sloths were boring until you added 'pygmy three-toed' in front of them. Likewise, salamanders were nothing special until you added 'Chinese giant'. Run of the mill monkeys became

Peruvian spider monkeys. Admittedly there were some creatures I had positively never heard of even without their fancy prefixes. Rondo dwarf galagos. Chacaon peccaries. Hooded grebes. I was sure Kimberly would have known all of these creatures and a bit like Sandy back at the zoo, I felt that if I could just slip in some of these tongue twisters into regular conversation she would be impressed. That being said, saying their names was one thing, understanding their plights, or what or where they even were was too much to memorise in a couple hours.

It dawned on me to be bold and construct a cover story that I was working undercover for an organisation looking into illegally trafficked animals like the WWF or the EPA. That would win Kimberly over on an ethical level but again, it would be impossible to maintain the story all evening. I realized that in my mind it was becoming a case of pursuing the rare birds or pursuing Kimberly. I couldn't see how to do both. I should also add that I was moved by the plight of these creatures that were dying out but I wasn't sure what I alone could do to stem the tide. I was sure that the moment I denied Carroll and Mr Dee their request, they'd have another five people on the case if they didn't already. Therefore, I resolved to find a way to find out more from Kimberly whilst not alienating her.

Kimberly arrived only fifteen minutes late explaining that she was reading up on new methods of freeze drying animal carcasses and lost track of time. I ordered us a couple of vodka cocktails. Kimberly practically drank hers in two gulps. I sensed it was nice for her to get away from all that flesh and skin for an occasional night out. I began overthinking again how I'd broach the subject of my rare bird search and Kimberly was staring.

'Everything okay?' she asked.

'An American Robin,' I blurted out.

'Huh?'

'I've been thinking,' and that part was at least true, 'I hope we might have a long working relationship, and what better than for the first piece I commission you to make is the most common bird in New York,' I said, studying Kimberly's expression. She seemed to gradually deflate as the mundanity of my underwhelming request hit home.

'A Robin, sure, of course, yes, I'd be honoured,' she said.

'Wonderful. Now I didn't scrutinize your rates online. How much would a Robin be?'

Kimberly stared at me a moment as the vodka seemed to hit her, or perhaps she was wondering why a superficially wealthy collector was quibbling over a mere Robin. 'I'd say three hundred and fifty.'

I tried to nod casually. I really had no idea the amount of time and effort it took. 'Have you got a good supplier of Robins?' I added, before flagging the barman down for two more vodka cocktails.

Kimberly nodded. I waited for her to elaborate but she just smiled enigmatically. We drank up the cocktails and I felt the attraction growing with every mention of taxidermied small birds. I couldn't tell if it was mutual and Carroll popped back into my head again. He'd be expecting an update soon.

'I was curious Kim, with the rarer birds, do you have sources for them too?'

She smiled. I could see she was already a little drunk.

'It's a bad world out there Peter. Some of these species are nearly gone. You know, I had some Russian guy, or European, I don't know, turned up at the studio unannounced last week pretending he wanted to commission me, but started asking if I had access to a Cebu flowerpecker,' she said shaking her head. 'I mean, you know how rare those are? Before I even answered, he took out all this cash like a gangster and was all sandpipers this and flufftails that, it was crazy.'

I shook my head in genuine shock. She seemed to be describing Carroll. I realized that meant he knew about Kimberly and I started anxiously looking around the bar.

'Peter? What is it?' she asked, innocently.

'I'm just disgusted, I guess he was after a spoon-billed sandpiper and a white-winged flufftail?'

'Yes!' said Kimberly, elated at my superior knowledge. 'You know your birds, Peter. They're endangered. Who knows what he wanted them for?'

The Taxidermist

'Kim,' I said, spontaneously going in for the metaphorical kill, 'I've not been entirely honest with you. I'm actually sort of working unofficially for the WWF. I'm a keen birder anyway, but I also look for people like that man who are illegally dealing in rare birds and animals. We try to shut down their supply before they have a chance. You didn't tell him where you might source such birds, did you?'

'No way Peter, and anyway, I wouldn't be sure. I mean I have some people sure, but never birds that rare. You weren't after birds that rare when you first contacted me, were you?'

'Oh no, no,' I said, vigorously shaking my head, 'I mean, as it happens, I've always loved the Cebu flowerpecker and of course, spoon-billed sandpipers and white-winged flufftails are both stunning creatures, but you know, I was intrigued to know if you knew where I could visit any white-rumped vultures? I've always been a fan, along with Seychelles sheath-tailed bats and of course, the Philippine eagle. I'd never commission a taxidermist, but just to see them in the flesh would be wonderful.' I could see Kimberly was genuinely moved. Finally, a young man who knew his sandpipers from his flufftails. 'And don't get me started on what's happening to those poor Chacaon peccaries or hooded grebes.'

Kimberly's mouth fell open.

'I don't know what those are but d'you wanna get out of here?'

*****

It turned out Kimberly's apartment was just above her workshop so we made sweet love with the faint aroma of formaldehyde and drying dog hide. I knew there and then that I would either have to bark up another tree for sources to these rare birds or refuse Carroll and Mr Dee entirely. I woke early in the morning to an empty bed. Downstairs, Kimberly was hammering a loose tooth into the mouth of the Greyhound over her first coffee. She said she would get on with the Robin commission and I smiled and said I'd give her a call. On my way out, I remembered something and turned back to tell her if that strange European ever contacted her again, to let me know right away. Then I went home to shower and change.

*****

I arrived back at the office to find Dina had returned early from her honeymoon. She said there was a hurricane in Bali and was surprised I hadn't heard about it. I told her I'd had a busy couple of days.

Dina made some strong coffee and I grabbed a cup, then settled at my desk and took care of some calls to my other clients. After several minutes of my trying to figure out what to do next, Dina stuck her head around the door and glared. I quickly realized I had forgotten to ask her about her trip and she recounted five days of Bali sun and wonderful wildlife. I smiled but didn't tell her the specifics of the Carroll case, only that we had a steady flow of cash. I knew it would soon be time to call him back with an update but I wanted to do an overdue background check first.

I called an old NYPD contact and he agreed to run both Carroll Benning and Mr Dee through their database. Nothing returned on Carroll but my contact suggested Mr Dee was an alias of known organised crime boss Giancarlo Alberto D'Angelo. At this point, I was scared. If it were him, he wasn't someone to disappoint. Carroll was likely a killer. They also knew about Kimberly Raffle as Carroll had already visited her once.

I sat thinking for an hour whether to warn Kimberly which would entail my revealing my true identity and motives. I thought about whether I could continue the search for these rare birds and what I could say to Carroll. I hadn't been paid yet for the previous few days' work either. It was clear they would pay cash which meant I'd have to meet Carroll in person at least once more. I Googled D'Angelo. He was half-Sicilian and supposedly floated between New York and Moscow. One thing didn't make sense to me. If he were a rare animal and bird collector, why did he come to me? Surely he knew everyone there was to know? It got me thinking. Were they really after the birds themselves? Or was it something else? Maybe it was just my paranoia.

With these worries plaguing me I went out to tell Dina to inform any callers I was out but she wasn't there. I noticed her computer screen was open on a bright picture from her honeymoon. I leaned in. Dina and her husband were in some private alcove. It was idyllic. The pink sand was rich and the sky was a luxurious turquoise. I couldn't help imagining one day being there myself with Kimberly Raffle. I clicked on the next picture. There were palm trees and again it seemed like some private beach where Dina posed alone. I studied the image as something seemed familiar. Up perched in some palm trees were three small birds with black and red backs. I swallowed hard. Dina had gone to Bali in Indonesia. It was under two thousand kilometres from the Philippines where the Cebu flowerpeckers resided. They were miraculously perched above Dina`s head.

'Wes, this man says he`s a client,' said Dina, holding two coffees in the doorway.

Next to her stood Carroll looking worse than before, with an unsettling smile on his face.

'Carroll, I was about to call you,' I said, sweating. 'Come to my office, I`ll be right in.'

Carroll grabbed one of Dina`s coffees and walked through to my office with an envelope sticking out of his jacket pocket. Dina looked at me curiously. I studied her holiday image again and quickly had her explain the precise location of that photo and print it for me. I returned to my office thinking fast. Carroll was holding up the photo of myself and my father.

'Fathers and sons, the same wherever you are, huh?' he said, not looking up.

'Right,' I said, my heart pounding.

'It`s been nearly a week Wes. Why you not call? Mr Dee very unhappy,' said Carroll, putting the picture down on my desk, before sitting and lighting a cigarette.

'I have good news for you. You met my assistant?'

'Good cleavage,' said Carroll, exhaling a lungful of smoke.

'I had Dina do some research,' I said trying to ignore his comment and placed down Dina`s vacation picture. 'You can clearly see here at least three Cebu flowerpeckers.'

Carroll studied Dina`s form before finally squinting at the birds. 'What is this, a joke?'

I took out a magnifying glass from my desk and handed it over. He grabbed it, studied the birds and smiled. 'You have them, yes?'

'Not exactly. I've given it some thought and these are very rare. I didn't think it would be right.'

'You didn't think it would be right? You know who I work for Wes McGraw?'

At this moment, my last week flashed before me, from flirting with Sandy at the zoo and her terrible dyed hair, to the ethereal Kimberly and her magic taxidermy. I fell back on my resourcefulness and formulated an instant response which kept me out of danger, was ethical and allowed me to have renewed contact with Kimberly. But first I needed the cash.

'Is that payment for the work I have done so far?' I said, looking at his pocket.

Carroll grudgingly took out the envelope and threw down the several thousand dollars on my desk. I would count it later.

'I have a solution which can work for us both Mr Benning. You said Mr Dee was prepared to accept dead birds as being better than nothing?'

Carroll's eyes narrowed. He nodded, unconvinced.

'I shall call you with news soon.'

Carroll shuffled out in a haze of smoke. As soon as he was out the building I checked the images of the rare birds again. The Cebu flowerpecker. The spoon-billed sandpiper. The white-winged flufftail. The white-rumped vulture. The Seychelles sheath-tailed bat. The Philippine eagle. It was Dina's picture which finally confirmed to me that I couldn't aid in removing these beautiful creatures from their natural habitat. It was Sandy at the zoo and her badly dyed hair which made me surmise that most of the birds could be doubled if their feathers were recoloured, except the spoon-billed sandpiper's unique beak and body combination and I didn't risk the unique looking Seychelles sheath-tailed bat.

So I set to work ordering Kimberly to taxidermy me a Common Starling, a vulture, the largest eagle she could find and attach the punk like feathers to its head so that it resembled a Philippine. I would collect them along with the Robin already ordered. I enlisted Dina to find a top local graffiti artist who could spray paint the taxidermied specimens to precisely resemble their rarer counterparts.

*****

I visited Kimberly three times over the next month and paid her in advance in cash while she ethically sourced and worked on the commissions. We talked more of her life as a taxidermist and I said, in some seriousness, that I would gladly give up my job on Wall Street to help run and expand her business. She was delighted with the paid work which meant she could forego any further stuffing of deceased pet dogs for a while.

I told Carroll on the phone that I would secure a perfectly preserved Cebu flowerpecker, a white-winged flufftail, a white-rumped vulture and a Philippine eagle. He told me Mr Dee would accept these and agreed the fee as initially slated for the creatures delivered dead; a quarter of fifty thousand dollars for the flowerpecker and the flufftail and a quarter of twenty five thousand for the vulture and eagle.

Dina negotiated a very reasonable fee for a young man called T-Dog to visit our office exactly a month after my last meeting with Carroll where he meticulously spray painted the four taxidermied birds to resemble the four endangered species so closely, I couldn't tell the difference. Carroll arrived the next day, inspected the stunning handiwork of Kimberly and T-Dog, and paid thirty seven and half thousand dollars in cash. I told him the month's additional daily rate was unnecessary but he insisted and threw in somewhere around an additional twenty thousand. All in all the whole affair had earned me around sixty thousand dollars. I was happier though that no rare birds were illegally trafficked or killed and I had met a truly wonderful taxidermist called Kimberly Raffle.

Some weeks later I read that Giancarlo Alberto D'Angelo and many known associates had been arrested in South Africa on multiple drug and animal trafficking charges, whilst an unseemly Eastern European had been caught trying to steal one of the last known families of white-winged flufftails breeding in Zimbabwe. By then I had already told Dina that I was closing shop and moving to Brooklyn to open a taxidermy gallery with my fiancé who still called me by my middle name. I was going to hang that photo of myself with my father at the zoo by the entrance as I think he would have approved.

Bad Apples

A Jaye Jordan Vermont Radio Mystery

Nikki Knight

Part 1 – Harvest Time in New England

When I first came to Vermont, I thought leaf-peeping was something dirty. Little did I know it could be something deadly. I found out the hard way on the first Columbus Day Weekend of my new life as a single mom and small-town radio station owner.

The Green Mountain State is at its picture postcard best just then, the maple and birch and oak flaming into glorious pink, yellow, and rust for the tourists sweeping up I-91 in their big shiny SUV's. Of course, the locals are waiting for them and all their lovely money.

In Simpson, that takes the form of the Apple Festival, a sweet little craft fair at the high school. We've got everything: cute grandmas selling quilts, the local orchard pressing cider and giving out samples, Sunday School kids dipping candy apples, petting-zoo cows accepting wary strokes…and of course, Your Hometown Radio Station broadcasting live.

Yep. That's me.

Jaye Jordan, nice to meet you. I only use the "Metz" from my ex at our daughter's school. And yes, I was in fact born Jacqueline Jordan. People always wonder with DJ's.

Thank God, my pal Rob Archer was riding shotgun. He'd been willing to dust off his old morning-man skills for a share of the miniscule fee the Chamber of Commerce was paying to sponsor the remote. (He would have done it for free, but I wouldn't let him.)

For a while, that Saturday was the best day I'd had in a couple of years. My daughter Ryan and Rob's son Xavier had helped us set up the remote kit, and then the two tweens had taken off to explore the event, already fast friends and partners in crime. The broadcast was going smoothly, without any of the technical glitches that we had every right to expect with our decrepit equipment. Friendly folks — actual listeners, not just relatives — had come up and told us they were glad we were back.

I even looked pretty good, in my favorite pair of thrift shop jeans, my Uncle Edgar's old black leather moto jacket and a vintage Apple Festival shirt from the station promo merch closet. I'd matched my red lipstick to the apple, and my black hair, with the wide platinum streak, was staying in the clip where I'd put it. Nobody agreed with me, but I liked the bony frame that came with being too stressed to eat much – as far as I was concerned, it was one of the few positive surprises of the last year or so.

Walking on Sunshine was playing on our big speakers. Perfect. Everyone in the place looked happy, from the sweet older folks, to the kids just barely *not* running up the aisles to the food corner, even the tourist couple with the wife's determined smile and the husband's sharp gray face that suggested serious illness. The sun was streaming through the big windows high in the gym walls, giving everything a little glow, and the warm scent of apples and cinnamon filled the room.

Too good to be true, but enjoy it while it lasts.

"Here, have some cider!" I looked up from checking the next hour's commercials to see Orville and Oliver Gurney, town pillars, my ex-husband's uncles, and classic Vermont characters, standing in front of me.

"Maybe she doesn't want one, Little Brother." Oliver, hardware-store owner and head of the select board, told Orville, who'd spent the last seventy years paying for a three-minute lag.

"Everyone wants cider." Orville, a lawyer and school-board member, held out a paper cup. I did not, in fact, want the cider, but I would never have dreamed of giving one brother the advantage over the other.

"Thanks." I took the cup. "I'll drink it after our next hit."

Orville beamed. Oliver sighed. As far as they were concerned, they were the designated protectors of Ryan and me, which was a little sexist and weird, but mostly cute. They looked like every Vermont male stereotype: plaid shirts, barn jackets, jeans – Oliver's in shades of green,

Orville's in blue. My guess is their mother started it, to tell them apart, but these days it was easy enough, with Orville rounder and intense, and Oliver wiry and wry.

"Where's Ryan?" Oliver asked. "I want to know which 'Who Was' book to get her next."

"She's over there with Xavi." I nodded to the fudge stand just past the cider place, where the kids were clearly considering how to spend their allowances.

"Fudge," Orville's tone was almost reverent. The Wife, as he always called her, tried to discourage sweets in hopes of banishing his little pudge.

"Never mind that." Oliver's spouse didn't have to worry about a sweet tooth. "I have to be in Brattleboro next week and I want to go to the big bookstore there."

"Oh, fine." Orville turned back to me. "See you later, Jaye."

Oliver had barely finished his own goodbye before his little brother started suggesting books.

"Bye." I stepped back to find a safe spot for the cider, chuckling as I heard their fading bickering about the biographical merits of Sonia Sotomayor versus Sacagawea.

"You are *killing* it," said a happy voice behind me.

I put down the cup and turned to see one of my best friends standing at the booth. Maeve, otherwise known as the Reverend Collins, is pastor of the Episcopal church in town, and has surprisingly good taste in liquor and expletives for an ordained priest. She's also a makeup maven – my red lipstick today came from her sample stash – so it was no surprise to see her eyes lined in the perfect deep-green shade to highlight their hazel irises. For this informal event, she'd traded the clericals for a forest-colored UVM fleece, a show of pride for her husband, who was finally finishing his Master's there.

"Hey!" I said, leaning in for a hug that was only a little bit comical because I'm more than a foot taller than she is. "So glad you came."

"Oh, I had to supervise the Sunday School kiddies, but I wouldn't miss you guys for the world."

"Reverend!" Rob took off his headset mic fast enough to muss his brown hair and came over too, his light blue eyes sparkling and spare face lighting up with a smile. She married him and his husband Tim, and they're regulars at Saint Gabriel's. I would be too, if our family weren't relatively observant Reform Jews, Ryan by birth and me by conversion.

Rob and Maeve hugged hello, too. Usually born Vermonters like Rob aren't huggy, but he makes an exception for Maeve.

"Looks like it's going well." She nodded to the nearly full box of raffle tickets for a gift certificate to Rob's restaurant. It wasn't just good promo; the tickets also gave us a great start for the online newsletter that Ryan had suggested and set up as the station's new webmaster.

"So far so good," I said.

"Really good." Rob shot me a little glance.

Plenty of subtext here. WSV, once one of the most revered stations in the state, and one of the oldest in the country, as you can tell by the three-letter call sign, had been a satellite drone for years. Then the former owner sold it to me at a discount because I promised to bring back live local programming.

A few of the dead-enders who missed their daily dose of third-rate hate hadn't been pleased, and I'd gotten some pushback in the form of nasty letters and more…but nothing serious enough to rise to the level of a real threat. So far.

The Apple Festival was our first remote since the change, and I'd been just a tiny bit worried that some of the people who'd been telling me I was going to hell for the last month would show up and try to send me on my way. But Maeve was right; the response had been wonderful.

And the joke was on the dead-enders anyhow. I wasn't *going* to hell. I was already there.

Two years ago, I'd had a damn near perfect life with a part-time gig as the happy friendly midday DJ at New York City's top light music station, plenty of mom time with Ryan, and a decent, if not romance-novel, marriage. I can't say David's cancer ruined everything. He survived, and Ryan still has a father. That's all that really matters.

But David decided that life was too short not to do the things he wanted. Mostly blonde things. Right about then the big NYC station went all-sports and paid off the DJ's, and Orville called us and said WSV's owner was looking to sell. So, I bought WSV, and Ryan and I moved into the little apartment above the studios. David took over the English Department at the community college across the river in Charlestown, New Hampshire, and settled with his parents. Close enough for Ryan, far enough apart for us.

Not easy, but it worked.

"I'm starting to feel pretty good about this," I admitted. "At least today."

Maeve grinned. "Today's enough."

"Sure is." Rob had been running the little restaurant in the town plaza, right next door to the station, ever since WSV went satellite. He was happy and good at it. But he'd missed radio, and he jumped at the chance to record bits to air in the mornings, even for the pitiful sum I could offer. "I love getting out the old remote kit."

"So did our engineers." I shared a wry glance with Rob. Both kids were STEM fiends, and loved having the run of the radio station with all of those interesting electronics and computers.

"Just keep 'em busy," Maeve said, nodding toward the Sunday School booth. "I'd better get over there…it looks like the confirmation class is going Mean Girls over the caramel apples."

"I'm glad ours aren't that age yet," Rob observed.

"Coming soon to a house near you."

Maeve had just turned away, and the record (irony alert: it was *How Am I Supposed to Live Without You*) was starting the final fade when we heard the crash.

Part 2 – Never Mind That Apple A Day Thing

"What?"

"Where?"

"Get the Chief!"

"Get an ambulance!"

For maybe thirty seconds, the room was a swirl of confusion and yelling. It looked like whatever had happened was at the cider booth, two spots up from WSV, in the food corner. I couldn't see much more, and neither Rob nor I could leave the booth because we had to go on the air and get into the next song. Despite the apparent disaster several yards away, we managed a surprisingly happy and calm break, noting that we were at the "Wonderful Apple Festival" without actually urging anyone to come down and join us in the middle of whatever this hot mess was.

Only when Rob fired the next song, one of those long Chicago extravaganzas with the horns in the middle, did we get a chance to step a few feet out of the booth and get a view of the scene. By then, there was a crowd by the Bell Orchards stand. Well, a bigger crowd. The Bells had already been doing good business selling apples and handing out cups of cider freshly brought in from the press at their exhibition in the parking lot, between the petting zoo and the new ambulance.

From the WSV stand, we could see the fire chief kneeling in the aisle, working on someone who appeared to be male and wearing a brown barn jacket. That was about all I could tell.

"Looks bad," Rob said. "Should we go over?"

I shook my head. "We'll just be in the way."

"Probably right."

A couple of EMT's ran in with a stretcher. Everyone pulled back for them, with faces stunned by the ruin of their happy festival day. The rescuers had the look too, and no wonder. Until two minutes ago, they were showing off the new ambulance to curious kids and enjoying the coffee and company of the PTA moms.

No party now. Rob and I exchanged a quick glance. Like everyone else, we were trying to figure out what we should do. His phone buzzed.

"Now what?" I hissed.

"Never ask that – the universe might answer." He managed a wry chuckle. "Oh, yeah. Text from the governor's office."

"Why?"

He shrugged. "Sally at the Chamber of Commerce called somebody. Gov's got some big event in Burlington and can't put in an appearance this year, but they offered him for a phoner in half an hour. Want to take it?"

There was a definite bad-brother gleam in Rob's eyes.

If the EMT's had not been trying to save someone's life a few feet away, I'd have slugged him. As it was, I just replied with a cool nod.

Not going to give him the satisfaction.

Yes, I'd had a crush on once and current Governor Will Ten Broeck back in the day. No, I hadn't done anything about it. He was blond, blue-eyed and absolutely lousy with That Thing, as reporters describe political charisma. He was also married with a couple of kids, and I'm not that girl. Full stop.

Besides, even when he was Governor the first time, even before the Cabinet post and the big national career, he was smart, charming and all grown up, not to mention committed to a lovely adult woman. Me? Barely out of college, overweight, under-styled and all *wrong*. I wouldn't grow into my voice, my cheekbones, or myself for years after Vermont.

But Rob had known about my crush and taken wicked glee in it then, and within ten minutes of my return, taken yet more pleasure in telling me that Ten Broeck was back too, and single. I knew it was only a goof.

"Sure," I said, with just enough edge in my tone. "I'll take the interview if you don't have time."

"He's calling on the remote kit landline at four o'clock straight up. Let him ramble a little about apples and foliage…and maybe you can get a soundbite or two about the construction work on Route 11 for the Monday morning updates."

"Works for me."

"The Gov's always good for a bunch of bites." Rob's eyes twinkled a bit more brightly at his mildly smutty double entendre. "Sally told me his office asked her about the station."

"What?"

"Someone apparently heard we were back."

"Shut up. Our stick is good but not that good." The original owners had put up a very powerful transmitter – *stick* in radio parlance — by Vermont standards.

"Comes in clear as a bell in Montpelier." He shrugged. "If somebody didn't have anything to do at night, they just might hear it."

"I'm sure *some*body has plenty to do at night."

"Never know."

The sound of the stretcher rolling past stopped us – and everyone else. One of the EMT's, a woman not much taller than Maeve, was working the breathing bag, and the man was steering and holding an IV. It did not look good.

Those faces that had been glowing with golden autumn sunshine and fun just a few minutes ago were stark and pale with shock. Even the Sunday School Mean Kids (not all girls!), who'd been having one of those little hissing fights a few minutes before, were silent.

Behind me, there was a rustle, and a hand slipped into mine.

"Ma." Ryan's pale-green eyes, just like her father's, were cool and steady, but her voice gave her away.

I squeezed her fingers. "We're okay, sweetie."

"What about him, Dad?" Xavi had appeared next to Rob, his face a good bit more troubled than Ryan's. He didn't have her experience of staying calm in the chemo suite, which had made an already good kid into a truly amazing one.

"Don't know, buddy." Rob patted his son's arm. "But if anyone can help him, it's those two."

"Okay."

"Where's Papa?" Rob asked him, referring to his husband Tim. Though he was an assistant district attorney, the very definition of a serious professional, Tim took the same boyish joy in the Apple Festival as his son. The last I'd seen him, Tim was at the woodworking booth, studying a very elaborate puzzle that I strongly suspected would end up in a certain young man's Christmas stocking.

"Not sure. He's around."

People were still milling about, most with the unfocused stare that suggested they weren't sure where to go. I noticed the tourist couple with the sick husband again. Even by wealthy flatlander standards, she was very "done," with a nice French manicure and a really good highlighter catching the sun as she pulled her buttery burgundy suede barn jacket around her. I don't get to judge anyone for how they handle this kind of thing, but I caught a flash of annoyance in her expression as her gaunt husband walked with painful determination.

Maybe they fought earlier, I thought.

But no matter how bad it got with David, I had never looked at him like that.

"Hey, Jaye."

Despite the casual delivery, there was no mistaking the deep magisterial voice, even before the faint trace of New York accent. Police Chief George Orr was cultivating his usual friendly and low-key demeanor, to dilute any concern that the sight of a six-foot-three Black man in a leather trenchcoat and Indiana Jones hat might spark in the white-est state in the union.

Chief George was standing at the other side of the booth, his expression carefully neutral. He did his 25 years at the NYPD before coming up here and bringing some professionalism, not to mention diversity, and he was surprisingly good with small-town ways. "How are you folks doing?"

"Well, it *was* a fun day," I said.

"Us too." The chief sighed a little. "Alicia actually had to run home, she bought so much stuff. The last straw was one of those fuzzy throws."

His wife Alicia, a bank vice president and fast friend of mine, was about as fond of the cold as I was. No surprise that she'd decided to pick up a heavy creation in thick chenille. Me either. I nodded. "I bought one last night when I was setting up. What color did she get?"

"Purple. It's pretty nice, actually."

"I got a red one."

"Blue," Rob said.

Small, at least mildly inappropriate, shared smiles.

"So," the Chief asked, his voice returning to professional cool, "do you folks mind keeping up the remote broadcast for a while? Everyone has to stay till I can clear the scene, and it would help a lot."

"Of course," I said. Rob gave me a tiny glance of agreement, and nodded too.

Chief George's eyes widened a little. "That's it? No demand for an exclusive on the details, nothing?"

I laughed. "We both know the rules in the City. But this ain't that."

"True that. I'll owe you one."

"Hope I never need to collect."

"Thanks, Jaye. See you later, Rob." He nodded to the kids, too, acknowledging them with respect a lot of adults don't trouble to give.

"Well, looks like we're going to be here a while," I said.

"Won't have to bail on the Gov's interview anyhow."

"Shut up."

"That's not a nice thing to say, RyansMom," Xavi chided.

It was actually stupidly soothing that he called me the same thing Ryan's friends in Westchester had. More that he stood up for kindness, even to grownups.

"Yeah, Ma! Not cool." So does Ryan.

"True. I am sorry," I turned to Rob with exaggerated courtesy. "May we please not discuss our esteemed executive?"

Rob stifled a laugh. "For now."

Part 3 – Every Town Has One Bad Apple

Maybe ten minutes later, we were back into the groove of the show, and the kids had gone off in search of fudge, when Rob's aunt, Town Clerk Sadie Blacklaw, stopped by. Sadie, who's also one of my yoga buddies, is the real power in town, partly because she knows where all of the bodies are buried – and also quite possibly because she put some of them there.

When I was first here more than a decade ago, she was friendly enough, but we didn't know each other well, partly because of the age difference and partly because I was just coming through. Now, as a grownup clearly committed to a future in Simpson, I was in a much different place, and we were becoming real friends. Which didn't prevent her frequent and persistent lobbying to start a real AM drive show again, so Rob could return to his rightful place as the town's beloved morning man.

Neither he nor I had the heart to tell her that times and radio had changed a lot, and it was unlikely that we'd ever make enough money to do that kind of show…or that he would never give up the restaurant. Sadie would not have heard it anyway.

"Well, this is a pretty pickle," she said as Rob and I took off our headset mics.

Rob leaned down and planted a careful kiss on her cheek, and I hugged her and admired her ash-blonde hair, in a fashionable short cut that looked far better on her than the Oscar-winner who popularized it.

"Horrible thing," Rob agreed.

"I'll say. That Cuthbert Storey nearly ruined the town, and now he's nearly gotten himself killed in the middle of our chance to show off to the world."

I blinked.

Rob didn't look particularly shocked. "Well, I doubt Cuthbert collapsed on purpose."

"I doubt he collapsed at all. If I were Felicia Bell, I'd have given him a nice cup of poisoned cider."

"Aunt Sadie!" Rob hissed, glaring at her.

"Maybe you shouldn't say that…" I suggested.

"You know as well as I do what that fool did to the town, Robert."

Rob shrugged.

Sadie turned to me, with fire in her eyes. "You know that eyesore on the road into town?"

"Um…" I was sure I was not supposed to ask which eyesore. The minimart wasn't elegant, but it was clean and busy, so I knew that wasn't what she meant. And the motel was no longer a chain, but it was still decent enough, though I definitely did not want to know what might happen there.

Maybe the old machine tool factory. It was the most dilapidated of the two or three former industrial sites in town, probably too far gone to reuse or revitalize. But I didn't think she would speak of the shell of a beloved local business in such rude terms.

"That broken-down old Dollar Depot, of course, Jaye." Her mouth, brightened in the perfect berry stain to pick up her boiled-wool jacket, pursed in disgust. "A chain dollar store is repulsive enough, but a failed one? Ugh."

"I never heard about this," I admitted.

"Didn't keep up on our little town zoning matters in the big city, eh?" Her tone was teasing and her eyes sparkly, so it wasn't the slap it could have been.

"No reason to," Rob said. "It was a big deal here, but not even statewide. Unfortunately it happens too darn often these days."

"Big box store coming to town?" I asked.

Sadie nodded. "Will Ten Broeck and the woman after him were really tough on land-use… but the next guy wasn't."

"Bring in development at any cost," Rob agreed. "It's not that we don't want business, but it has to fit the town, you know?"

"And without state officials backing us up, things got through." Sadie shook her head. "Like that store. Cuthbert sold his grandpa's land for a bundle because it was zoned commercial for their old farm stand and had road frontage."

"The holy grail for a store anywhere," I agreed.

"But especially in Vermont." Sadie looked like she wanted to spit. "And what kind of store? Not even one of those nifty Swedish furniture places. No, a nasty, tacky dollar store…run by the only discount chain that could manage to go under in a growth economy!"

Sadie sighed. Rob shook his head.

"It would have been better to have an adult bookstore," she continued in a truly waspish tone. "At least we could have ignored that!"

"They've ignored the one in Ascutney for fifty years, after all." Rob's eyes were twinkling and I knew he was trying desperately not to laugh at his aunt's fury.

"You don't really think that nice Mrs. Bell did anything, though," I said. Bell Orchards had bought ads a week after we came back, and Felicia Bell had seemed genuinely thrilled to have us – me – in town.

"I certainly would have. He ruined the approach to the town, not to mention leaving that mess right by her drive. And he stays in his nice big house while she's stuck running that huge orchard alone."

"She has a son and a daughter who pitch in, Aunt Sadie, and everybody just ignores the old dollar store," Rob reminded her patiently.

"Not everybody." Sadie scowled. "The state development director mentioned it when he came to town to talk about the old mill last month."

"The development director's a snotty flatlander." Rob coughed. "All due respect."

I swallowed a chuckle.

Rob mistook my amusement for offense, and the ends of his ears turned pink. "You know we don't think of you as a flatlander."

"She's not a fool, Rob," Sadie patted my arm. "My rude nephew is right about the development director, though. He's from Long Island, thinks he knows everything about everything."

"One of those."

"Yup. Coming up to save the poor Vermonters from themselves." Sadie sighed. "But he *has* done a nice job bringing in environmentally conscious businesses... so Will Ten Broeck and the rest of us put up with his nonsense."

Rob shot me a little eyebrow at the mention of the Gov's name. "Ten Broeck doesn't put up with nonsense, usually."

"Good guy for a Knickerbocker." Sadie's approving tone only slightly diluted the intended insult. Even though he'd been in Vermont since he came up for college decades ago, the locals would never forget that he was actually from a very old New York family. (Knickerbocker as in Dutch settlers, not free throws.) "Smart and sensible."

I nodded. The only adjectives I could come up with were not the kind I would share with anyone, and certainly not these two. I offered something nebulous, knowing full well that nobody would believe it: "He was always nice to me."

Rob very deliberately blinked fast a couple of times.

Sadie's gaze suddenly sharpened on me. I felt like a misbehaving teenager.

Then she grinned. "You know, he *is* single now. And you're probably the only pretty girl in the state who could keep up with him. He's almost as smart as you are."

I wasn't sure whether to be amused or offended by the characterization of my scruffy fortyish self as a pretty girl, but figured it was best to just play it off. "I'm sure he's wonderful. But I've got a lot of work to do right now."

"Well, dear, you know that deliciously vulgar old saying about the best way to get over someone..."

I did indeed, and I was honestly rather stunned to hear it coming from Sadie.

Rob was suddenly studying the raffle ticket box with great intensity, a brighter pink tinge at his ears and a little shake of his shoulders the only sign that he was trying desperately not to howl with laughter.

"Oh, calm down, Jaye dear. Sooner or later, you'll stop mourning over your marriage and decide to get back into life." She patted my arm, and I remembered that she had a very quiet "friendship" with Fire Chief Frank Saint Bernard. We young things were not allowed to acknowledge it, but it existed and we were actually very glad for them.

"In the meantime," Rob reminded us both, "it sure looks like death is our problem."

"Chief George's problem anyhow," Sadie said, nodding as the man himself approached the booth.

"Ms. Blacklaw?" he asked. "Wonder if you might be able to supply a little background?"

"Cuthbert Storey?"

"Not Mr. Storey as much as the Dollar Depot and why folks in town hate it so much… and how it got built in the first place?"

"Well, Chief," she said as she turned from us. "The state development director is one of those arrogant flatlanders…"

Rob and I smothered chuckles as they stepped off deeper into the gym, toward the crocheted doily booth, putting a few more local artisans between the Chief's background conversation and the orchard investigation. As I returned to the commercial log, I felt eyes on my back and glanced catty-cornered, to the gun – sorry, outdoor sports – store's spot. Two grubby guys in tractor company gimme caps with cups of cider in their hands were taking a break from poring over the deer jerky and the latest in orange camo vests to glare at me.

I straightened my spine and glared right back.

"Oh, it's Harold and Howard." Rob gave a derisive snort. "Well, at least they're not protesting."

"Not now, anyhow."

Harold and Howard were the loudest and most unintentionally comical of my dead-enders. Every Tuesday night, at the former air time of the Edwin Anger show, they demonstrated in front of the station in bad Revolutionary War getups, complete with Gadsden flag t-shirts under their greatcoats, and tube socks and New Balances with the knee breeches. It would have been downright hilarious except that they were also carrying muskets, and I had no idea whether they were functional.

The muskets, that is, not Harold and Howard.

On the first night, Chief George had quickly come out to remind them of the rules of peaceful protest, and me of the protection at hand. Soon, it became nothing more than a routine, if rather unnerving, part of my already stressful week.

But that didn't mean I was thrilled to see them, or they me.

Rob folded his arms and joined the glare. It was a little bit silverback gorilla for my usually low-key friend. But every once in a while, he felt the need to remind folks that the local power structure, to which he belonged by birth and business ownership, liked having me here.

I was not ungrateful.

Vermont men somehow manage to be both protective of women and respectful of our independence. Guys from other states should come up here for lessons.

For a fraction of a second, Harold and Howard returned Rob's gaze with poisonous stares. Then they broke eye contact and swaggered over to the other corner of the gun store booth, to inspect the latest trends in duck calls.

"Creepy." Rob shook his head. "You shouldn't have to deal with that."

"I deal with it every Tuesday."

"I know. Free speech is not an unmixed blessing."

"Still the best we got." I shrugged. "Sure is." His scowl lightened a bit. "Look – we're getting a visit. Wonder what's up with this?"

Some of the Sunday School kids were coming toward us, and by the looks of them, not the usual A/V club geeks who were the only people under 50 who thought radio was cool. This might be interesting.

Interesting in terms of coming attractions, anyway, since these kids were sixteen-ish, and Rob and I were both absolutely terrified of what actual teenager-hood would bring for our little – well, medium-sized angels.

"Can we make a request?" asked a dark-haired girl, who carried herself with the confidence of one who'd skipped awkward teen and gone straight to nymphet. She was dressed that way, anyhow, in jeans that were a better fit and quality than most of the kids wore, and a fuzzy deep blue sweater with a low neck only partly filled in with a lighter blue lace tank, picking up her eyes, which were indeed blue, though probably not nearly as striking as she thought they were.

"They don't have anything you'd want, Shannon." The other girl was cultivating the far more common scruffy goth look, if that's even the right word for it these days. Her oversized burgundy plaid shirt was so perfectly wrong with her coppery hair that I wondered if it was deliberate, and she had troubled with only one cosmetic: black eyeliner, and plenty of it.

Shannon had a face-full of makeup, but none of it stood out: a little shimmer on the lips, lashes darkened a bit, something to even out the skin, whatever girls used now.

"*Do* you have anything new?" The blond boy asking the question was close to my height, and still getting used to his size. He had the droop I remembered from my cousins when they'd started their big growth spurts, and the faint air of apology for his size that they'd had for a while.

So had I. Until my grandfather looked at me one day and snapped: *You're not going to get any shorter, you know. Stand up and be proud of it.*

He'd been dead for 20 years, but I still heard his voice sometimes, gruff but affectionate.

"Depends on how you define new," Rob said. He was picking up something from the kids. I wasn't sure what – or which kid – but there was definitely something going on here.

"Anything that we'd recognize." The last one looked like the classic class clown type, a little shorter and a little pudgier than average. But there was a real taunt in his voice that suggested something more serious than the usual teen messing with the olds.

Rob smiled. Not the friendly one that I get, but the very cold one he saves for people he wants to back off. "Not my fault if you don't appreciate the classics. Jaye here likes her Beyoncé, though, so I suspect she might be able to find something for you."

"No thanks." The kid's expression of disgust once again struck me as more than necessary.

"You should be nice to Jaye," Rob said, with a wicked little sideglance. "She's the one who tells you school's closed."

The kids had no way to know, but to me it felt like the passing of a torch. When I was up here all those years ago, Rob had been the hero of every Career Day because he opened with: "I'm the guy who gets to cancel school."

Now my dubious honor.

"I'd rather be at school than shoveling snow," said the blond guy with a nervous smile.

"Me too," I said. "I hate cleaning out the satellite dish."

"C'mon, Shan," the clown cut in, with a too-carefully casual pat on the girl's arm. "We have to cook up some more apples."

"Let's go, Cooper," she said, pulling away just enough to discourage – but not insult – him. "C'mon, guys. Yummy apples."

I caught something, just enough to register, but not enough to pursue, because right then, everyone jumped at the sound of a new crash. This time it was from the pottery booth next to us.

What now?

If nobody else was smart enough not to ask the universe to answer that question, I sure should have been.

Part 4 – He Knows How to Pick 'Em

"I'm so sorry, sir." It was the sick man, the one with the very done and very annoyed wife, taking a genuinely apologetic tone that most tourists couldn't manage. "She didn't mean to knock it over."

"How could you even suggest that?" the wife snapped as they both tried to prevent any unpleasantness with George and Jennie Wray, the couple who ran the pottery studio on Rockingham Road. "Of course we'll pay for it."

George Wray, who was still a big gruff Brooklyn guy despite his graying man bun and turquoise mandala sweatshirt, nodded slowly. "You bet you will."

The item in question was a sizeable earthenware platter with a glaze that shaded from amber on the outside edge to burgundy in the center. I'd noticed it when we were setting up, and briefly considered it as a possible gift for my mother and Uncle Edgar, who were enjoying a very late-adolescent rebellion as the feisty sister-and-brother act of a Florida condo complex. They would have appreciated the workmanship and colors.

I, however, could not afford to spend *three hundred dollars* on a tchotchke for the fam.

Our visitors, apparently, had no trouble with that, or at least wanted us to think so, as the man pulled a platinum card out of his wallet, and the woman glared at him.

I hoped she was glaring because he'd given her attitude, and not because of the slow, painful way he was moving. I'd seen that careful precision before, in the waiting room at the chemo suite. Combined with the yellowish-gray tone of his skin, it meant only one thing. Even so, his expression was the classic annoyed husband, just possibly a bit more intense.

Pretending to be very interested in my commercial log, I watched them closely. Something was off.

"I'm sorry, do you mind if I take a pen?" The woman was in front of me now, those perfectly manicured fingers reaching for the old merch from the promo closet.

I managed a chuckle. "That's what they're there for."

"Thanks. Can't believe I was so clumsy." She tried for a self-deprecating laugh.

"Happens more often than you'd think." My tone was probably overly cautious, but I don't wear my experience as The Cancer Wife like a tag on my wrist, and I wasn't sure I wanted her to know I was a paid-up member of the club nobody wants to join. "I've already picked up that cup of pens three times."

She returned my wry smile. "I'm Alana. Alana Harmon."

"Nice to meet you. Jaye Jordan."

"Sorry if I don't shake, I'm trying not to bring any germs to Mitch."

I nodded. Held her gaze an extra beat longer than entirely necessary. "Makes sense to me."

Alana Harmon got the right vibe if nothing else. "This trip really mattered to him. We come up a couple of times every year."

"Normalcy is a big deal," I agreed. "The more things you can keep while other things are being taken away, the better."

Alana's brownish hazel eyes sharpened on me. "What's yours?"

"Remission divorce." I shrugged. "It happens."

"I couldn't ever leave Mitch."

My cheeks flooded red. In all the months of admitting to the failure of my marriage, not one person had ever suggested, even obliquely, that I was the one who'd left. If I hadn't been so infuriated and humiliated, I would have wondered why she went there. "Um, no. I saw him through treatment and then he decided there were other things he wanted to do."

Never insult someone who talks for a living. My voice was cold enough to freeze off body parts, and Alana Harmon visibly shrank back.

"Mrs. Harmon," Rob said, in a tone clearly intended to pour oil on the waters. "Glad you two got up here for the foliage."

"Rob, dear. How nice to see you. You haven't quit the restaurant for radio?"

"Nope. Just helping my pal Jaye here and there." Rob's face and voice were absolutely friendly, even if he punched the 'my pal' a little.

Just enough to let Alana Harmon know that I was part of the circle.

"Terrible thing about that Cuthbert Storey."

A rusty cough, or attempt at a laugh, followed the comment and we all turned to see Mitch Harmon, carefully placing his credit card back in his wallet. From the satisfied expression on George Wray's face, I had no doubt that Mr. Harmon had covered his wife's mistake and then some.

"Are they sure it was him?" Alana Harmon asked.

"Of course they are," her husband said. "Everybody knows everyone else up here."

"Isn't that the truth," I said. "I'm Jaye Jordan, owner of WSV."

"Mitch Harmon. I'm a writer."

He offered a hand and I shook it, mildly surprised after his wife's insistence on not touching. She didn't look concerned, either, or shoot him a mild little glare, as I'd been known to do to David when he bent safety precautions.

While his hand was bony, and the fingernails had a strong yellowish cast, his grip was strong and he made eye contact like a businessman or politician: direct and assessing, holding my gaze longer than I expected.

For a second I thought it was something creepy. Then I realized he was waiting for me to recognize his name.

Unless you're Hemingway, dude, you gotta give me more than just writer.

"Mitch is a *screen*writer, dear." Alana gave a derisive chuckle. Not making fun of me, but of her husband. "He thinks everyone knows who he is."

Mitch Harmon wilted visibly. Alana stood a hair straighter. Ugly dynamic there.

"Ah, well," I said, covering as kindly as I could. "I've been working weird hours or mom-ing for years. I don't even know what won the Oscar last year, let alone who wrote it."

The screenwriter managed a light laugh. "Well, it wasn't me. But I do write the occasional thriller too, and I'm working on a cancer memoir."

Of course he was. So was David. There was something about men and cancer memoirs. Women get through it, take care of their families and move on, and often don't feel the need to tell their story until someone suggests it might be interesting. Men just assume that their lives and pain are worth a book.

"She doesn't care, dear. She's in the middle of a broadcast." Alana's dismissive tone shocked me. There was a level of casual cruelty that had never been part of my relationship with David, no matter how bad it got.

"Broadcast? Ah – it's a remote." Mitch nodded to the setup. "All these years visiting and I didn't know there was a local radio station. We listen to NPR."

I forced a graceful smile at the comment I'd heard far too often up here, and kept the focus on WSV. "There wasn't, really, until a few weeks ago."

"Jaye used to work here years ago," Rob explained. "She was a DJ in New York when the station went up for sale, and she bought it and took it local again."

"Really." Mitch Harmon blinked a little, as most reasonably savvy people do when they realize just how successful I was before my return to the sticks. "Come back for family?"

"Something like that." I sure didn't want to tell my family's story with its happy, if complex, ending to this man who was staring down a much worse outcome.

"Nice state. Nice people. We spend a week or so in Manchester every year, but get over here for the Apple Festival. Love to eat dinner at

Janet's."

Janet's – as in Rob's supportive mother – was the name of his restaurant.

"Mac and Cheese Night is a very good thing," I agreed.

"You do a Mac and Cheese *Night*?" Mitch Harmon asked. "How'd I miss that?"

Rob shrugged. "It's Tuesday. Good way to fill the seats early in the week."

"It's a little too much cholesterol, dear. Why, I couldn't take enough kickboxing classes to make up for that." Alana literally inserted herself back into the conversation, moving in and taking her husband's arm. As she did, the light caught an ID bracelet on her right wrist, a copy of the one on his.

It had the grayish cast of platinum, bore one word, **Survivor**, and stopped me cold.

After the three-month checkup came back clear, I'd given David a black leather cord bracelet with a silver bar engraved with the same word.

It would never have occurred to me to buy one for myself.

His war wasn't mine.

"Cholesterol isn't my problem." Mitch said, his voice matter-of-fact, but his eyes cold and sharp on his wife.

"You know how important diet is, sweetheart." His wife's tone wasn't soothing at all, but hard. As if the helping was about her. As if everything was.

"Not so important that I'm not going to enjoy my dinner in Vermont."

I knew that tone too, but not the intensity. The main reason that David and I had ended up in divorce court instead of on a second honeymoon was the Mean Guy. I didn't blame David for being angry and mean and combative. I didn't even blame him for taking it out on me; it's like the toddler who's perfect at preschool and a terror when they get home – you let go with the people who love you. But it all got into my head, and I heard the Mean Guy even when he wasn't there.

Mitch had a Mean Guy, too. A *really* mean one.

"Well, fine." Alana pulled on his arm, just a little too hard, and Mitch winced. "Come on, let's go look at those lovely quilts."

"Let's."

He could have been gritting his teeth with pain, or annoyance, but either way, it was their business, and they took it with them when they left.

"Come back here." Rob, watching me a little too closely. "Too much like you and David?"

"No. It got ugly, but not that kind of ugly." I shook my head, took a breath. "I never forget that he gave me the best thing in my life…and neither does he."

Rob smiled. "Kids make up for a lot."

"Always."

Part 5 – Not So Sweet Talk

My phone buzzed, making the whole remote table vibrate. An unknown number with a Montpelier exchange.

Rob nodded to it. "I gave the press secretary your number."

"Of course you did."

"Just prepping for the interview, I'm sure. She's a pro."

"I'm sure she is." I picked up. "Hi, it's Jaye Jordan."

"Hi! Mary Alice Winterbury. Glad to hear you guys are live and local again."

Her voice was friendly and warm, with the crisp diction and flow that suggested she'd been on the air, at least a little, sometime before she crossed the line into the Press Office.

"Thanks," I said. "Doing our best."

"Are you doing the interview shows and all that again, too?"

"Not yet, but we will be." So far, our Sunday morning public-affairs shows had consisted of old recordings and a couple of sit-downs Maeve had helped me scramble with the food pantry director and a pal at the Salvation Army.

"Good. When you're doing it on the reg again, let me know. The boss loves that sort of thing... and we have plenty of commissioners and secretaries and whatever who like to talk too."

"Thanks. I'll be taking you up on that."

"Hope you do. And just so you don't think I'm up to anything nefarious, I have lunch every week with the Majority Leader's guy, and I'll tell him to give you a buzz. She's a terrific interview, too."

Majority Leader Charlene Allen, a magnificent legislator from Shelburne (not to mention the other political party), would have been quite offended at the thought that she was anything other than a good interview. I had only spoken to her a few times in my first hitch; she was Appropriations Chair then, but I'd always admired her.

"Great. Thanks. You can give him this number – it's my cell."

"Will do. Is this the right number for the interview, too?"

"No, that'll be on the remote-unit landline. Let me give it to you."

"Landline." She chuckled.

So did I. "Only a little old-school."

"Aren't we all. Better that way."

"I like to think so."

It only took a few seconds to set it up, and we broke off with a cordial farewell and understanding that she'd have the Gov call in the next ten minutes.

Yes, there were a few butterflies flitting around in my stomach. No, not one of them was related to the idea of talking to Will Ten Broeck again. I was worried about the tech; I doubted the remote kit had seen action in more than a decade, and now we were asking it to hold up for a live phone interview.

With the top "get" in the state.

Of course we were.

Well, hell, if you're going to fall, fall from a great height so you're unconscious when you hit.

An NYPD officer had told me that once, and I never forgot it. Good advice both literally and figuratively.

Rob smirked only a little as he showed me which buttons to push and assured me that everything would work. And that he was already running a cassette tape on the ancient boom box we kept in the kit. Ryan and Xavi had also set up a digital recording of the whole remote back at the station, but I was stupidly glad to see that ancient cassette.

"You worry too much," Rob said as he put the boom box back under the table. "It's just a basic phone hit. We've done it a million times."

"No. We *did* it a million times. We haven't done it here – or now."

He shrugged, met my worried gaze squarely. "That's fair. But it's going to be fine. Really."

"Rob? Jaye?"

We turned to see Felicia Bell. Though she was the matriarch of the Bell Orchards clan, she wasn't much older than Rob or me, attractive in that clean and unfussy New England way. Wiry rather than slim, with smooth, lightly-freckled skin and almost certainly natural strawberry-blonde hair, she was actually rather stylish in her weathered black barn jacket and peach pointelle henley, her jeans tucked into good, if not new, riding boots instead of the green rubber ones she wore in the orchard. The parking lot and gym were probably a very nice change from the compost and manure required to produce those lovely organic apples.

But her gold-flecked green eyes were troubled.

"Hi, Felicia." Rob shook his head. "Terrible thing."

"Hi." I was closer, and I held out a hand. "How are you?"

"Not good." Her grip was a little shaky, and so was her small smile. "Cuthbert's in rough shape, and if he makes it, he'll probably sue me."

Neither Rob nor I said anything – we had nothing for that.

"I'm really worried it's going to be my fault somehow."

"Surely not." I patted her arm. "Just because he collapsed at your booth?"

"He was drinking cider when it happened." She coughed. New Englanders don't sob in public, but she sure looked like she was thinking about it.

"That doesn't mean anything," Rob said.

"I know." She sighed. "I'm probably just scared. It's been a really tough couple of years, with the economy, and that horrible shell of a store just sitting right there at the turnoff…"

Rob and I exchanged glances. He was the one who should say it to her.

"Um, Felicia, don't say anything like that around Chief George, huh?"

"Of course not." She looked sharply at him. "You don't think…"

"Nobody thinks anything." I kept my tone cool and definite. "But Chief George was on the NYPD. It's his job to look at things a certain way. You don't have to give him a reason."

Felicia nodded slowly. "You'd know, working in New York."

"I would."

She took a breath. "Okay."

"Anyway, it was probably just a terrible coincidence." Rob thought for a moment. "Didn't Cuthbert have some kind of health problem?"

"No." Felicia shook her head. "His brother Newton had the heart attack last year, not him."

"Maybe it runs in the family." Rob's jaw tightened a little at the mistake, which was very unusual for him. As a son of one of the local clans, he knew everything about everybody. "Anyway, Jaye's right. Just keep your head down and stay calm. Chief George is a good guy. If you don't give him a reason to look at you, he won't… so don't give him a reason."

"Exactly," I agreed.

Felicia took another deep breath, and it caught. "Ugh, in addition to everything else, allergies. I'm living on menthol cough drops."

I shook my head. "I think I have some peppermint tea somewhere."

I always have some because it's good for the voice, and my mom instincts make me want to tend to everyone, though I try not to be obtrusive.

"I'm fine," she said a little too quickly, taking another breath, and then speaking more to herself than us: "We don't know anything yet, anyway."

"No, we don't," Rob agreed. I just nodded.

She turned to walk back to her booth.

Rob and I exchanged glances.

"Sure hope Cuthbert makes it," I said finally.

"Sure hope it was natural."

Another slow, shared nod.

My phone buzzed.

"Hey, Jaye. It's Mary Alice. Gov's going to call you on the landline in a couple of minutes."

"Cool." It came out in a teenybopper squeak, and I could feel my cheeks flaming red under Rob's amused gaze. Another wonderful thing about fishbelly white skin.

With an irritated wave, I shooed Rob back to the music.

I cleared my throat. It was dry, and the last thing I wanted was to squeak like a fifteen-year-old in my first talk with Will Ten Broeck as an adult and yes, all right, a single one! I reached for the cider Orville had given me what seemed like a year ago. It was cool, but still fresh, and I pulled the cup close enough to smell the heady wonderfulness of freshly mashed apples.

And something else.

Something off.

Not off like a bad apple. Medicinal. Maybe chemical.

Except that Bell Orchards was proudly organic.

Oh, dear God. The cider.

I carefully brought the cup away from my mouth, but didn't put it down. Chief George needed to see this. Smell this.

Who? Who did it – and who was the target? Felicia Bell had no reason to poison me. My only actual enemies – Howard and Harold – weren't really smart enough, were they? I'd never even heard Howard speak; Harold did all the chanting.

If Cuthbert was the target and not me, then Felicia was still in the frame. But why *two* tainted cups?

None of it made sense.

Rob was staring at me. *What the hell?*

I held up the cider.

His eyes narrowed. He understood immediately, and started the next song. "Having a Party" was clearly intended as the perfect way to take out a fun little talk with the Gov.

But of course, this wasn't a party any more.

"All right, Jaye, the Governor is ready." The press secretary's cool voice cut right through my spinning thoughts.

"I'm sorry, Mary Alice –" I managed to return as calm a tone as I could, but even I'm not perfect after probably coming within a quarter-inch of poison. "I can't right now – something's come up…I-"

Mary Alice Winterbury, Lord love her, heard it. "You're okay, right?"

"I am…things just got a little – complicated – here."

"I heard about the guy who collapsed…is this part of it?"

"Maybe. Anyhow-"

"Of course. We'll set it up for later. Are you back at the station tonight?"

"Yes, yes. I can tape anytime after seven if he's not busy…" Why, holy hell *why*, did I have to say it that way?

She chuckled. "He'll be delighted to. Maybe you play him a request."

"Um, sure. Thank you for understanding."

"Absolutely."

If there was a tiny dry trace of amusement in her voice, I sure didn't have time to process it. I clicked the phone off. "Chief!"

Part 6 – Poisoned Apple, Anyone?

Rob stared at me as I marched across the aisle and a couple of booths down to Chief George, who was being buttonholed by one of the nonagenarian Cutter sisters at their crocheted doily booth. He looked almost relieved to see me coming.

"I'm sorry, Miz Cutter. I'll absolutely look into it."

A twitch at the corner of his mouth gave him away. I didn't need to hear the conversation to know that Bette and Babe had been bending his ear about their pet concern: bicyclists downtown.

I happened to agree with the ladies; I didn't like rounding a corner as I sped up to Ryan's school for pickup and finding myself way too close to some fool on two wheels, either. But the sisters harped on it at nearly every selection board meeting.

"Those darned cyclists," the chief said to me as he cleared earshot. Then he saw my face. "What?"

"Smell this." I didn't want to prejudice him.

"Do you know how many cups of cider I've looked at in the last hour? Everybody thinks they were poisoned and-"

"One more, Chief."

He sniffed. His eyes widened. "Okay, you win."

"What's my prize?"

"Well, you didn't drink it."

"That's enough of a win for now."

"It sure is. Storey is still unconscious. They gave him Narcan, and sure enough, he's breathing on his own now. But..." He shrugged.

"Narcan?" I was surprised that the opiate antidote was used – and more that it worked.

"It's a good guess around here, unfortunately."

"I suppose."

"But it's no guarantee – and it took a couple doses to get him breathing. So you're really glad you didn't drink that."

If I hadn't been such a hard-boiled professional, I might have been a little wobbly in the knees.

"Ma! What-"

Ryan was suddenly right on us, her usually cheery face tight and troubled. "What's with the cider?"

"Chief Orr is looking into everything, sweetie," I said in a soothing tone, as the Chief nodded.

I don't lie to Ryan, but I'm not above keeping back a scary or upsetting fact.

"He should look at the cider." Xavi was right behind Ryan, and no surprise, since we rarely saw one kid without the other.

"Why?" Chief George asked.

"We saw somebody moving the cups around." Ryan squirmed as she said it.

"I thought it was a game," Xavi added. "You know, like that shell game that we did at the school carnival, or something."

The chief's gaze sharpened on them.

Mine too.

"Tell me exactly what you saw." Chief George pulled out his notebook. "Who moved the cups?"

"We were over at the fudge booth," Xavi explained. "So we didn't get a good look."

"No?"

"All I saw was a hand." Ryan thought for a minute. "And something on the wrist. A bracelet. Not silver, like your star, Ma, but silver-y…or grayish."

I wear a silver starfish necklace as a nod to the Star of David. I don't feel worthy of a full-out one, being a convert and a bit sloppy about observance, though we light candles every Friday and mark the major holidays.

"Grayish?" the chief asked.

Xavi nodded. "Exactly. Not as gray as solder, but grayer than bright silver."

If it hadn't been such a serious matter, I would have laughed. Only these kids would have even known what solder, the base metal used for metal-to-metal bonds, was – never mind what it looked like. They'd watched with great interest when our contract engineer fixed one of the old studio boards, which required a little bit of solder to reattach some wires.

"Like this, maybe?" The chief held out his hand, with the platinum wedding band. I knew, because Alicia had told me, that they'd upgraded for their twentieth anniversary. Renewed their vows, too. Nice.

The warmth and love that was always so visible between the chief and his wife reminded me of where else I'd seen platinum today. On two much less happy partners.

"Exactly like your ring, Chief." Ryan spoke, but Xavi agreed.

"It was shiny, but not the same way as RyansMom's star."

"Thanks, kids. So we need to talk to someone who's wearing a platinum bracelet." He glanced over the crowd, looked to me with an annoyed scowl. "Any other day in this town, that would be a pretty good clue."

"I think it is today, too," I said.

"How so?"

"Both of the Harmons are wearing platinum bracelets."

"The screenwriter and his wife?"

"The very sick screenwriter and his wife." I held his gaze.

"What are you thinking?"

"I'm not thinking anything, Chief." I nodded toward the Harmons, who were, bizarrely, at the gun shop booth across from the cider stand. Howard and Harold were there again too, but I expected that…and the poisonous looks they gave me.

Ryan and Xavi caught the glares from the dead-enders and returned them with their own, not that the men even acknowledged their existence.

Alana Harmon reached for a duck call, and her jacket sleeve slipped back, leaving her wrist to catch a bit of sun.

"Is that the bracelet?" The Chief kept his tone to a whisper.

"Yes." Ryan nodded. "But-"

"But what?"

She and Xavi both shrugged. Neither looked happy, but I thought it might just be a child's normal reluctance to get an adult in trouble.

"All right. I think I'd better head over there and talk to our visitors." He looked down at the cider, held it out to me. "Keep it for a little while, all right? It's evidence and I'll have to pick it up later."

"Will do." I turned to the kids as he walked away. "It's your job to make sure nobody else touches it."

"We can do that." This time, Xavi spoke and Ryan nodded.

We walked the few steps back to the booth, where Rob was in the midst of an impressive display of denial, using the latest break to talk up all of the fun on offer at the Festival without one word about anything else. I found a spot for the evidence: right where it had been before, on the little table where Rob and I had left the commercial log and a few other things. I grabbed an extra Apple Festival program, marked it with a big X, and put it over the cup.

"Here, put these on other side." Ryan handed me two cellophane-wrapped treats from the Sunday School booth.

"Candy apples, really?" I asked.

She blushed, blessed – cursed! – with the same fishbelly skin as me. "Well, they were having so much fun making them, I figured they had to be good."

Tweens don't always have to make sense.

"That's right, RyansMom," Xavi added. "The Confirmation Class said this year's recipe is special."

"Special, huh?" I could not imagine what was so great about melted cinnamon candies and questionably clean apples, but that wasn't my area. I sighed. "Maybe if you're going to finish a car with it."

"All right, so what happened?"

Rob's tone was sharp and angry. I'd expected him to tease me, not attack me.

I cringed, took a breath. "Something wrong with the cider… I had to take it to the Chief."

"You didn't—"

"Nope. Smelled it just before I took a sip."

He let out a breath, patted my arm with unexpected care. "Good."

That's when I realized he hadn't been angry at me, but worried about whether I – or even possibly his son – might have been in danger. I needed to stop assuming everyone was attacking me.

Except that a few people actually were.

"Chief's on it," I assured him. "It's all good."

"Does he know who did it?"

"The kids saw a hand with a platinum bracelet switching cups… I don't know if you noticed, but-"

"The Harmons wear the same one." Rob didn't need to start finishing my sentences. We were already close enough to sibs for a couple of onlies.

"Yes."

"Who do you think?"

"I don't think." I shrugged. "More accurately, I don't know what to think."

"I still have a hard time seeing Felicia poison anyone, even Cuthbert Storey." Rob pushed back a few strands of hair disheveled by the band of the headphones. "And why now, anyway?"

"Maybe she knows something we don't about the site… or the plans?"

"Probably not. If anyone knows anything, it's Sadie, and if she thought Felicia had anything to do with it, she would have said so."

"True." I looked over at the cider booth again. "It would be easy enough to move cups around. Look at the way they just leave them sitting out."

"No reason to do anything else."

Rob checked his watch and looked back at the remote unit. He waved at Tim, who was buying that puzzle I'd seen him studying at the woodworking booth. "We're out of this for now, anyway."

"What do you mean?"

"We're going to interview a cow."

Part 7 – Take a Bite Out of Crime
(You knew that was coming!)

Since Tim was within arm's length, it was, despite potential poison and all other hazards, safe enough to leave the booth to the kids for a couple minutes as I followed Rob out into the parking lot. Especially when I realized that Chief George had asked the Harmons to come outside for a moment.

That made sense; even if the town fathers and mothers hadn't made it very clear that the Apple Festival must remain fun for the tourists, the Chief would not want to confront possible suspects in such an uncontrolled situation.

"Jaye!"

"Slow down, Little Brother, can't you see she's working?"

Orville and Oliver, were puffing toward us, looking quite upset.

"What was wrong with the cider?" Orville asked. "Ryan said she and Xavi were watching it?"

"Smelled medicinal."

Both stared. I could not remember when they had both been silent for more than a few seconds.

"Only when I got right up close." I said quickly, not wanting to hurt them. "You would never have known."

"Should have expected trouble. "Those two crazies with the muskets are here today." He glared over at Howard and Harold, who'd moved to the parking lot displays, checking out the town's new snowplow.

"Oliver." Orville, the lawyer, snapped. "We don't know anything."

"We don't *not*, either."

"The chief is handling it," I said, with enough force to hold back the bickering for a moment. "I'm fine, and it's all good."

"And I'm here, too," Rob said.

The three men exchanged glances. I knew they were doing one of those silly "menfolk protecting the women" things, and I decided to let them, because we still had to interview that cow.

Orville and Oliver took off, apparently arguing about whose idea it had been to hire Chief George. Actually, I knew from Rob it had been Sadie's, but I wasn't going to make the argument worse.

Rob and I moved toward the petting zoo, passing Chief George and the Harmons, who seemed to be having a very intense conversation in the small empty space between the gym door and the exhibits. It was probably the Chief's best bet for a quiet talk, but it automatically made the cows the good cop.

Or maybe the llamas. Certainly not the goats.

Pushkin Dairy had a couple of everything at the petting zoo. Fine by me. I've always liked big ruminants.

Actually, I just like big animals, period. Ryan's cat (he's allegedly mine, but let's be honest!) Neptune is a twenty-pound ball of gray fuzz with a permanent air of offended pride. It has not been an easy time for Neptune. Just ask him.

Anyway, the llamas seemed to be cultivating the feline aloofness I usually associate with them, and the goats were chasing each other around the pen and making the kids giggle, but the Guernseys regarded us with at least mild interest.

"Hey, Rob!" Olga Pushkin, who'd gone to the same style school as Felicia Bell, walked over with her hand out and a sparkly smile. If she'd bothered, she could have rocked the blonde bombshell look, but she was much happier in jeans and a denim chore jacket open over a bright pink tee.

"Olga!" Rob shook and motioned me up, too. "Have you met Jaye Jordan?"

"Nice to see you."

Her handshake was firm and friendly, like Felicia's.

"So you got this guy out of the kitchen to play radio again, huh?" Olga grinned. "Good thing."

"I sure think so." I returned the smile, sensing a kindred spirit – another woman running a business on her own. It was only when I saw the dairy's winking double-headed eagle logo on the booth that I realized who she was. Her grandfather Oleg Pushkin was a high-profile Soviet dissident who'd somehow managed to escape and settle quietly in the next town over. I'd watched on the news the day he left Chester for his triumphant return to Russia, never knowing that years later I would end up working nearby. Some of the Pushkin family had gone with him, but other branches hadn't.

Olga, clearly, was happy in Simpson, and from the looks of that cheeky logo, enjoyed tossing out playful little callbacks to her heritage. Good for her.

"Nice to finally meet you," Olga continued. "I've been listening at night for a while. Like having a local voice again."

"Really?" Even now, after a couple of decades in the business, I was still surprised and pleased to meet happy listeners. People on the radio are invisible, and invisibly famous: it's rare that anyone remarks on our existence, and rarer still when it happens in a good way. "That's wonderful."

"Yeah. All of that Edwin Anger talk stuff was exactly what we DON'T need."

"I'm not going to argue," I said. "It wasn't talk, it was yelling… and we'll never accomplish anything by yelling at each other."

"Hate speech." Rob's tone was cold. "Almost ruined a good radio station."

"Yeah, and some of those haters are still around." Olga shook her head. "Those two guys who picket in the Plaza are right over there."

"They're harmless, Olga." Rob held her gaze, clearly trying to get her to stop scaring me.

Not that I really scare.

"You want the truth, I'm not too sure about that. They creep me out." Her face was tight. "It's a type. Men don't always see it."

"Creep me out too," I admitted. "And it's tough to tell the difference between just creepy and really dangerous."

"Especially these days," Rob said reluctantly. "Still, I don't think they came after you today, Jaye."

"Came after…" Olga started.

"Almost drank a bad cup of cider. Chief George is sorting it out."

"It's the kind of juvenile thing people like that would do," Olga said. "But what happened to Cuthbert Storey was serious. And I really don't think Felicia would do that."

"Me either," I said it, but Rob nodded too.

"I'm in a farm group with her, and she's a good lady. Total standup woman." Olga sighed. "Be nice if the bad guys were always the bad people, wouldn't it?"

"Too easy," Rob observed.

"And nothing in this world is easy."

Olga and Rob both heard the note in my voice; he knew what it meant, and she knew enough not to ask.

Better to just move on to interviewing a cow.

"So you're going to talk to Empress Alexandra," Olga said, turning us toward a Guernsey so beautiful she might just have been Imperial. Actually, based on what I'd learned of Alexandra Feodorovna in my college history classes, I had to suspect that the bovine version was friendlier. Certainly more approachable.

The cow was immaculate, her roan and white flanks freshly brushed, the patches of color around her velvety brown eyes giving her a surprisingly impish expression, like a little girl who'd been playing in her mother's makeup.

"Great." Rob pulled the small digital stick recorder out of his jacket.

"So, how are we going to do this?" I asked, putting my hands in my pockets because I wanted to pet the Empress.

Olga chuckled. "You can touch her if you want. She's friendly."

"Um, okay." I reached out and very gently patted the cow's head. She made eye contact and what seemed to be a happy noise. "Nice to meet you, your Imperial Majesty."

"Well, we're not REALLY going to interview the Empress," Olga said. "I'm going to tell you a little about her, and the cheese that we make with her milk, and she's going to contribute her thoughts."

I gazed into those deep bovine eyes. "Looks like she has interesting thoughts."

"Many. Sometimes when things get really weird in my life, I like to go out and talk to the cows."

"Probably better company than the llamas," I said. "They look like divas."

"They are." Olga nodded to Rob. "Okay, Radio Dude, roll 'em."

Rob hit the button, just in time to capture a shriek from the cider-making exhibition.

"HOW DARE YOU? DO YOU KNOW WHO I AM?"

We never did find out what the Empress thought of that comment. Right then, we turned to see Alana Harmon follow what cops like to call the magic words with an attempt to throw a punch at Chief George.

In other parts of the world, that could have ended extremely badly.

Not in Simpson, though, and not with Chief Orr.

Instead of reaching for his gun, he simply stepped aside with a resigned twist to his mouth, and let her take care of herself.

Which, of course, she did. Whatever Alana had learned in those fancy kickboxing classes, it wasn't how to throw a punch. She put too much force behind it, and not enough effort into keeping her balance, and over-rotated right toward the huge vat of discarded apple pulp.

There was an instant where she tried to catch herself, and hovered above the rim, struggling, as if she might manage to do it. But no.

Alana went right over, flipping into the pulp with a surprisingly low splash… and just a quiet splat.

How do you like them apples?

Part 8 – (Apple) Pulp Fiction

Llamas do not like drama.

We discovered this the hard way, as Olga's two (Rama and Dali Lama, if you're wondering) reacted to Alana Harmon's unexpected dip with a guttural sound that was a lot like a mocking laugh. The goats jumped in with some distressed baas…and Empress Alexandra and her sib added a mooing bass line.

Olga stepped in to calm the stock, while Rob and I ran toward the vat of apple pulp.

At first, it sounded a lot like there was some kind of animal in there, a huge, nonverbal howl of rage.

Nonverbal it may have been, but the noise was so loud that most of the Apple Festival came running. Rob and I were in the first wave, since we were so close, but people quickly came pouring out of the gym, too.

Among those people, the kids, who reached us before Alana even took a breath to start another howl, partly because they're young and fast, and partly because they were scared by the sound of screaming from where their parents had just gone.

"Ma!"

"Dad!"

They cannonballed right into us with twin tackle-hugs, nearly knocking us over the rail and into the pyramids of cider bottles.

And wouldn't that have just added to the fun?

The ruminant chorus, by the way, was still at it, slightly quieter, but undeniably unhappy and wanting to make sure everyone knew it.

By the time Rob and I got ourselves steady and sorted out, Tim had joined the group, at an only slightly more deliberate pace, as had Felicia Bell, Sadie, and who knows who else. They all got quite a show, between the angry animals and the splashing and shouting from the vat. Alana's protests had started to form words, if not especially coherent or polite ones.

Actually, I hoped the kids weren't listening too closely.

"You couldn't say any of that on the air, could you, Ma?" Ryan asked.

"Not a word," I said firmly. The rule in our house has always been: *If Mom can't say it on the air, you can't say it, period.* Saves a lot of aggravation and explanation.

"Off your list too, Xavs." Tim's tone was similar to mine, except he looked a whole heckuva lot better saying it.

"Yes, Papa." Xavi drooped a bit, exactly as Ryan was doing, as our tall tweens will do when they're feeling deflated.

"You two okay?" Tim asked, giving his husband, and then me, a quick damage assessment.

"We're not the ones you're going to be prosecuting," Rob replied with only a little amusement.

Tim allowed himself a wry grin. It only made him cuter. He's the very definition of tall, dark and handsome, and people sometimes underestimate his intelligence, which makes him extremely dangerous in the courtroom. "I might just enjoy this one."

"You probably will," Rob agreed. "Flatlander tries to kill husband..."

"At the Apple Festival, yet," I added. "Made us all witnesses."

"Even the llamas," Tim said.

Rama Llama or Dali, who knows which, let out a particularly piercing cry as Alana Harmon's butter-blonde head poked above the line of the waste barrel. She cringed and her wild eyes raked over the crowd that had clearly already convicted her... of bad behavior if nothing else.

"Keep up like this and she'll get a change of venue," mused Tim.

"What are you looking at?" Alana shrieked, as the pulp flowed in chunky waves down the top of her head. She spat out some of the lees and took another rough breath.

Rama and Dali let out their weird cries again.

"Orgle."

I glanced sharply to Rob. His eyes were just a little too sparkly.

"That's the name for the llama noise."

"Good to know."

"Yup."

Despite llama drama and apple pulp, the Chief had maintained his NYPD game face through it all. Now, with only a little twitch of the muscles in his jaw, he nodded to the only patrol officer on duty, Laroche, to help his suspect out of the vat.

Alana understandably took that as an effort at arrest, and shrank over to the other side of the tub, shrieking again.

"I'm telling you, I was sick of it all, but I didn't try to kill him!"

A few minutes ago, she'd been one of those overly perfect women who make me – and a lot of other scruffy females – extremely uncomfortable. Now, though, she looked like a walking serving of applesauce, as the pulp oozed down her face and upper body like some sort of bizarre beauty treatment. Probably full of natural fruit acids… I should ask Maeve.

Maeve.

Beauty.

We might indeed be making a terrible mistake.

I turned to Ryan and Xavi. "That hand you saw, was there nail polish?"

Ryan scrunched up her face. "All I saw was the metal bracelet, the one they both have."

Xavi shrugged. "The nails were kind of shiny, but no color."

"Not even white on the tips?"

"Not white. More like a yellow color."

Yellow. Like a man whose body was slowly failing, say.

"Chief," I said. My command presence tone works on or off the air.

Even the llamas turned the volume down a little. That was kind of cool.

Everyone looked at me. That wasn't so cool. I'm on the radio for a reason. *Shake it off, it's not about you.*

"What's up, Jaye?" He turned from supervising Mrs. Harmon's extraction from the barrel.

"It wasn't her."

His eyes narrowed a little.

I stared hard at Mitch Harmon. "They'll figure it out. There will be fingerprints on the cup."

"Mitch!" Alana shrieked again as it hit her. "You son of a b—"

Halfway out of the vat, now, she tried to escape from Laroche, fighting to get at her husband. The cop held her around the middle like an angry toddler, as she kicked and squawked, pulpy apple bits splashing from her boots and her hair.

"You shouldn't get to go on without me." The sick man's voice was quiet, weary, but no less poisonous for it. "I've seen it in your face. Wishing it was over. Wishing I was gone."

"I didn't wish you were gone."

But she did wish it was over. I knew that feeling. You can only watch someone you love suffer for so long. And if it was less about love than status and money? More, if there was real animosity there, not just the daily struggle and the sudden appearances from the Mean Guy?

She might well have been wishing for the end.

"Close enough," Mitch Harmon said. "If I have to leave, you do too."

As if she were the wife of some ancient Pharoah waiting to be walled in his tomb with him.

"So you admit you put your painkillers in the cider?" Chief George asked Harmon, his voice calm but very hard.

"Of course I did." He shook his head, and something very much like despair came into his face. "I didn't mean any harm to come to Cuthbert Storey. Is he going to make it?"

"The Narcan worked, but it's going to be a while until they know." Chief George held his new suspect's gaze with cold intensity. "Why here?"

"Why not?" Mitch shrugged, one of the few people in the world not intimidated by the Chief. "I figured people would think it had something to do with the dispute over the orchard and the dollar store… and there'd never be enough evidence to figure it out anyway. Some folks would probably give that uppity orchard woman a medal."

"Just another bad thriller plot," his wife spat, with at least a little actual spit and apple bits. Laroche winced in revulsion. "And it didn't even work."

"Too bad." Amazing how much hate Mitch managed to pack into those two words.

Enough hate for more than one killing.

Maybe more than one attempt, I thought suddenly, remembering my cider.

"What about the second cup?" I asked. "Insurance?"

"I didn't do a second cup. I told you I didn't want to harm anyone but her."

For a moment, we all stood there staring at each other.

"You mean the cup Orville brought to you?" Felicia Bell sighed, with a sheepish head shake. "Oh, that was me."

"What?" For one hot second, there was a real possibility that I might cry.

"I'm sorry. It wasn't anything really bad," she said quickly, reaching around Tim in an effort to pat my arm. "It was just stupid. I'm so sorry. All I did was spit my cough drop into it. For Cuthbert because we're in real trouble. Thanks to that mess at the end of the road. I put the cup down for him, but then Orville picked it up and started walking over to you and I couldn't—"

Felicia Bell was the one who burst into tears, which shocked me nearly as much as the fact that *I'd* almost done it.

Tim turned to Chief George with a dubious shrug. "I don't know how you would charge it, but I would have a really hard time getting a conviction for a stupid prank – especially when nobody got hurt."

He and the Chief both looked at me. I shrugged. Why make her life any harder than it already was? I knew for tough and I didn't need to pay *that* forward.

The Chief nodded gravely, then favored Felicia with the NYPD hard look for a full twenty seconds because he knew that was all he could do.

"It's not going to help, you know," he said finally, in a quieter tone than I expected.

"No, but I'm going to have a word with that snotty development director," Sadie put in, stepping into the middle of the scene. "Let's just see what we can do before we start giving up. Assuming Cuthbert comes through, he may not have the energy to fight any re-use plans. Come along, Felicia."

Sadie's tone left no doubt. She put an arm around Felicia and led toward the door. As they passed Orville and Oliver, Sadie nodded to the two and they joined her. Looked like the town was taking care of its own.

Everyone stared for a few seconds.

"What about these two?" Chief George asked Tim, indicating Mitch and Alana, who despite their status as the principals in the only felony case, had almost been forgotten.

"Oh, you've got a solid attempted murder charge for him anyhow." Tim returned the Chief's cool gaze. "Let me know what you need."

Rob shook his head. So much for happy family time tonight. He gave his husband a wry little smile. "Guess I'm watching *Law and Order* and you're living it."

"Something like that," Tim agreed. "Maybe a bad movie."

"Mitch would know about that!" Alana snapped, clearly wanting to get a few more licks in.

Chief George tensed. "Mrs. Harmon."

"How about it, Mitch? Write another script that you can't sell," Alana taunted her husband.

"Sold enough to keep you in overpriced shoes!" Mitch shot back.

"Till you decided that everybody had to care about your damn cancer story."

For what seemed like an eternity but was probably only about ten seconds, they stared at each other, the poison and hate almost shimmering between them like heat rising from pavement in the summer.

My stomach twisted. David and I could so easily have ended up there. If the treatment hadn't worked, if we hadn't been able to keep our focus on Ryan's needs and not our own pain...

Mitch took a ragged breath and turned to Chief George. "I'll be dead before you convict me. But I'll live long enough to change my will so *she* doesn't get anything."

"Joke's on you." Alana Harmon hissed, shaking her head to send more apple splatter onto poor Laroche. "I've still got the money from my trust, so I'll be fine after that man or his family take every penny of yours. I'll be on a beach with some hot cabana boy when you die in prison."

It might have been a stupid and unoriginal comment, but it hit Mitch hard. He seemed to crumple from the center. Chief George stepped in and grabbed his arm.

"We can arraign you just as easily in a hospital bed." The Chief's tone was surprisingly gentle.

Alana Harmon's wasn't. "I hope you *rot*."

"I'm rotting already." Mitch took a breath and winced. The malice and anger suddenly drained from his face, and he looked like the dying man he actually was. "I really didn't want to kill anyone but Alana."

The Chief nodded. "Doesn't change anything, but it's good to know."

We all stared as he led Mitch away.

My Hebrew is too basic for me to offer any kind of proper prayer for the dying, but I was more than happy to ask God to be good to Mitch… and thank Them (Maeve's pronoun habits are rubbing off on me!) for sparing David and me that level of poison.

When your life is consumed with *not* dying, you forget that there are things worse than death.

"Let go of me! I'm going back to my hotel right now!" Alana Harmon snapped.

"I don't want to spend another second with you people and your damn apples!"

No one pointed out that we didn't want to spend another second with her. Always be polite to the tourists.

Part 9 – Just Deserts

"Hey, Ma, want some candy apple?"

I was pulling commercials and music for the first hour of my evening all-request show. The email box had been loaded with requests, which suggested that the Apple Festival remote was a success, despite the untoward events. My favorite request was from Olga Pushkin: Mary J.

Blige's "No More Drama," for Rama and Dali. You bet I was going to play that – in a prominent spot after the first break.

Neptune, our giant gray cat, was sitting on the old turntable cabinet, half asleep. He preferred Ryan's company to mine, but had a hard time resisting the opportunity to doze in the warm corner, though he periodically woke up to disparage the locals' taste in music. He'd been known to howl along with Celine Dion.

Supply your own joke here.

Ryan walked into the studio, wearing her favorite faded pink sweatshirt, which read **DO THE MATH** in holographic glitter, her hair damp, smelling of buttercream frosting body wash, the signature scent of the tween – and often enough, her mom. She had a book in one hand, the bio of Sally Ride she was finishing for a report, and her vile purchase from the Sunday School booth in the other.

"Ugh. I can't imagine how you eat that stuff." I looked at the hard, shiny red finish. Fine for cars, but not food.

Everybody buys them, but I doubt anyone actually EATS them.

"I don't want to eat all of the fudge tonight," Ryan said as she sat down in the guest spot, cultivating a virtuous expression. "So I'm trying to be healthy. Sort of."

"Really sort of. You know what's in those things?"

"I should – I saw the Sunday School kids making 'em on the hot plate. They were laughing and having a great time."

She sounded a little wistful. Her Hebrew School was at the Hillel at David's college twenty minutes away, and she didn't get to many social activities. Neptune heard the note in his girl's voice and walked right over the board, which thankfully wasn't on yet, to lick her nose.

Ryan giggled and scratched under his chin. "Good kitty."

His Majesty graciously accepted tribute for a full thirty seconds, purring like a jet engine, and then noticed the apple sitting on top of the book. *What's this? Something new to explore?*

Like many cats, Neptune likes to chew on cellophane, so he happily crunched away at the wrapper for a moment, then sniffed at the apple itself.

He let out a squawk and backed off.

"See? Neptune doesn't like it either."

"What's so horrible about the red shell?" Ryan took a closer look as Neptune ostentatiously cleaned himself. "It's just melted cinnamon candies and a bottle of something clear. Flavoring, right?"

"Maybe corn syrup. What kind of bottle?"

"Looked like something from the drugstore."

I remembered Xavi saying the Confirmation Class had told him that this year's apples were special. Surely not that kind of special.

Ryan caught my expression and put down the apple. "You don't think…"

"I don't know. But after this day, we're not taking any chances." I picked up my phone and hit Maeve's number.

Thirty seconds later, we knew that the — thankfully — very few people who'd actually taken a bite of those beautiful apples were spending the rest of the weekend in the bathroom… and Cooper the class clown and his willing accomplices were in very serious trouble indeed.

Plus Tim had yet more affidavits to write. Good thing Xavi liked hanging out with Dad during dinner service.

The Sunday Schoolers didn't need to worry about the law or the Lord, though. They needed to worry about Maeve.

Ryan's apple went in a bag at the bottom of the filing cabinet until I could give it to Chief George in the morning. She took the rest of her choco-peanut butter fudge and her book up to the apartment, while I started the night shift.

At long last, we had restored order, such as it was.

The show was still new enough that I got a kick out of picking my own songs to mix in between the requests. In the City, the desk jockeys and consultants tell you what "tests well" and that's what you have to play. If you want to keep the nice union job that feeds the kid.

Not here.

I did my open, reminded everyone that I was here to take their requests, and hit my song. The first one is always my choice; it's my announcement that I'm here, my little statement. After this insane day, I was in the mood for some 80's cheese, so I started out with Night Ranger. It's so overwrought it makes me giggle… and it's in my key so I can sing along.

Which I fully intended to do. Once the mic was off, of course.

But no. The phone lamp blinked right after I fired the song. The ringer is only audible upstairs, to prevent nasty little surprises during the show.

"WSV, Good Evening. What's your request?"

"You answer your own phone."

I couldn't help laughing, even though I thought I recognized the voice. "Who else would pick up?"

"Well, your staff…" Governor Will Ten Broeck broke off in a chuckle. "You *are* the staff."

"Since my assistant is doing her homework, yep, it's just me."

"I should know better."

"Probably. But you were in the big leagues, so you get a break." He'd been a Cabinet secretary at one point, after all; he probably hadn't answered his own phone the whole time.

"Double-A ball is more fun."

"Go Lake Monsters." I remembered that he was the Burlington team's highest-profile fan.

"Absolutely. Always love a good game."

I was sure that I wasn't hearing what I thought I heard in his voice. Better not embarrass myself here. I pulled my tone back to friendly, but not too warm. "Anyway, I'm really glad you called back. The folks at the Apple Festival will be happy to hear from you."

"Glad to. Too bad I can't be there this year. Maybe next."

"We'll look forward to it."

"Good. Everything okay down in Simpson?" His voice turned

serious, professional. "Something about tainted cider?

It is a very small state. No surprise that he'd heard the highlights. "Chief Orr will probably put out a release in the morning. Looks like a dying man accidentally poisoned a local because he was angry that his wife was going to outlive him."

I still talk like a reporter sometimes.

The Governor gave a low whistle. "Tough stuff."

"Not much tougher." I definitely did not want to go there. "But the suspect's in custody, and no one else was hurt. Cuthbert Storey is hanging on—"

"Wait. Cuthbert Storey? The guy who sold land to Dollar Depot?"

"Um, yeah." I'd known Will Ten Broeck was a detail guy, but wow. "Why?"

"Let's just say my friend in the U.S. Attorney's office will be glad to know he survived."

"Well, then." I'd been a reporter long enough to know that the phrasing meant he wouldn't say more. And that Cuthbert Storey might soon wish Mitch Harmon had been a better poisoner.

"Nice." Will Ten Broeck sounded downright admiring.

"What?" I asked.

"You didn't ask anything else. Smart. You know how they play in the big leagues."

"No point in making it to the show if you don't learn the rules."

"Isn't that the truth." A pause, as if he were thinking about something. "Thanks for the info."

"My pleasure," I said, and immediately regretted it. From a typical female with a high, brittle voice, it would have been a mere pleasantry. Not from me, a classic Queen of the Night, as radio people sometimes call a woman with a low, husky sound.

"Sounds like you're all going to come out okay, then." Thankfully, the Governor ignored the mild double entendre, but his careful tone suggested he hadn't missed it.

"All's well that ends."

"Not quite the way Mr. Shakespeare put it, but I get you."

"Yeah."

For probably a full twenty seconds, we were both silent. Not uncomfortably.

Then, he took a breath as if he were shaking something off. "So I shouldn't take up too much of your time…"

"It's fine, I'm in a song. Let me do a quick consent to tape." It had been a few years since I'd done one on the phone, and I almost referred to myself as Jaye Jordan Metz. I could tell he caught it, but he didn't say anything.

"All right," I said, keeping my voice as cool as I could, "let's talk up those lovely apples. What's your favorite?"

"Macoun – they don't ship well, so you don't get them much outside Vermont, you know."

Maybe two minutes later, the interview done and duly checked (no point getting tape if it didn't record), we wrapped up, keeping a nice civil tone, though it still felt like something was simmering underneath.

Yeah, right it was. Get over your damn self, girl.

"Well, good luck in your new endeavor," Governor Ten Broeck said, his phrasing maybe just a little too careful.

"*Too Late to Turn Back Now*…and other bad power ballads."

He laughed. Not the big, jovial one I'd heard when people joked with him in public, but a softer, more intimate sound. More real. "Maybe you could play me a request sometime."

"I could probably spin something for 'a friend in Montpelier.'"

"Ms. Jordan," he said, in a low, warm tone that made me think of maple smoke and things I wasn't ready to hear yet, "you always have a friend in Montpelier."

Good to know.

The Black Glove
Issy Jinarmo

DI Mark Whitehead examined the black soft leather glove in the plastic evidence bag handed to him by his sergeant, Rob Archer. It looked like the kind of glove someone would use for driving, rather than stable work.

"Where was this found?"

"Near the ransom note on the stable door. Do you think one of the kidnappers dropped it by mistake?"

"We'll let Forensics worry about that. In the meantime, let's find the two victims."

A frantic Triple 0 call had been received from Susannah and Roger Fortescue, owners of an extremely successful South Australian vineyard. The first inkling they had that something was wrong was when they had found the ransom note. It demanded $150,000 be left in their roadside mailbox by the next morning if they wanted to see their 10 year-old son, Adrian again. He and his instructor, Amanda Gillis, had failed to return home from a ride around the family's vast vineyard that morning.

Handing the glove back to Archer, Mark asked, "How's it going with the interviews?"

"I've still to get in contact with the stable staff. I've phoned the manager's mobile, but it went straight to voicemail."

"Keep trying. He can't be far away." He pointed across the stable yard. "I believe that's his 4x4 over there."

"Will do, boss. Where will you be when I'm done with him?"

"I'm going to take a walk around this place and have a think. It's all too smooth to be an impulse crime."

*****

DS Archer finally found the stable manager as he was returning from the lower paddock. He was a short, stocky man, sun-tanned complexion and sun-bleached hair. He reminded Archer of several failed jockeys he'd known in the past. *Those that can, do. Those that can't...become stable managers.*

Archer wasted no time on niceties: "Charlie Coleport?"

"Who's asking?"

"DS Archer. I want to talk to you about the kidnapping this morning."

"What's to talk about? Amanda went out with the boy for their regular mid-week ride around the property at 8.30am. They're usually back by 10.30 to 11 at the latest. When their horses returned to the stables rider-less, I knew something was wrong."

"You raised the alarm?"

"I told the Fortescues, then rode out to see if I could find them. There's a river running through the bottom paddock, and it wouldn't be the first time the boy has found himself in trouble trying to cross it."

"And they were carrying phones?"

"Not sure about Amanda, but Adrian's never away from the thing. Anyway, I've already shown your lot where they'd gone. What more am I expected to do? Find them for you?"

Archer ignored the animosity, but noted the man's body language; overly defensive and obviously nervous. *What are you hiding? Are you protecting someone?*

He pulled out the evidence bag with the black glove in it.

"You wouldn't happen to recognise this, would you?"

"No."

Archer offered it to him again. "Perhaps you should take a proper look at it?"

Coleport snatched the black glove, gave it a quick glance, immediately handing it back. "I'm sure it doesn't belong to Adrian, or Amanda. Now are we done?"

"For the moment. But don't stray too far. We'll probably have more questions as the investigation continues."

*****

The kidnapping was having a disturbing effect on Mark. As he walked round the vineyard a vision of his 2 year-old son, Joel kept playing on his mind. *What if someone kidnapped his precious child?*

The thought of this happening was beyond belief. How agonising this would be for him and his wife, Jenny. How unbearable must the uncertainty be for the Fortescue family?

As he met up with DS Archer, he shook his head and promised himself the missing boy and his riding instructor must be found 'alive.'

Archer held up his smart phone. "I checked and Coleport's got previous for theft. Mostly petty stuff, but...."

Mark sensed the uncertainty in Archer's voice. "You think he's good for small stuff, but not for something as full on as kidnapping?"

Archer nodded. "He just seems too nervous to be reliable."

"Okay, keep him on the suspects' list until we can rule him out completely. Maybe he helped by providing a layout of the stables, staff timetables, or when the two go out riding."

"Will do."

"Right, I'm off to interview the house staff. Stay in touch with the station, we need an initial report from Forensics about the glove as soon as possible.

*****

There was something about the housekeeper DI Whitehead thought when he was greeted at the front door of the Fortescue's large home, situated a fair distance from the stables. She looked to be in her early forties, mousey brown hair pulled back neatly, and a face that seemed vaguely familiar.

Half squinting, Mark said, "I'm DI Whitehead. Excuse me, but haven't we met before?"

She tried to mask her surprise. "I don't think so."

Of all the bad luck, she thought. *The same bloody cop who put me away five years ago for Extortion.*

Mark blinked several times. "Actually I do remember you, Megan Fields. Two years for obtaining money with menaces. Do the Fortescues know what you've been up for?"

The Black Glove

"They didn't ask, and I've not told them. Anyway, I've got nothing to do with this kidnapping, so don't think you can pin this on me."

"You're still a subject of interest, Megan, so don't think about doing a runner."

He paused for a moment adding, "You've still got a couple of years before your conviction's classed as spent. Play nice, or I might be forced to tell the Fortescues about your past."

She gave a low groan. "Look, I've told you, kidnapping is way out of my league. Anyway, Amanda's always been good to me — we sort of look after each other. And the boy's not bad either."

"You've not seen any strangers hanging around? No old mates from your days living up in Darwin?"

"I moved interstate to make a fresh start. I'm not going to mess that up, however, oddly enough, I recently did get a visit from an old acquaintance from Darwin — John Fitzgerald. He was looking for work, said he was short of money. I told him to see Mr. Fortescue and not bother me again. Charlie has since told me he picked up some casual work here and is hanging around with Amanda!" She paused. She sensed DI Whitehead was about to interject. "….and, before you ask, yes, I did warn Amanda to watch him!"

"Well, Megan, thanks for that information. Obviously, you can account for your whereabouts?"

"Are you serious? Of course I can. I've been here sorting out the week's deliveries and making sure the Fortestscues are fed and watered. The agency cleaner comes on Thursdays, and Mrs. Fortescue follows her around to make sure she doesn't pocket anything.

"So, there's just you, Amanda Gillis and Charlie Coleport?"

Behind Mark Whitehead came the hiss of air brakes as a Kenworth semi-trailer carrying a Mobile Incident Room arrived in the stable courtyard.

*****

Sitting at a plastic desk in the main section of the MIR, DI Whitehead said, "Interesting, eh?"

Archer looked over his computer screen. "What is, sir?"

"We've been re-acquainted with a couple of 'old friends' but we both don't think this kidnapping would be their style."

A motorcycle courier stepped into the demountable, took off his helmet and looked around until he spotted DS Archer.

"Evidence box to go over to Forensics?"

Archer picked up a package the size of four house bricks. "There you go. We need a rush on the DNA and a trace from the glove. Also, if there's anything on the ransom note. The other samples are included for elimination."

Package in hand, the courier put his helmet back on and departed, motorbike lights flashing.

Mark checked the digital clock on the wall, 16.20. The ransom note said the kidnappers would call at 16.45. He looked at Archer and inclined his head towards the door. "Come on, let's update the poor parents."

*****

The main lounge of the Fortescue's house was styled in tasteful designer opulence. Floor to ceiling glass doors made up an external wall, high polished floor, and lighting that dropped 3m from the ceiling, yet still remained 1.5m above head level. Sofas replaced chairs. The back wall had several doors leading off, and against it was a well-stocked bar. At the far end of the room a glass staircase and banister led up to the bedrooms.

Susannah Fortescue sat on one of the sofas holding a glass of red wine. Roger Fortescue was standing near one of the glass doors. Since their arrival Mark had observed Roger knock back several straight Chivas Regals with only a slight pause for breath.

He waved his glass at Whitehead. "Let me guess, you've found nothing so far?" He made it sound more like an accusation than a question.

"We've a few things we're looking to follow up on." Mark didn't want to give too much away — especially as Megan Fields and Charlie Coleport seemed to be making new lives for themselves. At least that was the initial impression. "However, we should know more once the kidnappers call in." He pointed to the smart phone which was plugged into a Wi-Fi repeater. "Our tech boys are on standby back at headquarters. Once the call comes in, give them five seconds to start chasing the signal towers, then answer the phone,"

"And then what?" Again, there was a tone to Roger Fortescue's voice — something that irritated Mark, but he tried not to let it get under his skin.

"Then we find out what the demands are, and work on getting your son back safe and sound."

"You need to ask for proof of life before you start any bloody negotiations and not just for Adrian, there's also Amanda to worry about as well," Susannah was close to tears.

Roger glared at her. "Do you think I don't know that? What do you take me for?"

"At the moment, a half-drunk idiot."

Thankfully, the mobile phone on the coffee table burped into life before the conversation had a chance to develop into a full-scale argument.

Archer said, "Five, four, three, two…" then, silently, pointed to the phone.

Roger picked it up, placing it on speaker. "Hello?"

The voice at the end of the phone sounded like someone wearing a Darth Vader mask.

"Mr. Fortescue?"

"Yes."

"We've someone here who would like to talk to you. Say hello to your dad."

The sound of the phone being handled was closely followed by a child's voice, "Dad? Are you there?"

Susannah's glass slipped from her fingers and smashed on the floor. "Adrian!"

"Mum is that…"

The phone was pulled back, and Darth Vader's voice returned.

"Mr. Fortescue, you've been a very naughty man."

"Sorry, what?" Roger sounded genuinely confused.

"You invited the police to our little party."

"No, I…"

"DON'T LIE TO ME! We saw their demountable arrive earlier. That wasn't part of our deal, was it? You need to be punished." The sound of Adrian screaming in pain and terror came from the phone at full volume, generating a scream from Susannah, and causing Roger to almost drop the phone.

The screams died into sobbing and the voice said, "That's what happens if you keep a teaspoon in a cup of hot coffee for a minute, then hold it to the back of your son's hand. The next time it will be a kitchen blow torch. Do I make myself clear?"

Susannah sat on the couch, nodding and whimpering. Roger kept staring at the phone in disbelief, "I…"

"Do. I. Make. My. Self. Clear. Or do you want your son hurt some more?"

Roger looked at the phone in the palm of his hand. "No!"

"Now, because you've involved the police, the ransom's increased. We're putting it up to $200,000. Leave it in your mailbox by tomorrow morning or we'll start mailing Adrian back to you, piece by piece."

Roger glared at the phone. "We don't have that kind of money to hand!"

"I'm sure you have some assets you could sign over to the bank."

"At this time of day, what on earth are you talking about?"

But the phone had already gone dead.

*****

Mark and Rob returned to the Mobile Incident Room. Rob checked his computer. "The tech boys have located the phone the kidnappers used. It was strapped to a battery power two-metre radio. One number, on voice recognition. The radio transmitter could've been anywhere — SUV, back of a ute, or a covered truck. Call the receiver, say the name to the smart phone and the thing dials out regardless."

Mark shook his head. "So we've no idea where they were calling from?"

"No, but …." He stopped as his mobile started ringing. "Hello?"

"Forensics here, Sir. We'll have the DNA results from the black leather glove found at the Fortescues' back to you as quickly as possible. We've found something interesting though. It matches a glove found at the scene of another crime which was sent to us for profiling several months ago. That profile fits one John Fitzgerald, wanted for extortion and murder in the Northern Territory. Our sources tell us he is believed to be hiding out somewhere in South Australia. He has, so far, escaped detection."

Rob Archer relayed the news to Mark Whitehead.

"John Fitzgerald? How interesting. That's the bloke from Darwin who visited Megan. He's been grape picking for the Fortescues and hanging around Amanda!"

Mark immediately called Roger Fortescue. "What do you know about a guy named John Fitzgerald? Evidently, he's been spending time with Amanda Gillis."

"Not a lot," replied Roger. "Bit of a surly chap. Tall, good-looking though. I guess that's why she's taken with him. Me, personally, I don't like him but he's a good worker. I believe our housekeeper, Megan Fields knew him when she lived in Darwin. He came down to South Australia looking for work. He's been doing some casual work here with the back-packers who travel round the area picking grapes. Why do you ask?"

"His DNA was found on a glove that matches the one found near the ransom note. By sheer luck, the same lab is doing our profiling and let us know. Makes him a suspect!"

"My God," roared Roger. "I said I didn't like him. Maybe he dropped the glove when visiting Amanda in the stables?"

"I've a couple of calls to make then DS Archer and I will be over to your place. We need a sample of everyone's handwriting." He looked at the clock. Time was moving fast; abduction cases were notoriously less likely to have a happy ending the more the time passed.

He phoned Megan Fields. "I will be perfectly frank with you, Megan. Time is running out and we've received evidence your *friend,* John

Fitzgerald, could have something to do with this crime."

"What do you want me to do, confess to the kidnapping?" Megan replied in a loud voice. "I told you earlier I now nothing, absolutely nothing."

"Fitzgerald is wanted for extortion and murder in the Northern Territory."

"What?" Hang on, I know nothing about what he's been doing up in the Territory."

"We have evidence that links your friend to the disappearance of Adrian and Amanda."

After a few seconds of silence, Megan replied, "Look, he's not that much of a friend."

Mark's long experience told him he wouldn't completely exclude Megan from his investigations but he was nearly 100% convinced she was telling the truth.

"That's all for now. You're not off the hook yet. I would appreciate you letting us know if you catch sight of Fitzgerald."

Rob Archer smiled at his boss in support. "Shall we…" His mobile rang. He smiled. Forensics had found traces of Cabernet Franc grape on the black glove.

"At last we could be getting somewhere, boss. The Cabernet Franc grape is grown in very few vineyards in South Australia. The Fortescues don't grow it, therefore, the traces didn't come from anyone living here so it lets the Fortescues, Amanda, Megan and Charlie off the hook for the time being. We're looking for someone who has been handling that grape."

Mark Whitehead stretched out in his chair. "Well, Rob I think…" His sentence was cut short by the arrival of a police constable. "What can we help you with, constable?"

"Sir, my sergeant thought you should know we observed someone in a hoodie loitering near the mailbox located on the vineyard approach road. Sorry, Sir, I gave chase but he was too fast for me. He ran into the vines and I lost him."

Mark groaned. "I appreciate your honesty, constable. Where does that leave us?"

"Er, er," stammered the constable. "It's not all bad news. My sergeant checked the mailbox. There was a brown paper parcel inside which he carefully opened, thankfully with gloves on," the constable hurriedly added. "He found this," He displayed a plastic evidence bag containing an old metal tobacco tin. "There's a lock of hair inside, and a note."

"Did your sergeant read the note?"

The constable gave Mark a sheepish look. "Well, he did sort of say we'd better get it to you as quickly as possible, Sir."

"Thank you, and thank your sergeant, too. I'll have a word with him later."

The constable left the room. Mark put gloves on and opened the tobacco tin. Inside lay a lock of light brown hair and a note — *As we said, there's worse to come. Pay the $200,000 by the morning or it will be Adrian's burnt hand next.*

*****

DI Whitehead and Sergeant Archer were welcomed at the Fortescue's house by Megan Fields. She escorted them to the lounge room where Susannah and Roger Fortescue were seated on one of the sofas.

"We've some good and bad news," announced Mark. "The good news, traces of the Cabernet Franc grape were found on the glove at the stables."

"Cabernet Franc!" exclaimed Roger. "Well, that narrows the field, doesn't it? Not many vineyards grow that varietal. It could mean Adrian and Amanda are where the grape is grown."

"Yes, Roger, it does to a degree," replied Mark. "The bad news is this." He handed the couple the evidence bag revealing the contents of the tobacco tin. "Is this the colour of Adrian's hair?"

Susannah burst into tears. "Oh no! They've cut Adrian's hair."

Roger was about to comfort his wife when his phone rang.

"Y-y-yes, we did," he stammered. Please, I beg you, do not harm our boy. Yes, I managed to secure the money you've asked for. It will be in the mailbox in the morning...."

Mark indicated to Roger to keep the caller talking.

"Please let me speak to him again. His mother and I need to know he's okay," Roger pleaded.

A shrill scream was heard followed by silence as the connection was broken.

Susannah's sobbing filled the room.

A few minutes later Archer's phone rang. "Yes, okay, I'll let him know. Thanks."

He ushered Mark Whitehead out of the room. "That was the tech boys. The call was traced to the *Galloway Arms Hotel,* coincidentally where the barman has just phoned Triple 0 to report a body has been found dumped in the car park. Accompanying the body was a bottle of Cabernet Franc!"

Mark and Rob made a quick exit from the Fortescue's home and drove to the *Galloway Arms Hotel.*

"No one is to leave the premises," Rob Archer informed the barman as he led Mark and Rob to the car park to examine the corpse.

"Did you see anyone using the bar pay phone?"

The barman shook his head.

"Did you notice anything suspicious?"

The barman responded again that it had been far too busy to notice the comings and goings of patrons.

"Do you know the deceased?" Mark asked.

"I've seen him. He's a backpacker. He picks grapes, that's all I know."

"The coroner is on his way. Looks like those gashes on his head caused his death."

"Stay with the body, Rob, till the Coroner arrives," Mark said. "I'll start questioning everyone inside.

The Coroner confirmed the body had suffered blunt force trauma to his head. Time of death 17.15.

With the body off to the morgue, Rob joined Mark Whitehead inside the *Galloway Arms Hotel.*

"Rob," said Mark. "This is Joe, a patron of the hotel. After the deceased backpacker made a phone call, he saw him arguing quite violently with a person wearing a hoodie. He's identified the backpacker as Sven Eriksson from Sweden. He doesn't know who the person in the hoodie was. But he also says he saw a bloke on a mobile hanging around in the car park. He was gone when your lot arrived. This all happened shortly before the bistro opened."

"Do you think the person in the hoodie killed him?"

"Highly likely, Rob," replied Mark. "He was probably murdered to keep him quiet. We still don't know who threatened the Fortescues while we were at the house. It could be the bloke on the mobile? The person in the hoodie could be the same person who put the parcel in the Fortescue's mailbox. We'll take Joe to the MIR for a statement. His description of a tall male of slight build is identical to that of the hooded person described by the police positioned near the Fortescue's roadside mailbox. "

"We are, of course, assuming it was a male. It could be a tall woman?" Suggested Rob.

"Good thought. Amanda fits that description. What is confusing, however, is that the DNA on the gloves is Fitzgerald's. Could she have set Fitzgerald up to carry out the abduction? According to the NT Police, he constantly denied he was implicated in the crimes he was accused of. Find out where he hangs out, Rob."

"If Fitzgerald wore riding gloves," pondered Rob, "Amanda could have planted them to involve him and what about the bottle of Cabernet Franc we found beside Sven's body?"

"That could have been planted to implicate Sven. We need to compare the ransom note writing with a sample of Amanda's but, more importantly, let's concentrate on locating Fitzgerald," Mark said as he checked his watch. Time was fast running out. The kidnappers were expecting 'payment' in a few hours' time.

*****

Susannah and Roger Fortescue spent a restless night. Sleep evaded them. They were both agonising about Adrian's welfare and safety. At dawn Roger could wait no longer.

"I'm taking the money to the mailbox now. Even though we don't know the collection time, after all our negotiations to raise the money, I don't want anything to go wrong."

"Didn't DI Whitehead say they would be here by 6am and to wait for him?" interjected Susannah.

"I can't wait, I am off now," Roger said, unlocking the safe.

"I'll come too," Susannah said, reaching for her clothes.

"No, No, Susannah. I don't want to worry about you too. You stay here. I'll be okay. I'll just place the money in the mailbox and come straight back."

Susannah sank back in bed, admitting to herself she was actually relieved Roger didn't want her to accompany him. She was terrified of seeing the kidnappers and even more terrified that she might recognise them. Suppose it was Megan's acquaintance, John Fitzgerald? He was a big man and the thought he may have terrorised Adrian was more than she could bear. His screams heard over the phone were still resonating in her ears and, more importantly, her heart.

As Roger slipped his camera equipment in his car, he speculated on how DI Whitehead and DS Archer would react when they arrived at 6am to find he had already left to deliver the money. He pulled off the road on to a grassy outcrop close to the mailbox, bringing his car to a halt beside a fence post. He got out of the car, looked right and left, then bent down as if he was checking his tyre. This provided him with the opportunity to attach a solar-powered Wi-Fi outdoor camera to the post. He stood up slowly. To anyone watching, including the police, they would assume he had assessed a possible tyre problem. He then drove a few metres further along the road, depositing the money in the mailbox. The only sound he heard, as he prayed Adrian would be returned unharmed, was that of the birds greeting the dawn.

*****

Meanwhile, Susannah had abandoned any hope of sleep, and was sitting on the verandah sipping a cup of tea as Mark Whitehead and Rob Archer arrived promptly at 6am. They were less than impressed when she told them what Roger had done.

"That is such an irresponsible action. Where is he now?" bellowed Mark.

"Didn't you see his car? He hasn't come back. I thought he may have waited to see if he could catch a glimpse of the kidnappers." Alarm bells began ringing in everyone's mind, Susannah breathlessly adding, "Oh, no! Roger could be in danger!"

*****

Meanwhile, his vehicle hidden, Roger was well concealed behind bushes on the grassy outcrop he had checked out earlier. It was 6.45am. In the distance, the roar of a motor bike engine broke the silence of the morning. His palms were sweaty. *This could be it,* he thought, praying the camera would capture a good image of those involved in his son's kidnapping. His shoulders slouched with disappointment as the motorbike sped by. False alarm! Susannah would not approve of what he was doing. He knew she would have told him to leave the surveillance to the police, but where were they?

Just after 7am a furniture truck trundled slowly up the road and stopped at the roadside mailbox. A hooded figure emerged from the passenger seat, looked around furtively then, quick as a flash, snatched the bag containing the money from the mailbox and ran to the rear of the truck where, to Roger's utter amazement, down the ramp sped a motorbike. Within a nanosecond, driver, passenger and Roger's money disappeared in a cloud of dust!

Stunned at the slickness of the pick-up, Roger sat for a moment in his hiding spot before standing up and walking over to collect his camera. Still in disbelief, he began disconnecting the camera as a police car came to an abrupt halt beside the mailbox. Roger was confronted by Whitehead while Archer walked over to inspect the furniture van.

"Mr. Fortescue, may I ask what the hell you are doing here?" Mark was angry that Adrian's father had taken matters into his own hands.

Roger looked forlornly at Mark; suddenly his expression changed. He screamed loudly as he saw DS Archer escorting Adrian down the ramp of the furniture van.

"Adrian! Adrian! Oh, son, are you hurt?"

Adrian ran into his father's open arms. "No Dad, I'm okay now. Amanda said we were having a fun night away and that you and mum were okay about it. When we arrived at the old house 'my' Amanda was tied up on a chair and I was very frightened."

"*Your* Amanda?" queried DI Whitehead.

"Yes, there were *two* Amandas. I was very confused."

"*Two* Amandas?" said a puzzled Archer.

"Yes, they looked exactly the same. The 'other' Amanda told me she was 'my' Amanda's twin sister, Lucy. I wouldn't have gone with her if I had known that. Honestly I wouldn't. She took my phone off me too."

Adrian's statement stunned everyone.

"It's okay, Adrian. You are safe now. I think we should get you back home to your mother and also let our doctor check you over," suggested Archer.

Mark Whitehead nodded. "Yes, young man. Off you go with Rob. We'll a get a statement from you later."

Roger was nonplussed by what his son had said. "Amanda is a twin. Maybe my camera has footage of her?"

"Your camera? What camera?"

"Um-m-h!" Roger paused for a second before replying. "I mounted a Wi-Fi camera on a fence post not far from the mailbox to, hopefully, record the kidnappers."

"You did?" Mark slapped Roger on the back and gave a laugh. "Good on you! Your son is safe mate, collect the camera for me then go home and celebrate his home-coming. Let's hope the camera footage will give us the break we are looking for. I'll call you later and we can all meet up in the MIR."

*****

Two hours later, DI Whitehead accompanied by DS Archer and a police woman, were joined by Roger, Susannah and Adrian Fortescue in the MIR.

"PC Marshall will look after Adrian for a while," explained Mark Whitehead as the police constable and Adrian left the room.

"We would like to bring you up to speed on where we are right now," he continued. "First of all, Amanda is okay. She's being interviewed at the police station and, as luck would have it, the motorbike duo ran out

The Black Glove

of petrol just out of town and are now in custody. Your camera footage identified the hoodie wearer as Lucy, Amanda's twin sister."

Susannah gave a groan. "Thank goodness. We are so relieved Amanda had nothing to do with the kidnapping."

Mark smiled reassuringly. "Lucy has been very co-operative. You will be very pleased to learn we have retrieved your money totally intact and she has actually confessed to the murder of Sven Eriksson who was found at the *Galloway Arms Hotel*. She and Fitzgerald were struggling cash-wise while living in Darwin. Fitzgerald, according to her, had plenty of ideas of how to get some easy money. He also knew it would only be a matter of time before the NT Police caught up with him. The fact that your housekeeper had helped him out years ago and Lucy's sister was here, prompted them to come to South Australia. Megan wasn't as co-operative as he hoped but he did get work on your grape-picking crew. Lucy, evidently, got in touch with Amanda but she told her to get lost. It was Lucy who cut off the lock of Adrian's hair and Fitzgerald who threatened you over the phone."

Susannah and Roger shook their heads in disbelief.

Mark continued, "We can't link Megan or Amanda to this crime. It was Lucy who struck up a friendship with Sven Eriksson at the backpacker's hostel. The inside information about local vineyards was passed on by Sven to Lucy and Fitzgerald. That's what led them to target you and kidnap Adrian. Lucy, after our constant questioning, admitted she had been jealous of Amanda her entire life and she saw this as a way to 'get even'"

Mark paused for a moment giving the Fortescues the opportunity to digest what he was telling them.

"The black gloves with the traces of the Cabernet Franc grape belonged to Fitzgerald. Lucy told us she and Fitzgerald did some grape picking at *Classique Wines,* the only local vineyard growing that grape."

Roger nodded his head. "Thank goodness for that."

"Yes, exactly," replied Mark. "Fitzgerald promised Sven a share of the ransom money. Sven became extremely impatient and threatening, so Lucy decided to 'quieten' him permanently. She then conned another backpacker who was temping for a furniture removal firm, to drive her and your son to the mailbox. Luckily, you had left the money there, Roger, as I don't think Lucy would have hesitated killing her sister and Adrian if the mailbox was empty."

Susannah shook her head in horror. "Have you arrested Fitzgerald?"

"He's proving to be slightly elusive right now," admitted Mark Whitehead. "I suggest you collect Adrian and go home. If you like, we will drive Amanda to the vineyard. This will give you the opportunity to thank her. Adrian is resilient, I feel sure he will settle back into family life quickly after this horrendous ordeal. We will leave a couple of our best men on duty at the vineyard. It will only be a matter of time before Fitzgerald shows up. After all, he is short of money."

*****

Twenty-four hours later, Roger received a phone call from DI Whitehead. "I'm happy to inform you we've apprehended Fitzgerald. He's spilled the beans regarding his part in the kidnapping and he's also providing the NT Police with information about his crimes up north."

"Thanks for letting us know. Had he got far away?"

"No, funnily enough, he hadn't. An attendant at a servo near Port Pirie called Triple 0, following which the Highway Patrol picked Fitzgerald up for failing to pay for his fuel, theft of a couple packets of sandwiches and, would you believe it, a pair of black motoring gloves."

Danger at Death's Door
N. M. Cedeño

Standing on the deck of the two-masted schooner *Donna* sailing across Death's Door towards Green Bay, Lars shoved his gloved hands into his coat pockets and hunched his broad shoulders against the icy wind. His thoughts were on his children. While he'd grown up in Copenhagen, a large city by any standard, the children had never been to a large town, let alone a city, and could have no idea of the dangers abounding in such places. Washington Island, where they knew everyone, was their home. Lars had done all he could to prepare his son and daughter for the perils they might face in bustling Marinette, Wisconsin. With the booming lumber industry, many unsavory and unscrupulous characters had moved to the Great Lakes region, including many men haunted by memories of the Civil War that had ended just six years earlier, around the time of his own arrival in the country.

Please God, the children's stay in town would be brief.

Lars regretted having to leave Sarah and Robbie with his half-sister Adele and her husband. But the children were too young to be left alone, and he couldn't care for them while working to feed them. Since Maggie's death in mid-winter, the children had grown substantially and now looked like ragamuffins in ill-fitting clothes. Five-year-old Robbie's jacket was too small, exposing his wrists, and the back of four-year-old Sarah's dress wouldn't button. Lars had tied the dress closed with ribbon stretched across the gap and then covered his makeshift closure with a round shawl.

With no ready-made clothing on the island, most mothers made their children's clothing. Without a mother, his children would soon have nothing to wear. The island women had enough work handling with their own families and couldn't help. They advised him to remarry quickly. Lars had no choice but to deliver Sarah and Robbie to his half-sister Adele in Marinette while he went about finding a new wife, though it was hard to imagine anyone replacing Maggie. His heart still ached for her.

Where he would find an unattached woman willing to face the starkness of island life and willing to marry him without being properly courted, he didn't know. However, he needed to find a bride quickly, before Robbie and Sarah became accustomed to their aunt's home and resented having to leave it to return to him. Maybe Adele would have some suggestions on where to find an appropriate bride.

The schooner *Donna* was an eighty-foot-long cargo ship meant for carrying cordwood, not a passenger ship. The captain, Olaf Olsen, was a friend from the island who was aware of the problem Lars faced. Olsen had offered them transport since he was already carrying loads of timber to the mills in Marinette. Lars and his children were the only passengers aboard ship so the captain had given them the aft cabin for their personal use during the passage.

The wind stung Lars's eyes, and he turned to verify that his children, whom he'd left snug in the cabin, hadn't ventured outside. Though April had come, the wind was frigid, and storm clouds were massing in the distance. Having worked along the lakes, Lars was wary when cold winds descended from Canada. He'd seen enough early fall and late spring blizzards to always be alert for changes in the weather. He studied the slate gray clouds hoping they'd reach Marinette before the storm caught them.

Lars noticed a flurry of activity on deck and realized the ship was changing course. He scanned the horizon and spied another ship, a three-masted schooner, in the distance. As the *Donna* drew closer, Lars noticed that the other ship was signaling distress. He couldn't immediately identify any trouble. Then a gust of wind carried the smell of smoke across the water. Fire! Every muscle in Lars's body tensed. Fire aboard ship during a voyage was deadly. Spotting no smoke, he breathed a sigh of relief. The crew must have managed to extinguish the flames.

As the *Donna* came alongside the damaged vessel, the *Fleur*, Lars crossed the deck to hear what was happening. The captain of the *Fleur*, which was double the size of the eighty-foot-long *Donna*, asked to move a few passengers to the *Donna*. He also asked for escort to the closest port, Marinette. He'd been sailing from Canada for Green Bay when the fire occurred.

Lars heard the *Donna*'s Captain Olsen ask, "What caused the fire?"

"Pirates attempted to take the ship. A tipped kerosene lantern caused the fire. We lost two crewman and had another injured during the attack," the *Fleur*'s captain replied.

Lars gripped the rail tightly. Pirates had been a problem on the Great Lakes, plundering docked ships, and trying to capture ships on the lakes, and working with moon-cussers who moved lights on shore to cause wrecks so they could scavenge the wreckage. Lars wished his children were safe at home with Maggie watching over them. A pang of grief washed over him. Maggie was gone or he wouldn't be out on the lakes with the children.

After a brief discussion, Captain Olsen agreed to escort the *Fleur* to Marinette, to take on the passengers displaced by the fire, and to send one of his own sailors to help the depleted crew handle their damaged ship.

Lars watched as the passengers from the *Fleur*, two men and a woman, were rowed to the *Donna* in increasingly rough waters. The ominous cloud front he'd observed earlier had raced closer to the *Donna* while the captain was responding to the *Fleur*'s call for aid. The wind rose causing the schooner to dip and rise on growing waves. The two male passengers climbed aboard the *Donna* before helping to lift the woman by rope onto the deck.

One of the men, a middle-aged clerk by his clothing, was expostulating officiously about the disposition of his trunk and his company's cargo on the *Fleur* and about the delay in reaching his destination in Green Bay. The woman, dressed in a modest, but inexpensive, dove gray traveling costume and straw bonnet, clung to a younger gentleman as if she might collapse without his assistance. The young gentleman, a youth barely in need of a razor and wearing a well-cut, expensive wool suit and overcoat, patted the woman's hand nervously, discomfited by her distress.

Lars retreated from the blustery deck to the cabin where he found his blanket-wrapped children sitting on a bench. "Robbie, Sarah, more people are coming to share the cabin. Shift to the floor and leave the chairs and bench for the others." Sarah clutched her rag doll and Robbie collected his carved wooden boat as they moved to the floor. Lars replaced the blanket around his children. "Stay here and be quiet. The people are upset."

"What happened, Papa?" Robbie asked.

"Another ship ran into trouble, and we're helping them. Be polite, but be cautious of the strangers."

Sarah snuggled close to her brother and nodded.

The cabin door opened, and the three new arrivals squeezed into the small space.

The querulous clerk stopped short on seeing the children. "Hmph."

"Excuse me," the young gentleman said, leading the woman around the clerk to seat her on the bench the children had vacated. Once he peeled her clinging hands from his arm, the young man hastily retreated, almost bumping into Lars in the tight space. "Pardon me, sir."

Lars, knowing his six-feet-three-inch height and broad shoulders could be intimidating, moved a step toward the children and said, "Think nothing of it. I'm Lars Pedersen, and these are my children, Robbie and Sarah."

The young man, lanky, but well-grown, tipped his fur hat to the children, "Pleased to meet you, Miss Sarah and Master Robbie. I'm Rupert Graham. Please call me Rupert." He slipped off his overcoat and folded it over his arm.

"Hello, Rupert," Robbie replied as Sarah hid her face in her brother's shoulder. "Sarah says hello, too, but you might not hear her. She's shy."

"That's quite understandable," Rupert said in an easy manner. He turned and extended a ready hand to Lars. "Sorry to crowd you like this, Mr. Pedersen."

Lars shook his hand. "It's not as if you had a choice."

"No, we didn't. I'll have a tale to tell when I get home. Mother may not let Father send me out on business alone again. Who'd have thought we'd encounter pirates?" He said the words with a relish that emphasized his youth.

Lars, estimating Rupert couldn't be more than eighteen-years-old, realized belatedly that the young man's words had caught Robbie's attention.

"Pirates? Where?" Robbie asked.

Rupert, after tossing an apologetic look to Lars, said in a reassuring voice to Robbie, "The pirates fled when the captain fired a cannon at their ship."

"Ooh, a cannon." Robbie's eyes grew as big as saucers.

"Children should be silent," the clerk said in a dampening tone with a look of reprimand for both Robbie and Lars. "I'm Mr. Friberg. I'm on important business for my company, G.L. Iron Ore. I shall be lodging a complaint with the authorities. Pirates should not be free to harass private vessels on these waters."

"No, they should not," Lars said in a placating tone as his eyes found the only passenger yet to be introduced. The woman sat on the bench with a handkerchief pressed to her mouth and nose. She was in her forties with a full figure. Her shoulders slumped as if she were exhausted. "Is there anything I can do for you, madam?"

"I'm Mrs. Beale. No, thank you, sir." Her voice sounded weak with fatigue. She inhaled, expanding her impressive bosom and opened her brown eyes into a wide, frantic stare. "It was terrible. I want to go home to my husband in Green Bay, but now we're going to Marinette."

The cabin door opened, and Captain Olsen appeared in the doorway. "Madam, gentlemen, welcome aboard. We will get you to Marinette as soon as possible." His eyes sought out Lars. "Lars, could I have a word?"

Surprised, Lars nodded and said, "Aye, Captain."

*****

Stepping outside, Lars followed the captain a few yards from the cabin door.

"Lars, we have a problem."

"What's that, Captain?" Lars braced himself against the icy wind and the rolling of the deck.

"Captain Jacques of the *Fleur* says the fire started before the pirates attacked. His men were distracted, putting out the fire, and didn't see the pirates approaching. They were lucky to fight the pirates off. The damage to the ship isn't severe, but he didn't want to risk continuing with a saboteur aboard."

"Someone set the fire to aid the pirates?"

"Ja."

Lars was stunned. "A passenger or one of the crew?"

"One of these passengers. The crew was accounted for when the fire started." Captain Olsen set his mouth in a grim line. "Can you keep watch on them? They shouldn't be able to cause trouble in such close quarters, but I don't want to take any chances."

"Aye, Captain, I can watch them. Who does Captain Jacques suspect?"

"He can't decide. Each one claims to have been alone when the fire started."

"So it could be any of them."

"One more thing." The captain leaned closer to Lars. "Captain Jacques was warned by authorities about passengers smuggling goods from Canada to the United States. He found no unreported cargo, but he thinks whichever passenger is in league with the pirates might be carrying contraband. I want you to find out if one of the passengers is carrying smuggled goods."

Lars stared at the captain, aghast. "I'm not an investigator or an officer of the law. Surely you are the best person to resolve this. You are the captain. You could search them. You have complete authority on your ship."

"I'm shorthanded, and we have to set watch for the pirates. You are an intelligent man. Well educated in the old country before you immigrated, weren't you?"

"Ja." Lars couldn't deny he was an educated bastard. His father, who wouldn't publicly acknowledge him, had paid for his education back in

Denmark. While the circumstances of his birth had limited Lars's life in Europe, here on the frontier, a man's capabilities earned him status and respect.

Captain Olsen clapped Lars on the shoulder. "You can detect the guilty party. Captain Jacques searched the passengers' luggage and found nothing. If there is anything to find, the smuggler must have it on his person. I trust you to handle this."

Lars rubbed his bearded chin, wondering where to begin. "I'll see what I can discover."

"Thank you, Lars." Captain Olsen left, returning to the foredeck.

Lars entered the cabin and found his children in conversation with Rupert, who was showing Robbie how to make a whizzer from a button threaded through a piece of string. Rupert demonstrated how to loop the button, twisting the string, and then pull sharply to set the button spinning. The clerk, Mr. Friberg, had taken a chair at the table by Mrs. Beale, who still sat hunched on the bench against the wall.

Lars considered the passengers from the *Fleur*. Young Rupert in his tailored, wool jacket and black trousers looked like a perfect young gentleman. If he were carrying contraband on his person, where would he hide it? In his hat and coat, perhaps, which he'd placed on hooks on the wall? Mr. Friberg wore a navy greatcoat over his clothing. He could have something concealed in it, perhaps sewn into it. And Mrs. Beale's dove gray traveling costume could hide anything beneath the voluminous skirts.

Lars joined Mr. Friberg and Mrs. Beale at the table. "The fire must have been terrifying. Were you very close to it, Mr. Friberg?"

"I'm lucky I wasn't burned alive. When I opened my cabin door, the passage was filled with smoke. I'd have perished if a sailor hadn't pushed me to my knees and directed me to crawl. My clothing still reeks of the smoke."

Lars made a sympathetic noise. "And you, Rupert? How did you escape?"

Rupert looked up from instructing Robbie on operating the whizzer. "My cabin was by the ladder to the deck. As soon as I heard the shouts of 'Fire!' I ran out."

Lars turned to Mrs. Beale. "Weren't you scared, madam? How did you escape?"

Mrs. Beale's eyes filled with tears. "Someone pounded on my door, shouting 'Fire.' I almost swooned with fright before I reached the deck."

"The crew must have responded quickly to extinguish the fire," Lars said.

Rupert left Robbie and stepped to the table. "They worked like fiends on the bucket brigade. I helped in the line."

"Good for you, lad. Your father will be proud."

Rupert's cheeks flushed and his eyes brightened. "I hope so, Mr. Pedersen."

Lars asked Mr. Friberg, "Did you help with the buckets, too, sir?"

"Me? Carry buckets? Certainly not. I was stricken by coughing. In any case, that's when the other ship appeared and pirates swung aboard." Friberg's nose flared at the memory.

"Your company would have lost their cargo if the ship had fallen to the pirates. I've heard of men ruined by such losses."

Mr. Friberg shuddered. "The loss would have been tremendous."

"Would your company have paid a ransom for your safe return?" Lars asked.

Mr. Friberg sputtered, "Ransom? Do you think the pirates would have held us captive?"

Rupert rapped his knuckles on the table. "Certainly they would. They're pirates. I'd wager my parents would have paid my ransom."

Lars said, "And you Mrs. Beale? Would someone send money for your release?"

"None of my connections would have money to spare to buy my freedom. My dear husband is only a hotel manager. What would have become of me?" Her round face crumpled and she twisted her handkerchief in her hands.

Rupert said in an encouraging voice, "I'm sure they'd have released you. They know they can't get blood from a stone."

Lars asked Rupert, "Does your father's company have cargo on the

Fleur? Is that why you were aboard her?"

Rupert threw a long leg over the remaining chair at the table. "No, sir. My father owns several lumber mills at the major ports. I was sent to learn the business, traveling on ships carrying the timber from the logging camps to the mills. I even traveled with Captain Olsen on one leg of my trip, since he carries timber from logging operations on the islands to the mainland regularly."

Lars realized why the captain hadn't wanted to search these people. The captain, who dealt mainly in timber, didn't want to risk insulting a mill owner by searching his son. And he didn't want to alienate Mr. Friberg, who represented a company with shipping interests on the Great Lakes. Captain Olsen had business relationships to maintain. And Mrs. Beale, the lone female, would certainly object to being searched. Lars said to Rupert, "Then, you've been aboard the *Donna* before?"

Rupert said, "Yes. My father was a sailor in his youth and felt I needed the experience. I enjoy being aboard ship. It's a fascinating life, calling at different ports every few days. The voyage on the *Fleur* was to be the end of my journey, taking me home."

Lars raised his eyebrows, considering the trouble a youth could find in ports on the Lakes. "Did you enjoy your shore leave? Sailors find a variety of entertainment at ports of call. The activities must have been eye-opening for a lad your age. I hope you kept out of trouble."

Rupert flushed in embarrassment, then picked his words with obvious care. "I learned not to participate in games of chance in the saloons. The gamblers see me coming and see a bird for plucking. They'd let me win a few rounds and then fleece me. I lost some money before I learned my lesson."

"That's an important life lesson," Lars said, as he wondered in which other vices the young man had indulged. Drinking himself unconscious? Opium dens? Prostitutes? Rupert was a handsome fellow with an open nature and guileless face. Could he have encountered the kind of trouble that might induce him to smuggle goods?

Mr. Friberg snorted in derision. "Saloons are dens of iniquity. You should have avoided them completely."

Mrs. Beale bobbed her head in agreement. "Think how your mother would want you to behave, Mr. Graham."

A burst of red spread from Rupert's cheeks to his ears, and he said, "Yes, ma'am."

Lars stood and walked toward his children. As he passed the hook holding Rupert's hat and coat, he allowed the rolling motion of the ship to cause him to bump them and knock them off the wall. "Oh, so sorry." He stooped down and collected the hat and coat, feeling in the hat's lining, and running the coat through his hands as if brushing off dust before replacing the items on the hook.

He found nothing unusual.

Lars knelt and touched his daughter's thin legs to be sure she wasn't cold. Sarah smiled at him, and he patted her head before standing. He needed to check Friberg's coat next.

Lars returned to the table. "It's getting warm in here. Mr. Friberg, are you uncomfortable in that coat? Would you like me to hang it on the wall for you?"

Friberg stood from the table and shed his coat. "Thank you, sir. That would be appreciated." He handed the coat to Lars.

Lars ran his hands over the coat as he hung it on the wall hook, ostensibly straightening it. He felt nothing hidden in the lining, though the coat did smell strongly of smoke and something else, another more elusive scent. Glancing at Friberg, Lars could see no unseemly bulges on the man's jacket or trousers as he resumed his seat. His clothing, while not top quality, was well kept and tailored to fit.

That left Mrs. Beale. Mrs. Beale wouldn't be the first woman to smuggle goods across the Great Lakes in her clothing. Lars had heard stories of women from Canada taking day trips across the border to buy goods that were cheaper in the United States, and women from the US bringing home goods from Canada. Many ladies had been caught hiding items under their skirts that they didn't wish to declare to customs officials: everything from jewelry, to nutmeg, to dress-making materials.

Searching Mrs. Beale would be harder to accomplish. Lars thought of a way to do it, but not in front of his children. He buried his suspicions behind a smile and hoped the woman read nothing in his posture. "The air is getting heavy in here, madam. Would you like to take some fresh air on the deck? I'd be happy to escort you."

Mrs. Beale hesitated as the ship lurched under them. "I'd like some air, but with the ship rolling so violently, I'm afraid I'll fall."

"I'll support you, madam. I got my sea legs long ago."

"Well, then, I would appreciate that."

Lars offered Mrs. Beale his arm for support as she rose from the bench.

Exiting the cabin, Lars led Mrs. Beale carefully across the heaving deck toward the rail. The sky was a mass of angry clouds. Mrs. Beale clung to Lars for support as the wind whipped at their coats and reddened their faces. Lars patted Mrs. Beale's gloved hand on his arm.

When a gust of wind forced her to grab the rail, Mrs. Beale stopped walking. "I made a mistake, sir. We should return to the cabin. This wind is too strong for me, and it's beginning to rain."

"Certainly, madam." It was now or never.

As the ship dipped beneath them, Lars allowed himself to slip on the wet deck. He tipped Mrs. Beale to the deck and landed across her legs.

"Oh!" Mrs. Beale cried.

Scrambling off her, Lars's hands sank into the loose folds of her dress and matching coat. "My apologies, madam. My sea legs weren't as trustworthy as I hoped." Lars helped her to her feet, wondering how the woman kept her balance while walking with several bulky packages beneath her skirts. "Are you injured?" he asked in a solicitous voice.

"My backside may be bruised, but I'll survive." Mrs. Beale laughed ruefully. "Let's get out of this wind and rain."

Lars led the woman to the cabin without incident, then proposed a game of cards to pass the time. Rain lashed the ship. Waves crashed against the hull. The schooner creaked and rocked in the storm.

Shortly before the ship was due to arrive at Marinette, the rain died to a drizzle. The children, exhausted by their travels, slept under the blanket. Lars excused himself for a walk. He found Captain Olsen and reported his findings.

*****

Upon returning to the cabin, Lars found Rupert and Mr. Friberg standing outside by the rail, watching the ship coming into the dock. As he entered the cabin, Lars saw only Robbie asleep on the floor. Sarah's doll lay beside him.

Mrs. Beale was cradling his sleeping daughter in her arms, holding a knife a few inches from Sarah's face. She said, "You must have felt one of the packages I'm carrying. You were looking for them, weren't you? What gave me away?"

"I checked Rupert's and Mr. Friberg's coats. You were the only one left with the space in your clothing to hide smuggled goods." Sarah didn't move in the woman's arms. "Is my daughter hurt?"

"Not yet. If I walk off this ship without interference, she won't be."

Lars felt the ship come into the dock. The ship rocked and shuddered as forward momentum ceased. Lars moved with the ship to keep his feet.

Mrs. Beale braced herself on the table with the hand holding the knife. But she had it back to Sarah's face before Lars could take a step. "Don't try anything. Move out of the doorway. I'm leaving this ship."

Lars backed out of the cabin hoping Robbie didn't awaken. He found Captain Olsen and two of his men standing outside with Friberg and Rupert. "Mrs. Beale has Sarah."

They all retreated a pace as Mrs. Beale emerged carrying the sleeping child and brandishing the knife.

"Let me off this ship, or the girl dies."

"Clear a path," Captain Olsen bellowed.

Lars saw Sarah startle at the sound of Captain Olsen's booming voice. Her eyes fluttered open and widened when she saw her father.

"Please, don't take my Sarah," Lars said.

Sarah sank her sharp milk teeth into Mrs. Beale's hand. Mrs. Beale shrieked in pain. Sarah kicked, squirmed, scratched, and didn't release her bite until Mrs. Beale dropped her. Sarah scrambled into Lars's arms.

Bleeding, Mrs. Beale raised the knife. "Stay back, or I'll kill you!"

"Take her!" Captain Olsen ordered.

The sailors converged on Mrs. Beale. She swung the knife wildly but was soon disarmed.

"Good girl," Lars whispered into Sarah's ear, hugging her to his chest. Noticing that Mr. Friberg was unobtrusively backing away from the commotion, Lars turned to meet the captain's eyes and said, "Don't let him escape."

Olsen stepped quickly and laid a hand on Mr. Friberg's shoulder. "One moment, sir. I have a few questions for you, too."

Friberg tried to shake Olsen's iron grip, but couldn't.

A short time later, Lars and his children met his half-sister Adele on the dock. Behind them on the ship, Lars could hear Mrs. Beale protesting being searched and Mr. Friberg denying causing the fire on the *Fleur*. A crewman had already gone to fetch the authorities.

*****

Early the next morning at Adele's home, Lars spoke to a US Marshal regarding the incidents on the *Donna* and the *Fleur*. Lars and the marshal sat by the stone fireplace, and Lars explained how he discovered that Mrs. Beale was carrying contraband and that Mr. Friberg must have started the fire on the *Fleur*.

"His coat smelled of smoke and an abundance of spilt kerosene. I suspect he almost lit himself ablaze while starting the fire aboard the *Fleur*. He knew exactly what goods were being shipped by his company and their value. I reasoned that he might join the pirates for a share of the profits."

The Marshal said, "The company owner found inconsistencies in the cargo records and Friberg was under suspicion regarding cargo items vanishing in the past. This time, instead of stealing a few items, he worked with pirates to attempt to steal everything. We confronted him and he agreed to name his co-conspirators when we made it clear that the length of his prison sentence would be contingent upon his cooperation. As for Mrs. Beale, she had an enormous amount of opium concealed beneath her skirts, but we don't think she was in league with Friberg." He paused. "I understand your daughter freed herself when she was taken hostage. How did she know what to do?"

"My children are used to life on Washington Island, where they know everyone. I warned them repeatedly that in traveling they would see many strangers, and not all would be good people. I told them if anyone tried to take them from me, they were to bite, kick, scream, and scratch to free themselves. When Sarah heard me say that she was being taken, she bit Mrs. Beale on the hand."

"You trained her well, sir." The marshal thanked Lars for his assistance and left.

Adele entered the room. "Now that's resolved, you can put your thoughts toward finding a suitable wife. I asked around and heard about an unmarried woman staying at one of the outlying farms. She's staying with the Jensens."

Lars sensed Adele wasn't telling him all she had heard. "What else did they say about her?"

Adele hesitated, breaking eye contact. "One of her eyes wanders, but it's not that noticeable. Since she left school at a young age to care for her siblings, she can't read or write. But she sews, cooks, and cleans, and can tend your children and keep your house."

Lars inhaled softly, trying to stifle the grief welling in him. No one could match Maggie, but he couldn't be picky. Single men outnumbered eligible women in the ports and logging camps. "What's her name?"

"Kirsten Martinsen." Adele gave Lars a sad smile. "I'm sorry you lost Maggie, but I'm glad you're willing to move forward."

"Thank you, Adele. I'll walk to the Jensen farm today." With luck, the woman would be where Adele heard she was.

"I'll make you a packet of food. It's a long walk." Adele bustled out of the room.

As Lars walked toward the Jensen farm, he decided that he wouldn't ask the woman to marry him immediately. They would have to agree that they could work together and at least like each other before they crossed that bridge. He'd give her time – perhaps a month – to decide if she wanted to marry him after she saw what life on the island would be like. Such an arrangement would have been unacceptable in Europe, but not on the frontier, where social niceties gave way to practicality.

At sunset, Lars, exhausted from his walk, mounted the steps to the Jensen farmhouse's porch and tripped on an uneven board. He crashed like a cut tree at the feet of a trim young woman with brown hair curling at her temples.

One of her eyes lit on him in concern while the other wandered slightly. "Are you injured, sir?"

Lars colored with embarrassment, righted himself, and removed his hat. "No, miss."

As he introduced himself, he studied her face and found it to be firm but kind. She looked like someone he could get to know. "Might I speak to you? I have a situation which I hope will interest you."

The Tears of a Clown
Wendy Harrison

I knew it was a bad idea, even before I tripped over the dead clown.

"Seriously?" I said it out loud. In the category of one more thing to worry about, this never would've made the list.

I didn't expect an answer from the white face staring up at me, his dead eyes above the grinning red lips a study in contradiction. I had felt all along that something about this job felt off, but how could I say no to Dahlia Moonstone?

Alex and Dahlia Moonstone were at the top of the pecking order in Porta Larga's version of movers and shakers. I knew from the news coverage of their social life that Dahlia's pet project was the Purrs and Pooches Animal Rescue. Its thrift store was the primary source of funding beside Dahlia herself. The very thrift store where I stood over the dead clown complete with a jeweled dagger sticking out of his chest.

*****

The day began early in the morning with a call from Dahlia. "This is Dahlia Moonstone. It's urgent I meet you as soon as possible. I'll be at your office in an hour." It didn't surprise me that Dahlia assumed I'd make myself available. I wasn't even on the first rung of Porta Larga's social ladder.

We met in my tiny office with "Donna Channing, Private Investigator" stenciled on the door. After retiring from the Porta Larga Police Department under a cloud, it had been harder than I expected to make a go of it as a private investigator. A seal of approval from Dahlia Moonstone would be just the kick in the career I needed to attract paying clients in the small Florida city I called home. I was tired of avoiding the pile of overdue bills that filled the top drawer in my battered old desk.

The meeting had been short. Dahlia asked no questions before agreeing to hire me to plant cameras and listening devices in the storeroom of the thrift shop.

"Things have been disappearing," Dahlia said as she smoothed her expensive blond hairdo with a carefully manicured hand. "I need to know who's stealing from such an important charity. Did I mention I'm on their board?"

I nodded, just as I had the last two times Dahlia had asked the same question.

She handed me a key. "This will open the back door. It leads to the storeroom. Be there at 7:00 tonight, when there's no chance anyone will be around. I don't want the staff to know about this." She stared at me with fire in her eyes. "I want whoever's doing it to be caught and punished to the full extent of the law." Her Botoxed face attempted to wrinkle with her righteous anger but lost the battle. "Spare no expense. Just be there at seven."

Pulling a thick roll of bills from her purse, Dahlia asked, "Will this cover it?"

I looked at the roll and the writing on the band around it. I could feel sweat forming on my forehead as if my red hair had caught fire. My bills would be paid for the rest of the year. I tried to sound cool, as if being handed a small fortune in cash happened every day. "I'm sure it will do for now. Let me make up a contract."

"No. No contract." Dahlia stood. "I'm sure I can trust you. Remember. Seven o'clock on the dot."

My cop radar was screaming a warning. The large cash payment and the refusal of a written contract weren't normal, but as long as Dahlia didn't expect me to kill anyone for the money, I'd find a way to make it work.

After putting together a shopping list, I headed out to buy the equipment I would need. By the time I arrived at the thrift store, promptly at 7:00 as required, I had made a small dent in the roll of hundreds. And now I found myself looking down at one of my many worst nightmares.

"I hate clowns," I mumbled and then added, "No offense meant."

As I continued to stare at the clown, I fought the temptation to turn and leave. This had all the hallmarks of a frame-up. Would the police be pushing into the shop any second now, after an anonymous call? What the hell was Dahlia's game?

But I was still a cop at heart, so I pulled out my cellphone and dialed the direct line to my former partner, hoping she was still working nights.

"Detective Fiona Sampson, I presume?"

"Donna? How are you doing?"

"I have a situation." I gave the bare details. "You're going to need crime scene and the ME. I'll wait for you at the back door. The front door is alarmed, and I don't have the code."

I calculated it would take at least fifteen minutes for Fiona to arrive with backup. Kneeling on the rough wood floor to take a closer look at the clown, I began taking pictures with my cellphone. What I had thought was makeup turned out to be a mask with a large red rubber nose in the middle. I took a close look at the handle of the weapon. It looked like an antique, with a jeweled hilt, and very expensive. Not something you'd expect to find in the Purrs and Pooches Animal Rescue thrift shop. The blood around it was dried and dark. I guessed the victim had gone to clown heaven hours earlier.

"Not your job," I reminded myself as I heard the sirens approaching. I started to stand and noticed a cellphone under a table next to the body, just out of reach of the clown's outstretched hand. Muscle memory kicked in, and I grabbed the phone with a linen napkin that was on the table. Stuffing it in my pocket, I gambled I wouldn't be searched. Fiona would kill me if she knew, but I couldn't resist. I told myself I'd find a way to return it where I found it and tried to ignore the echoes I could still hear of my nickname on the force. Cowboy. At least it hadn't been Cowgirl, which would've been more of an insult coming from the testosterone-driven police force.

I was relieved to see Fiona was first through the door. The two cops behind her had their guns drawn. I raised my hands slowly.

"You might want to calm them down," I told Fiona, who turned to see what I was looking at.

"Relax, guys, before you accidentally shoot someone. You wouldn't want a pile of paperwork, would you?" She turned back to me. "They're new."

"I could tell."

Once the weapons were safely back in their holsters, Fiona introduced them to me. "She's PLPD, retired. How about you search the rest of the store and make sure no one else is here."

They left through the inner door between the storeroom and the store. "That should keep them out of trouble for now." Fiona walked over to the clown. "Anyone you know?"

"Hard to tell with the mask, but I doubt it. Not too many clowns in my social circle."

"The ME and crime scene will be here in a while. They'll want to talk to you, but I'll take the condensed version for now."

I described the odd encounter with Dahlia. "I have all the equipment I bought in the car, along with the receipts, if you need to verify my story."

"I don't, but I'm sure the other detectives will. What do you think she was up to?"

I shared my theory and added. "I was waiting for the door to be kicked open after an anonymous tip with me in the frame for the murder."

Fiona said she'd check the tip line. "Wait out in the store until the ME gets here. When she removes the mask, we can try to ID the vic. Then you can leave. I'll see you at the station in the morning for a full statement."

I sat on a comfortable armchair in the store, watching the baby cops searching the place for bad guys. They were thorough, although I wasn't sure why they'd think anyone would be hiding under the furniture unless they were looking for Rubberman.

After hearing the rest of the team arriving, I got the call from Fiona to come back into the storeroom. They all stood around the body as the ME gently lifted the clown's head to slip off the elastic that held the mask on his face. I stared down at him and felt my knees give way. Fiona gasped.

"Is it?" She turned to me, and I nodded.

"Vaun. My ex." I knew it was going to be a long night.

I couldn't blame them for not giving me a free pass as a former fellow officer. Even I had trouble believing in the coincidence. Then it all got worse when Fiona called Dahlia to verify my story, only to have Dahlia deny knowing who I was.

When Fiona described the conversation, I felt my face redden, but before I could explode, Fiona shook her head. I struggled to stay quiet while she reminded the other officers about the roll of money I had shown them and the load of equipment in my car. The key helped as well, and so did my offer to have them come to my office and dust for Dahlia's prints. The woman had pulled the visitor's chair away from the desk when she sat, and the glossy wood probably would make a liar out of her.

The sun was coming up when they let me leave, but as tired as I was, I knew I wouldn't be able to sleep. The first order of business was the cellphone I had taken from the scene, the one I assumed belonged to the dead clown. To Vaun, my ex. It was still hard to accept.

Back at my office, I put on latex gloves and held my breath as I tried the one password Vaun had used for everything during our brief marriage. 1234.

I thought back to the last time I had heard from him. It had been at least a year ago, and he had been excited about his new job at Buster's Game Arcade. "I'm running it," he said. "This is it, Donna. I can feel it. I'm finally going places."

Vaun had always been on the verge of something big that managed to fizzle out. He was like an overgrown puppy, eager and friendly but not the brightest bulb in the litter. I had wished him well and hadn't heard from him since.

I had guessed right. 1234 was the password. Vaun's phone held a treasure trove of text messages. Some were with employees of Buster's and seemed innocent enough, but the most recent weren't innocent at all. Vaun had been exchanging sexts with someone who called herself Flower Girl.

V: Can't wait to see you.

FG: You know what I want.

V: That again?

FG: You know how hot it makes me.

V: Red nose too?

FG: The whole shebang.

Flower Girl. Could it be Dahlia? I couldn't imagine her getting it on with the hoi polloi. But Vaun was still a very attractive man, with or without a clown suit. Did the lovebirds have a falling out? The dagger looked valuable. Had Dahlia imperiled her manicure by sinking it into her lover? And then decided to use his ex-wife to take the blame?

Buster's was next on my list. I turned to Google, the cop's best friend after her gun. Buster's Game Arcade, Ltd., was owned by an offshore company, along with a string of similar businesses around Florida. As I tracked deeper into databases that didn't know I wasn't a cop anymore, I discovered the power behind the corporate veil was one Alexander Moonstone.

The plot thickens, I thought. Vaun was working for Moonstone and sleeping with his wife. Did Moonstone know? Did he care enough to kill Vaun? Or hire someone to do it?

I pulled tattered jeans and a BTK band T-shirt from my closet, my favorite outfit when I went undercover on the streets. With Chuck 70s on my feet and a well-worn baseball cap hiding my pinned-up red hair, I was ready to check out Buster's.

The game arcade was on the boardwalk along Porta Larga Beach. I'd been in the area over the years for disturbances, usually caused by drunk or high kids, and the occasional domestic violence call from a concerned citizen about a tough guy knocking his girlfriend around. Gangs weren't a problem on the beach. Maybe they were allergic to saltwater from the Gulf or had more urban territory to defend.

On this summer day, the arcade was busy with hyperactive kids playing the clanging, banging games that allowed them to pretend to be old enough to carry weapons and shoot them. There was a sprinkling of young mothers, showing off their almost bare bodies and deep tans. A sign in front required shoes but not modesty.

I wandered around, not sure what I was looking for, until I spotted a woman in a clown suit. I figured I must be in the right place. There couldn't be too many clowns in the entire city, and here I was, facing my second one in 24 hours.

"Excuse me." I had to raise my voice above the noise.

The clown turned to me. No mask, only a painted-on smile that contradicted the real tears in her blue eyes. "Can I help you?" Her voice trembled.

"Is there somewhere we can go to get out of this noise?" The girl nodded as the tears wore a path through her clown makeup. We walked to the back of the arcade and through a door marked "Employees Only," which led to a small kitchen with several tables. Once the door closed behind us, there was a sudden and total silence.

I looked at the name tag on the clown suit. A happy clown face on the left, "Hi, I'm Sydnie" next to it. "That's better, isn't it, Sydnie?"

Sydnie looked down at her name tag as if to be sure. "They were Vaun's idea. Happy tags for a happy place, he always said. Vaun, I mean Mr. Carson, made this room like, soundproofed, when he took over so we could get a break from the noise. He for sure cared about us." She started to sob. I sat her in one of the chairs and walked over to the sink to get a glass of water for her.

"Drink this." The girl nodded and sipped. "I'm sorry. It's been a very bad day."

"Would it help to talk about it?" I almost felt guilty, pretending I didn't know why the girl was a sodden mess. My bet was that Vaun was more than Sydnie's boss. The question was whether it was mutual or a one-sided crush. Sydnie appeared to be around twenty, which seemed too young for Vaun, especially knowing Dahlia was his latest cup of tea.

"What's upsetting you?"

The tears returned. "It's Vaun." No pretense of Mr. Carson this time. "He's dead." Sobbing. "Mr. Moonstone called to tell us." She stopped crying long enough to explain. "He owns Buster's, you know? His office is back there." She angled her head toward the back of the breakroom.

I patted her arm. How much might Moonstone have said? "Was Vaun in an accident?"

Sydnie blew her nose with a tissue she pulled from a pocket in the clown suit. "They're saying he was murdered." She shuddered. "It can't be true. Everyone loved Vaun."

"Including you?"

She nodded. "He was the most wonderful person I ever met, you know? I loved him. And he loved me back. He never said it to me, being the boss and all. It wouldn't have been right. But I could tell. We were gonna be together. I just had to be patient, you know?" The tears were gone, and the reddened eyes were flashing. Maybe she got tired of waiting for her Prince Charming to carry her off into the sunset. But why would she have been in the thrift store? And where would she have come up with the jeweled murder weapon?

My phone interrupted my silent list of unanswered questions. Fiona's name was flashing on my caller ID.

"Hang on a minute."

Turning to Sydnie, I said, "I'm sorry, but I really have to take this."

The girl nodded, and I braced myself against the wall of sound pounding into me as I opened the door of the breakroom and stepped out. I jogged through the crowded arcade to the relative peace of the boardwalk and turned back to my phone.

"What's up?"

"Where the hell are you? What's that racket?"

"Long story. What've you got?"

"You were right about someone wanting you left hanging in the wind. Just after I left the station last night, an anonymous call came in."

"Let me guess. A dead body at the thrift shop. Hurry. The killer may still be there."

"I see your crystal ball still works."

"Burner phone?"

"Naturally. Couldn't be traced. If you hadn't called me first, we would've caught you in *flagrante delicto*."

"Considering it was my ex-husband lying there, that's cold."

"Sorry."

I could tell she didn't mean it. That was the kind of friendship we'd always had. Bad taste reigned.

"Have they cleared the scene yet?" I figured there was a 50/50 chance they had.

"Forensics finished up an hour ago. Dahlia ordered the store to open. 'For the doggies and kitties sake.'" Fiona was a talented mimic. She captured Dahila's patronizing tone perfectly.

"Okay if I take another look?"

"I don't see how I can stop you. The place is open to the public. What are you looking for?"

"Anything to get me off the hook." Before Fiona could protest, I added, "You know I didn't kill Vaun, but right now, I'm a suspect. No way to get around it. Ex-wife finds body, upstanding citizen says ex-wife lied about why she was at the scene. It's okay. I know what it looks like. I'll tell you if I find anything, but someone should be taking a close look at the lying Dahlia."

I hung up and headed for my car. My first priority was to "find" Vaun's phone somewhere in the storeroom where no one else would think to look. I needed to be able to convince Fiona it had been there all along.

The thrift store was crowded. I suspected most of the people were lured there by the murder more than by the used furniture and clothing filling the room.

When I was sure no one was paying attention, I turned the knob on the door to the storeroom, hoping it wasn't locked. I was in luck. It opened and then closed behind me as I entered the space. The last time I had been there, I was focused on the body on the floor, but now I took a long slow look around. It was more orderly than it had seemed the night before. Large furniture pieces were stacked against two walls. The other two were covered with shelves bearing china and lamps and anything else that would fit.

The Tears of a Clown

I walked to the center of the room where I had found Vaun. There was a clear area where his body had been, with a variety of chairs and small tables surrounding it. I looked under the chair where I had found his phone. There wasn't any way the cops would've missed it, so I couldn't put it back and then pretend to find it. Crawling around the area, I judged how far the phone might have traveled if it had been dropped during a struggle. A rolled-up carpet caught my eye. This time, I had come prepared and pulled on latex gloves while saying a silent thanks to my instinctive reaction to use a napkin when I had first picked up the cellphone. At least I wouldn't have to wipe the phone's surfaces to get rid of my fingerprints. It seemed unlikely the killer had handled it, but at least Fiona might have a chance of finding prints that could help identify the clown killer.

I held the phone in my gloved hand and inched it into the side of the circling rug edges. Enough of it fit to make it plausible it had been missed on the earlier search. I took several photos, stuck the gloves back in my pocket, and called Fiona.

"I think I may have found Vaun's phone."

"Well hello to you too."

"Hello. I think I may have found Vaun's phone. I'll text you a picture."

After a pause, Fiona said, "Tell me the truth. How did you find it?"

"I crawled around the area where I found Vaun and tried to guess where it might have landed during a struggle." At least that much wasn't a lie.

"And you just happened to get lucky."

"I'm not sure lucky applies here. I'm the one who's being framed for her ex-husband's murder while he was dressed as a clown, remember?"

Fiona told me to leave the phone alone and wait for her to get there. "I'm in the middle of something so it might take a while. See if Wiggles and Waggles serves coffee."

"It's Purrs and Pooches and with Dahlia running the show, of course they have a coffee bar. Should I order you a latte or maybe a cappuccino?"

I laughed when Fiona hung up on me. I found a comfortable chair in a corner of the storeroom and settled in. Cops get used to waiting. At least this wasn't a twelve-hour stakeout.

After a few minutes, the door swung open. A beefy man who appeared to be in his late 50s moved into the room. He looked like a longshoreman but was dressed in designer jeans and a black silk shirt with a heavy gold chain around his neck and a Rolex on his wrist. We stared at each other. He went first.

"Who the hell are you?"

"Donna Channing. And who the hell are you?"

"Alex Moonstone." He paused. It was clear he was waiting for me to either swoon or curtsy. I hated to disappoint him.

"What are you doing here, Alex Moonstone?" I used my trusty voice of authority left over from the days of dealing with gangbangers.

He didn't hide his surprise at being challenged. "My wife misplaced her shawl. She thought she might've left it in here." His face showed the moment he decided he had the upper hand. "She's on the board." Dahlia must have convinced him it meant something important. "Why are you here?"

"I'm guarding evidence until Detective Sampson arrives."

"Are you a cop?" He looked at me, a slow scan from my head to my toes, stopping off at the good stuff in between.

Before I could answer, we had company. Not Fiona yet, but a familiar face.

"Alex? Are you in there?" Dahlia stepped into the room. "Did you find it?"

She skidded to a stop when she saw me. "You. What are you doing here?"

"I might ask you the same. Last time I saw you was when you hired me to come here at 7:00, so I could find the dead clown. Remember?"

Alex turned to her. "What's she talking about?"

"Nothing. She's a crazy person. I'm going to call the police."

I smiled. "Don't bother. They're on the way, and they'll have some questions for you. Better get your story straight before they get here.

Funny how much cops hate people who lie to them."

Alex continued to stare at his wife, who refused to meet his eyes. "Dahlia. Look at me. What the hell is going on?"

I decided to poke the bear. "You may as well tell him, Flower Girl."

The color drained from Dahlia's face. I'd never realized that was a real thing. Dahlia started to crumble, but I was faster than Alex and caught his wife before she hit the floor. There was still an outline where Vaun's body had been. If Dahlia had realized that's where she was about to land, she might've had a heart attack.

Alex pushed me aside and carried Dahlia to one of the couches against the wall. "Relax, sweetheart." His tenderness shocked me. It seemed out of character, but it was a useful reminder of something I had learned early on when I joined the force. Don't assume anything. Don't jump to conclusions. Follow the evidence even if, or especially if, it contradicts the mind you've made up.

"I'm so sorry." For a moment, I thought Dahlia was apologizing to me until she added, "It meant nothing. I swear."

I could see Alex had no idea what Dahlia was talking about so I decided to help.

"She means her affair with Vaun Carson."

Alex jumped up and I stepped back, wishing I had brought a weapon with me.

"What? The clown who manages Buster's?" He seemed more confused than angry.

"Well, if you put it that way, it does seem crazy." I realized I wasn't being helpful after all.

"Don't, Alex." Dahlia put herself between her husband and me. "I know what you did."

I was reminded of the jumping to conclusions thing. I had been sure Dahlia was about to confess to killing her lover.

"What I did? What do you think I did?"

"You found out about Vaun and me, and you killed him."

"What the hell are you talking about?" He looked genuinely bewildered.

"When I came to meet him, I found him dead. Stabbed with that jeweled dagger from your collection. I assumed you found out about us, and I panicked. I knew Vaun's ex-wife had been thrown off the police force and figured she'd be the first one they'd suspect. I went to her office and hired her to put security cameras in the storeroom."

I decided to finish the story for her. "Then you gave me a key, told me to be there at seven o'clock, and tipped off the police. Nice work." I added, "By the way. I retired. I wasn't kicked off."

Dahlia didn't have the grace to look ashamed. "Better you than my husband."

Alex's face twisted in horror. "You were having an affair with that loser clown? I can't believe it." He stared at Dahlia as if he'd never seen her before. "I didn't kill him. I didn't know anything about you two. If I did, I might've knocked him around some. I'm not sure. But one thing I do know is that I'd be sitting in a lawyer's office by now, figuring out how to cut you off without a dime."

Fiona appeared in the doorway. "Am I interrupting anything?"

I filled her in on the conversation while Alex glared and Dahlia wept.

"Is this all true?" Fiona looked at the about-to-be-unmarried couple. They both nodded.

Before she could say anything else, I jumped in. "One question. What about the dagger? Alex, Dahlia said it was from your collection. How did it get here?"

"Describe it for me. I have a lot of antique weapons. Which one are you talking about?"

I pulled out my phone and scrolled through the photos I had taken when I found the body. I ignored Fiona's scowl. This was the first she had heard about any pictures. I passed my phone to Alex who stared at the knife.

"That's mine, all right. It's a nineteenth-century Medici dagger. The jewels were real. Emeralds, diamonds and a large turquoise stone. A beautiful piece and very rare. I had it in a safe at Buster's, in the office I keep there."

"Why would you have something that valuable at an arcade?" Fiona asked before I could.

"I was planning to sell it. There was a magnificent antique emerald necklace on the market. I was going to use the money from the dagger to buy it as an anniversary present for Dahlia. I didn't want her to get wind of it, so I arranged for a dealer to meet with me next week at Buster's to make me an offer. I had no idea someone had taken it out of the safe."

At the mention of the necklace and her anniversary, Dahlia began to howl. Her life was crumbling, and she couldn't do a thing to stop it. But now I knew who killed the clown.

I rode with Fiona to Buster's after explaining how I figured out who murdered poor Vaun. Fiona called for backup, and the two rookie cops met us there. I didn't think they'd be needed.

The four of us walked through the arcade until we found the clown we were looking for. Before Fiona could say a word, Sydnie's tears began. Again.

"I thought he loved me." More tears. "Then I sneaked a peek at his phone and saw those horrible texts. I had to do something."

"How did you get into the safe?" Fiona and I asked at the same time.

The words poured out. "I knew the combination. Mr. Moonstone was opening it one day, and I watched over his shoulder. But please don't tell him. He'd be really angry. I was going to put the knife back. I just wanted to scare Vaun so he would see that I was the one for him, you know? I followed him to that stupid thrift store. He left the door unlocked when he went inside. He was real surprised when I followed him in, but he just laughed when I told him I knew it was me he loved. I got so angry."

She wiped at her wet face. "But I know we'll be together again. He'll be waiting for me, for sure." Her eyes went to the ceiling. I hoped she was right. Maybe there was a clown heaven where Vaun and Sydnie would live happily ever after.

Maybe…. But probably not.

Terrestrial Timeslip
Andrew Darlington

Spam. Delete. Spam. Delete. Spam. Delete.

Then he pauses. An email he doesn't recognize. His finger hovers over the delete key. But, just on a curious whim, he opens it instead.

An official solicitor's heading. 'Due to the unfortunate incident of your imminent death on the First of March we feel it appropriate to enquire if you have given sufficient thought to making out a Will? To ensure that your family and dependents are adequately provided for during this stressful period. We are qualified to offer a complete quick and easy Will-making service…'

Dependents? One embittered ex-wife. Does she count? He hit delete. This is a joke in very poor taste. He relaxes back in his studio chair. On the sloping drawing board with the angle-poise light there's the half-completed line-drawing illustration commissioned for the woman's fiction magazine. The full-face enveloped in ripples of hair. He likes the way the contour-lines cascade. She has a questioning look on her face. He's caught her expression quite well. In the background her husband is laughing and joking with the next-door-neighbour's wife. Maybe they are being just a little too familiar? They are not yet fully fleshed out. He needs to catch her doubts. The idea that their closeness is a little too suspect. Once he's caught the right mood he can scan it in, retouch and colour digitally. But these first stages still depend on sketches.

He picks up his pen, then lays it down again. Work is scarce. The woman's fiction market pays well. But his heart's not in it. There's an itch to get back to his Sci-Fi strip. His visualization of Arthur C Clarke's *Trouble With Time*, about the theft of the enigmatic Siren Goddess from the Meridian City museum on Mars, the colony that straddles two time-zones. It's for a crowd-funded start-up that probably won't break even. But that's where his heart lies. Damn. He stands at the studio window. Looks out over the nearby roofs and sparse Spring trees, newly budding, towards the Park and the River Wandle beyond. If you have to live in the London sprawl, life in Colliers Wood is as good as it gets, and convenient for tube-trips to potential buyers in town. But he's restless. And that email is irritating.

There's another later that same day. He opens it cautiously. 'Dear Mr Roberts, with commiserations for your death on First of March, we feel it pertinent to ask, have you considered an eco-funeral? With taste and style, and an entirely humanist service celebrating the deceased's life and achievements…' This time he checks out the email-address. It's a non-returnable that he doesn't recognize. Of course, he could respond to the click-box, but that would just be to play along with their stupid prank.

There were horoscope pages in the woman's magazines. They speculate about health and travel and intimate relationships. But they're never this specific. They never say you're going to be run over by the no.117 bus. Nevertheless, it's disturbing, unsettling. He's fit, in general good health, considering his age and take-out diet, his Fitbit documents his morning jogs. But the thought niggles. In these dog-days at the end of February, March is days away. He takes his pulse. It feels strong.

It's only when the third email predicts his death that he phones the local surgery for a full-MoT check. The receptionist is evasive. Why does he require an appointment? The Doctor has a full schedule. He can't bring himself to admit that he's been scared by some dodgy spoof emails. After a few moments he Googles for a private clinic, and it costs, but he gets a slot the following day. Following an uneasy night's sleep he showers and shaves, then sets out across the Park. A teenage slacker hurtles past him on a lethal skateboard. He dodges clear as it jets away oblivious to his presence. On the kerb-edge he steps out towards the tube station and a taxi misses him by inches, horn blaring, the driver yells and gesticulates obscenities. On the street he's wary of inhaling toxic exhaust fumes. The city is a dangerous place.

The test is efficient and thorough, with no intrusive questions asked, samples are taken and scans scanned, he's wired to this and plugged into that to read his various body-functions on screens and print-outs. There's nothing amiss. No threatening shadows on the x-rays. No abnormalities. The only pain comes when he has to swipe the card-reader to settle the bill. He feels better. It's only when he gets back to his flat and there are three new emails carrying versions of the same message. The dreaded black spot. He'd been singled out to die.

But wait. He was not going to die today, or tomorrow. He has until the first of March. And the city is a dangerous place. Thronged with the random hazards of reckless motors or random street-crime. It was then he decides. There was the time-share cottage in Grassington, part of a commercial artist's-collective project he'd subscribed to a few years ago. Safe in the splendid isolation of the north Yorkshire moors, nowhere could be safer. He makes the necessary phone calls, yes – it's free and available. He packs his ongoing artwork into cylinders, his clothes into his backpack, loads them into the Toyota, and leaves without a backwards glance. Around the M25, then north up the M1 and just keep going. Nothing can go wrong today. Today is not a day for dying. There was slight congestion through Ilkley, but once clear, climbing through between the fold of sheep-wandered hills and dry-stonewall enclosed fields he soon has the road to himself.

There's a Garden Centre with an adjoining café and hardware annexe. He pulls into the car-park and stops for a cappuccino. It's warm inside, there's muted nineties hits playing on a background loop and the young waitress is friendly. Inside the store he buys basic foodstuff in cans and microwavable packs, a number of animal-traps and trip-wire loops. He looks at a secure cabinet of hunter's rifles and shotguns, but decides against it. Pulling away back onto the road, from there he turns off the main carriageway onto a track between fields sheltered by the low foliage overhang of wind-swept trees, and eventually turns into the scrubby yard-space at the front of the cottage.

There's a single step down through the front door, and once inside he's enveloped by a tranquil feeling of security. He sets his artwork up on the table, makes a drink. Then puts the sleeping bag on the bed, and turns in.

It's a bright hard morning. There's a calendar hung inside the pantry door. It's last year's. But close enough. He pulls his coat on and makes preparations. Across a short overgrown rear garden there's a stream that chatters over white stones. He ambles some way up beside the stream's twisting course, ducking back from briar thorn-bushes and nettle-patches. There's a dead-end where the stream waterfalls down from some point steep above his head. There are no pathways or easy access points for miscreants with evil on their mind. Only a few dirty-looking sheep. He squats down beside the swirling pooling water, ice-cold to the touch. Life is good.

Back at the cottage he sites the animal traps in a half-circle, pulls the vicious jaws back and tensions them, then sets up the tripwires between each trap to form an encircling alert barrier, against inbred locals with murder in mind. Inside the cottage he locks and bolts the front and rear doors. Then prepares to isolate all the electricity. Electrical devices can attract lightning, they can short in violent power-surges and trigger a heart-attack. So no radio. No TV or internet. Like stepping back a century. Raw country living. He microwaves a final meal with hot coffee. Then turns everything off.

Everything safe. Nothing hazardous. He thinks briefly about knockout sleeping pills. But there's a chance of accidental overdose, of regurgitating and inhaling vomit while unconscious. He checks his watch, and turns in early. Tomorrow will be the testing time. The day of the email prediction.

He wakes warily and breathes deep. Still alive, he checks his life-signs. It's a long day. He doesn't go out, but dresses warmly. Drinks chill tap-water. Sits sketching while sufficient daylight endures, working on comic-book frames as the thief 'Danny Weaver' steals the mysterious Martian artefact, but gets trapped because he ignores the meridian time-shift. He's happy with the way it's shaping up. The moody shading, the bleak Martian landscape glimpsed beyond the colony domes. He feels the creative flow. He eats fruit. No knife. Nothing with a sharp edge. There's brief rain around midday. He pauses to watch the wind torment trees along the black skyline. He can see them scratching at clouds. Funny, he's never stopped to watch trees before. Life is a precious thing. Once the fateful day is over he crawls into the sleeping bag with a sense of relief.

The nightmare is over. Of course, it was a ludicrous idea from the start. Just some stupid email scam. He unlocks the door. Loads his stuff back into the Toyota. Deactivates the traps and tripwires ready for the next tenant. Then eases the car leisurely down the track between the rolling fields, back onto the roadway, through Ilkley and eventually back onto the motorway. He's humming tunelessly.

Accelerating, he casually thumbs the radio on to catch the news updates. Dateline First March 2024. Leap year. Yesterday was February Twenty-ninth! The one factor he'd ignored. He grips the steering wheel as the full implications sink in. At exactly the same moment the tyre bursts on an overtaking eight-wheeler striped with Netherlands regalia, it veers across the carriageway out of control, lurching, hurtling towards the Toyota…

The Ultimate Serial Killer
Larry Lefkowitz

Watching murder movies, reading graphic novels and cheap literature led to him developing a fascination for lurid crime stories.

First he began to focus on true crime stories, and then as his tastes became more refined, he further specialized in serial killer crimes. Especially he liked to follow true crime stories involving serial killers.

He became obsessed with the character of the serial killers, and their detailed profiles. How and why did they become not only murderers but serial murderers. He knew he should be horrified, but at the same time he knew he was becoming fascinated by them. And angry at them. In his mind, they were the number one threat to a harmonious society.

He began to watch factual TV shows, such as *The Forensic Detail* and *Kill and Chill* to learn all he could about serial killers. And many times, he thought to himself: *I could have done a better job of tracking them down than the authorities.* Eventually he felt that he could help solve many unsolved cold cases that were obviously serial killer crimes.

The day came when he said to himself: *Enough! — I will track them down and bring them to justice!*

But first he had to locate the serial killers.

To do this, he began to research the subject of serial killers. He learned that a serial killer is typically a person who murders three or more people — usually for some kind of abnormal psychological gratification — with the murders usually taking place with a slowly shortening period of time between them.

What he needed to know was the characteristics possessed by serial killers. Knowing their characteristics would help him identify them—help single them out in a crowd.

He learned the signs that would indicate if one would grow up to be a serial killer: being cruel or abusive to animals, especially pets, setting fire to objects or otherwise committing minor acts of arson, regularly wetting the bed.

He further learned about the four types of serial killers based on the type of crime they commit: thrill seekers, mission-oriented, visionary killers, and power/control seekers.

He learned the Zodiac signs of serial killers. Most of them were born under one of the four signs: Gemini, Virgo, Sagittarius or Pisces.

He, himself, was a Gemini, and had wet the bed. Yet although these might indicate that he might have a tendency to become a serial killer, he dismissed the thought, or even that such might make him sympathetic to serial killers.

But as he learned more about their modus operandi and methodology, he found himself becoming more and more disgusted and angry. So angry, he vowed to go beyond solving their crimes. He would locate and kill them, purely for the benefit of society.

And being a Gemini he felt he more than adequately equipped to tackle such a heroic task. Geminis are, by their very nature, curious, adaptable, with an ability to learn quickly and to solve problems. They like to talk with people with an almost sympathetic ear because Geminis often feel that their other half is missing.

He checked the biographies of notorious serial killers, concentrating on the modern period and the American serial killers for relevance in finding keys to their behavioral and personality patterns. In this way he succeeded in locating four of them quite quickly.

He discovered that one based his murderous system on the game of chess. Specifically, one game — Bobby Fischer's *The Game of the Century*, reflected in the placing of the victims' bodies according to its gameplay, as if on a chess board.

A second serial killer based his 'system' on a computer game involving a chase through the city's backstreets, and a third had based their M.O. on a very specific Aztec sacrifice ritual.

As it turned out, the third became the first to be investigated, and was more of a challenge. Our serial killer hunter labeled him *B*, borrowing the signature method of one another killer who used the alphabet to designate his victims. *B* for *beast* or *bastard* and also for *Beatles*, since he was dubbed by the media as The Beatles killer, because he apparently played Beatles' songs on his victims' audio systems during his murders or afterwards.

In keeping with this naming convention, he named the other three previously mentioned serial killers *C*, *D* and *E*.

Both *C* and *D* were found and duly dispatched by our man, which left *B*, and of course *E*. He eschewed the use of *A* because *Alpha* (the phonetic of the subject letter) began with this letter and an Alpha man is a man who takes charge, one who imposes his will on others and intimidates them — something of an anathema to a Gemini.

B had committed a series of murders of young women in the San Francisco area, and our man began to question relatives, friends, boyfriend and ex-boyfriends of *B*'s victims. He looked for a pattern to the crimes — a common thread that the Police, with their supposedly logical procedures, had obviously missed.

He discovered that all the victims were students of the colleges and universities in the area. They had all studied biology — microbiology, histology, genetics. He researched these subjects but nothing there turned out to be helpful.

Then, one day, a break.

One victim had worked in a lab. He sought out the lab instructor. The guy expressed "regret" about her death and that he would be "hard put to find a replacement of her caliber." He added that she was a good worker, but "too independent" in her judgments and "sometimes disobedient." The latter set off alarm bells that raised the suspicion that *B* was very much a control freak, one of the four identifiable types of a serial killer.

He went back and questioned the deceased's acquaintances about *B*. A friend of another victim told him that the victim had told her that she suspected that a man was following her. The man fit *B*'s description. A stalker, her friend had told her and had urged her to go to the police.

Sadly the victim declined, saying that the man was cute and guys

The Ultimate Serial Killer

usually weren't interested in her. Her friend asked her if she had spoken to him, or even tried to start a relationship. 'No,' she said, 'but maybe I will.'

That may have been her mistake, he thought, but did not say it to her friend.

Should he confront B and accuse him? Certainly not, that was dangerous. Should he tell the police? No, he didn't have enough evidence. And more to the point *he* wanted to kill the serial killer. It was *his* mission in life. He would apply the homeopathic principle: *like cures like*.

He had taken out a handgun license and practiced with the gun. Now the time had come to use it. He would dispatch B. On the true crime broadcasts, he would star as the successful killer of a serial killer. They would praise him as the ultimate serial killers' serial killer. Surely, it would bring him a gaggle of female admirers. He would choose one— one with an interest in crime. Maybe even the friend of the victim he had talked to. She was pretty enough and if she seemed not interested in him particularly, then that would change when he revenged himself (and her) on the killer. Maybe Tarantino would make a movie based on his success. Possible title: *The Ultimate Serial Killer* or *Pulp Nonfiction*.

He would probably become a legend in his own lifetime — if he wasn't killed in the process first.

He located and discretely broke into B's research facility. As if to confirm things, a Beatles' song was playing in the background, and he wondered if B played the band's songs as background when he murdered his victims, or as an afterthought, in order to help him calm down.

Regardless, he didn't ask B when he finally had the chance. He simply drew his pistol and dispatched B with a neat head shot.

By this time, after finishing off B, C and D in quick succession, he found he had become something of a legend in the media. Although they didn't know his true identity, he was sure they were talking about him – though using rather mundane names like *The Avenger*, and worse still, *The Justice Dude*.

His disappointment that those names did not approach the pinnacle of his own choice — *The Ultimate Serial Killer* — caused him to write and email the various news agencies, media outlets and websites, subtly (or so he hoped) suggesting the name as a replacement.

Although some did choose to use the sobriquet, his so being called brought about his undoing.

The remaining serial killer at large, number four, *E — The Computer Killer* as the media had baptized him — had read about this usurper, *The Ultimate Serial Killer*, and had vowed to track him down, turn the tables on him, and become, naturally, *The Ultimate Serial Killer's Killer*. But before he could find any viable trail, our man had tracked *E* him down.

Our hero (if such he can be called) had deduced that *E* was a Pisces from a number of aspects of his personality *E* had revealed in his crimes, and as a Pisces he was a would-be joker, a prankster, but one who ultimately fails in his risible efforts. Geminis possess a dry sense of humor, but he would overlook his disdain for the crude humor of a Pisces on this occasion. No, he decided. When he finally confronted *E*, he would put him off guard and allow him to put "finish" to *E* before *E* finished him, by laying on him the (possibly very tiresome) joke about the Zodiac killer who cut his victim into little Pisces.

Alas, the joke, as it happened, turned out to be on him, which some might say was rather fitting to a Gemini where the butt of their jokes is usually themselves.

E reacted to our hero's joke by telling one of their own—admittedly rude and sexist, and therefore best to leave it unprinted here. *E*'s joke caused our man to feign a laugh — a little too overdone in retrospect — and because of it, the pistol he drew from the shoulder holster under his jacket in order to help *E* pay his debt to society, fell onto the floor.

Enraged, *E* was quick to take advantage of the situation, picked up the gun, aimed it at him and fired, shouting that "Now I will be the Ultimate Serial Killer's Killer."

But as a Pisces, jokes were for *E* even more important than groundbreaking honorifics.

So much so, that *E*'s was indeed the last laugh, if such can be said, considering his final situation. After he was caught and strapped into the electric chair, just before the bolt struck him, he snarled: "And they say a Pisces can't tell a joke."

The Gathering Puddle
Jesse Aaron

Detective Weepy Willy Williamson, with watery eyes, looked across the cheap battered wooden table at the shooting team investigators and let out a series of painful and loud sneezes. He had a migraine that was barreling and pounding rhythmically behind his left eye like an overloaded freight train, and each sneeze drove the train deeper into the back of his eyeball.

He looked down and he could see that the psoriasis on the back of his right hand was angry and red, and that beads of blood were creeping out, as if they were prisoners trapped beneath the surface that had finally broken free. The patch of skin below and behind his thumb and forefinger was the color of a raw side of beef. Since the shooting two hours ago he had been unconsciously scratching this patch of skin over and over until it felt numb.

Now, as he sat in front of the investigators and got ready to tell his story he realized that the migraine was going to make him vomit. He excused himself and only just made it in time to the toilet. As he sat on his knees and wiped his face, he realized he could not remember what the man he had shot two hours ago looked like.

Once he had drawn his gun in the middle of the robbery, everything became distorted. It had seemed as if he had become another person. This day's events happened at two speeds-slow motion and fast-forward, and he honestly couldn't remember which part of the day fit into which category. As he slowly stood up, he realized he didn't know where his keys were, and it somehow reminded him of the moment just before the shooting, but he could not remember why.

As he stood in front of the chipped and rust stained sink, he looked at himself in the smudged bathroom mirror. His pale skin looked slightly yellow, and his wide and mostly hairless skull looked like a poorly decorated mannequin. His round eyes and meaty red lips completed the image of a broken and shaken man.

Willy also realized he saw the visage of a man who was alive. A man who had just taken another human life but now went on breathing, sneezing, coughing, doing all the things a moving piece of meat does, even though he had just ended this same type of existence for another living being.

Willy could still feel his ears ringing and he heard a slight buzz, as if he had been listening to music that was too loud for hours. For some reason he thought of the Circus. When he was just a small child, his parents had taken him to the Big Top, and he had sat in the second row.

The music had been so loud that close to the performers that Willy's ears rang for the entire car ride home. He did not know why that image came back to him so clearly, but at that moment he could vividly smell the foul odor of the animals and taste the salt of the peanuts on his tongue, and for a moment he was there. Then, in a flash, it was gone.

The door opened, and Riley, the larger of the two investigators he had just spoken with was peering in impatiently at Willy. Riley was holding the door open for him, demanding with his eyes that Willy return to the interrogation room. Riley's eyes commanded Willy to stop wasting time, to get this over with, and to stop being such a weakling. This was all stated in one glance in a way that only a cop could manage. Willy silently nodded and followed Riley back into the room and back into the memory of the first and only man he would ever kill.

*****

The day had started with a fifteen-minute tirade from Willy's Sergeant. Apparently, Willy's last DD-5 report was not satisfactory. Willy's Sergeant, a perpetually angry and impatient cop named Fignataro, did not approve of the report.

To show his disdain for the paper and Willy's writing style he had ripped up the report directly in front of him. He screamed at Willy for what felt like an eternity. Specifically, his complaint was that Willy's reports were "like God-damned college essays instead of actual police reports!" and that Willy should learn how to think and write like a cop and not a "God-damned pansy pinko college professor!"

This last statement was said with such disdain and fury that Willy had closed his eyes as he winced at the words. He had tried a technique that his deceased father had taught him, which was this: When things got really uncomfortable, just say to yourself: "That's-a-nice" and pretend you were someplace that you liked. Unfortunately for Willy, he had the misfortune of unconsciously saying this out loud while he closed his eyes and thought about his favorite comic-bookstore.

This only enraged Fignataro even more, until he finally told Willy to get out. He demanded that Willy have the rewritten report on his desk by the end of his tour or he would take away his Detective's shield and assign him to a permanent foot post as far away from the station house as he could get without falling into the East River.

Willy had just sat down to work on the report when his acid reflux punched him in the belly with a wave of nausea and gas all in one terrific spasm. He belched up a foul stream of acid into his throat and grabbed his side.

He decided to walk the two blocks to the local Bodega and buy the strongest antacid they had and a Ginger Ale to wash it down with. Ginger Ale always helped his nausea, and it was Gluten free, so he knew it would not aggravate his Celiac's disease and his allergy to anything containing even a trace amount of Gluten.

As he walked down the block towards the store, he realized the sun was shining brightly, and he closed his eyes and cursed as he had forgotten his sunglasses. His eyes immediately watered and burned. It was only a couple of blocks, but he hoped that the mid-day sun would not burn his skin.

He could receive a viscous sunburn on a cloudy day in the middle of winter, so he had to be careful. Plus, skin cancer was on his ever-growing list of terminal diseases that he was convinced would kill him far before his Sergeant did.

As he entered the store, he could see the Bodega was empty. The owner was a small and round Hispanic man and he happily nodded at

The Gathering Puddle

Willy as he made his way to the back to the cold drinks.

The layout was simple. The store was a long rectangle with the register located at the front right. The sides and the back wall were lined with the cold drink cases and in the middle were two narrow aisles of snacks and medications. Willy looked for his medication but did not see it on his way to the back.

Just as he opened the drink case, he heard the bell of the front door jingle open. A medium sized man with dark hair and dark skin looked briefly at Willy and then faced the owner. Willy removed the soda and opened it. He heard the release of fizz and then took a slow and long swig. The cold bubbly liquid felt soothing as it went down his throat in a rush of cool relief. As he drank Willy turned to face the front of the store.

The man reached into his pants and Willy somehow knew he was going to pull out a gun. He did not know how he knew this, but he did. It was some primal and hard instinct that came from the untapped primitive part of his brain that could only be accessed in times of extreme danger.

He dropped the Ginger Ale and heard some screaming, but he could not understand the words. He stared at the soda as it slowly crept out of the dropped plastic bottle and spread out to make a yellow puddle.

Then, without any thought or emotion he drew his gun. For a moment he felt the sudden terror of the forgotten item. It was a similar feeling to when you suddenly realized you had forgotten your keys and that you had no idea where they were or how you might get home.

But just as quickly as that fear struck him in the belly, he felt the solid handle of his automatic and realized he had not left his gun locked in his desk. As he drew the gun out, he could feel his hands trembling. He pulled his automatic up to eye level and walked towards the man at the counter.

The man did not see him until Willy was eight feet away. He turned to face Willy with the gun in his hand and Willy felt his own gun jerk several times in his hand and saw the man jump backwards, as if he had been punched in the body by a giant. Willy heard the shots pound into his ears, and he could not see or hear anything else but the man in front of him and the barrel of his own gun. He looked down through the sights and it seemed as if the end of his gun was miles away at the end of a dark tunnel. For a moment Willy thought he had been blinded as the rest of his vision closed in and around him.

Then, just as suddenly, the man was on the ground in front of Willy moaning and cursing. He had dropped his gun next to his body and Willy went to step on it. As he slapped his foot down, he felt the hard metal of the barrel slip out from under his foot and slide to the front door where it stopped against the wall.

The clatter sounded like the only noise left in the world. His foot started to come out from under him but then he balanced himself on the counter. He could hear screaming and crying, but he did not know where it was coming from. He smelled gunpowder, and he was reminded of the smell of wet leaves and fireworks on his childhood street during the summer. Slowly, he lowered his gun and stepped out of the store and into the light.

The street was empty, and it seemed to be too quiet. He could see people walking by and some of them were staring at him, but they still seemed oblivious to what happened. Willy stared at them as if they were not real. He realized that a difference of ten feet created the two completely different realities. Outside on the street life was normal. Inside the store there was a bizarre and macabre scene in which a man was dying on the floor in a bloody puddle.

Willy re-holstered his gun and went back into the store. He suddenly felt an unquenchable thirst. He stepped over the now gathering pool of sticky red liquid and the body of the man he had just killed, walked to the back, and drank down an entire fresh Ginger Ale.

As he stepped over the yellow puddle of the soda he had spilled minutes ago, he marveled at how similar the soda puddle was to the one now forming around the dead man at the front of the store. They both slowly spread out in all directions at once, like an eager explorer who has just seen a new land for the first time and cannot wait to see everything as fast as he possibly can.

The Gathering Puddle

*****

Willy looked down at his thin and pale hands and realized they had finally stopped trembling. He had the odd feeling that he was in someone else's body. He felt like he was an interloper, inside the body of this pale and weak man who had just murdered another human being.

He desperately wished that his partner Colin could be here beside him, consoling him, telling him what to say and how to handle the shooting team investigators. Willy knew Colin would most likely advise him to tell them as little as possible.

It was odd, as normally Willy was a talker. It was his way of interacting and at the same time integrating the crazy world of a police Detective into his otherwise mundane life. He had solved many cases by talking out the facts and allowing his brain to follow each piece of information the way a bloodhound follows an invisible scent. The more he talked, the more he learned and reasoned and explained until the facts finally all fell into place, and he could see the entire puzzle as a complete image.

However, in this instance he felt he had nothing to say. How could he explain the hollow and empty hole that was in his chest? How could he explain that the incomprehensible knowledge that he had just ended another man's life had left a deep and dark anxiety in the bottom of his stomach that felt like it had no end?

He could not find the words, and for the first time in a long time Willy realized he felt a vast and numbing emptiness in his soul. It scared him but also was reassuring and was a welcome contrast to his standard perpetual state of apprehension and anxiety.

Riley, the lead investigator, stared at Willy with a foul look on his face. Riley was one of the largest men he had ever seen. His red shaved head was the size of a large bowling ball and looked as if it was just as heavy. His wide body spilled over the sides of his chair the way a large piece of dough runs over the edges of the pan when it is kneaded too harshly, and his hands were the width of Willy's thigh.

He leaned forward towards Willy to express his impatience and he raised his massive hands into the air to express his frustration.

"Come on Weepy Willy. You're not telling us shit. We need to hear the entire story. You can't just sit there. You've got to talk to us Dammit!"

Riley's partner, a laconic detective named Steve Smith just nodded his White- haired head in agreement. Physically he was the absolute opposite of Riley. Smith was thin and demure, and he combed his white hair into an immaculate pompadour and wore expensive suits. People around the office had come to calling them Laurel and Hardy, but they were vicious and persistent investigators and not to be trifled with.

They viewed Willy's reluctance as resistance and immediately labeled him as an uncooperative witness. They had no patience or sympathy for the circumstance that many of the cops they interviewed were experiencing extreme forms of P.T.S.D., nor did they care. They had a job to do, and they meant to get it done as quickly and painlessly as possible.

Willy looked up at them with his watery eyes and just stared. He said nothing because he honestly could not think of anything to say. It was as if his brain had been tied in a loose knot. The harder he tried to think of what to say the tighter the knot of string got until it was balled up so densely that it could not be pulled apart.

Riley stood up, turned his back towards Willy, and then slowly turned around.

"Alright Weepy Willy, tell us that you at least identified yourself as a cop. At least tell me you did that much, please!"

Willy looked up at Riley's hulking form and finally was able to speak.

"I…I don't remember. I don't think so. No, I did not have time to…"

"Dammit Williamson! You didn't identify yourself? Jesus H. Keerist! You are really in it now!"

Willy finally stiffened up and realized he was starting to feel angry. *What right had Riley to come here and treat him like this? He had only done what any man would have done, hadn't he? For God's sake the man pointed a gun at him! What was he supposed to do?*

"Ask the store owner. He would know. I wasn't thinking about it, and there wasn't a lot of time."

"Look Weepy Willy. I'll just lay this out for you, and you tell me how it looks. A cop shoots a possibly unarmed man without provocation, does not identify himself, and then fails to secure the crime scene. You say there was a gun. We checked the scene, and we didn't find one. Now I believe you thought you saw one, I really do. But after you cap this guy, you grab a soda and then just wander off? What in the Holy Hell were you thinking? Now we have a shooting and only the word of the shooter that the victim was armed. "

"What does the store owner say? He saw the whole thing, didn't he?"

"He corroborates some of what you are saying. He does state there was weapon, but can't be sure it was a gun, and he didn't see the shooting as he ducked behind the counter and cowered there until the uniforms arrived. By that time, the weapon, whatever it was, if it even existed in the first place, was gone. This looks bad, really bad."

The rest of the interview consisted of Riley showing Willy a diagram of the store and some other questions that Willy just answered by rote. Once he had heard the information about the missing gun, he had tuned out everything else.

He knew there was a gun. There had to be. He could not be wrong about this. Someone must have taken it before the uniforms arrived. Willy cursed himself. He remembered kicking the gun across the floor, and even telling himself *I should pick up that gun and voucher it*, but his instinct to get out of the store and away from the body had overridden any common sense and he had wandered away.

As soon as Willy arrived home at his studio apartment, he fell into a deep sleep plagued by dreams of gunshots and screaming men. He dreamt of the shooting over and over until he woke up in the middle of a silent scream and drenched sheets.

He needed his partner. Thankfully, his phone had two voicemails, both from Colin. He had no idea how he had missed the calls and did not care as he anxiously waited for the call to connect.

His partner was on a two-week vacation in Barbados with his fiancé Jasmine, but somehow, he must have heard about the shooting. He desperately wanted to talk to Colin and when he answered on the second ring Willy felt some of the burning crater that was his stomach cool down.

"Will, that you? You okay? I heard what happened from the Sarge. Fignataro called me. As much as he hates you, he is also worried about you. He wanted me to check in on you. "

Just hearing Colin's voice calmed Willy.

"Yeah, I'm alright. I just don't know what to do, what to say, what to think. Was it like this when you had your shooting?"

"Yeah Will, it was bad. The most important thing to remember is that almost everyone wants to tell you how to feel and how to think, and those that don't know what to say will stay away from you. They just want to settle it in their own mind so that they can tell themselves *this could never happen to me*, but it's all bullshit. Just stop thinking so much. And don't scratch your hand."

Willy looked down at the back of his right hand and he was reminded he had already scratched away a full layer of skin.

"Colin, I don't know if I can take this. Now they are telling me there might not be a gun. After I did it, I didn't know what to do, so I kind of wondered into the street, and then I…I…"

Willy began to weep uncontrollably into the phone. Colin listened silently and let Willy pour out the pain and frustration into the phone. After a full minute of this Willy sucked in some air and gripped the phone solidly.

"I'm sorry Col, I just…I never thought this would be me. What the Hell should I do? Nothing feels right. Nothing feels real or normal. And my ears won't stop ringing and I've got a migraine that is killing me so badly…"

"Easy Will. Easy. I know and I understand. I know exactly how you feel. It's going to take a while to even begin to feel normal again, and in some ways, you will never go back to who you were before this, but give it time and you will settle down.

For now, here is what I want you to do. First, don't tell those buzzards in I.A.B. anything. Only talk to your D.E.A. union rep. and even with him, be careful what you say. Then I want you to turn that street upside down and find that gun.

I already talked to Fignataro, and he is willing to work the street with you if you want. Talk to every possible witness, every person you see and every damn human being within a square mile of that Bodega. Someone must have seen the gun or seen who walked with it. It couldn't have bounced very far. You will find it.

I don't want to you to go into one of your worrying fits. Take your migraine meds, get some sleep, and then hit that neighborhood with Fignataro until you find the gun. I'll text you his personal cell phone. He's waiting for your call. I would be there right next to you but even cutting my vacation short I can't be there for at least two days."

Willy let out a sigh of relief.

"Thanks Col. Thank you so much. You know you have saved my life here…I can't say…I mean I…"

"You don't need to say it Will. I know. By the way, Jasmine says she loves you and you are going to be okay. Text her if you need to talk. She's a wise woman Will. Take her advice. It's probably better than mine. One last thing Will. You don't need to feel a certain way.

The people at Psych. Services will tell you to get in touch with your feelings, and the other guys on the job will tell you that you are a hero, but you know what Willy? You are what you are, and you don't need to figure anything out yet. Just let this sit with you and sink in before you try to figure it all out. I'm here if you need me."

Willy felt tears of joy running down his cheeks.

"Thanks Col. Thanks. I'm tired, I think I'll take my meds and go back to sleep for a while."

"Okay, hang in there Will. I'll see you in a few days and Jasmine will cook us a big gluten free meal."

Willy ended the call, lay back, and fell into a deep dreamless sleep.

*****

Several hours later Willy woke up and his headache was gone. When he arrived at work Sergeant Fignataro was waiting for him and immediately called Willy into his office.

"Sit down Williamson."

Willy's Sergeant looked especially intense, and he unconsciously crept back in his chair waiting for the yelling to start. Sergeant Fignataro slowly walked around his desk and gently placed his hand on Willy's shoulder.

"Willy, I just wanted to make sure you are okay. Are you alright?"

Willy looked up in shock at his Sergeant. He had only seen rage and impatience every time he looked at him, and now he stood looking down at Willy like he was his favorite son.

"Uh, yeah, Sarge, I'm okay, I guess. I still don't know exactly what happened. It's like I'm walking through a thick fog, and I can't really see things until they are right in front of me."

Fignataro looked down at Willy with sympathy.

"Willy, I know I bust your balls and give you a hard time, and God knows you can be a pain in the ass. Your reports are terrible, and you whine more than my wife, but basically you are a good cop. "

Willy was in shock. Fignataro removed his hand and went behind his desk. He opened the drawer and strapped on his gun and his shield.

"Now, you and I are going to hit the street and find that gun. I'm actually looking forward to doing a little real policework instead of reading reports and signing overtime slips. We'll split up and knock on every door in a three-block radius until we find what we need. And I also have three other guys from the squad coming in early on their own time knocking on doors too. Everybody is chipping in for you. Now let's go."

*****

Four hours later Willy, his Sergeant, and the other Detectives had knocked on over a hundred doors between them and thus far had only come up with two witnesses who heard the shots. Unfortunately, the only thing they had seen was Willy wondering out onto the street.

After knocking on his tenth door Willy suddenly felt dizzy. As he walked down the stairs of the apartment building, he observed a dark-skinned man walking up the stairs towards him. The man reached into his pocket and Willy felt his guts tighten in terror. He reached down for

The Gathering Puddle

his gun and then saw the man was only pulling out his keys. He eyed Willy fearfully as he let him pass on his way down to the street.

Willy burst through the door and leaned against the building. His heart was racing, and he felt like he couldn't breathe. As people walked past him, they stared at him, and as these strange men and women passed him, Willy envisioned they were all reaching for weapons. They all looked like they were trying to kill him, and Willy staggered to the sidewalk where he sat down and put his head in his hands.

He just wanted it all to stop torturing him. He felt like the world was closing in on him and the air around him was a cold metal vice, moving in and clutching his body, until it had squeezed out all of the air and flattened him into a bloody mess of guts and bones and skin. He wanted to scream, but he knew he could not. Even if he did, no one would help.

They would look at him like he was crazy and call 911, and then Riley would show up and stare down at his pathetic form and shake his head saying "I told you so" over and over. He felt like his lungs were full of water and he could not get enough air. He was sure he was going to pass out when he felt a hand touch him softly on the shoulder. His jumped up at the touch and reached for his gun. Staring back at him was the sad and worried face of Sergeant Fignataro. Fignataro put his hands up in supplication.

"Easy Willy, easy. It's me, your Sarge."

Willy relaxed his body and then sat down again on the curb and put his face in his hands.

"Sarge, I think I'm losing it. I can't trust myself anymore. Everyone looks like they are trying to kill me. I don't know what the hell I'm doing. Tell the other guys from the squad they can stop. It's over, I'm finished as a cop, and now I really hope they don't find the gun. I don't care anymore. I just want it all to stop and be done with."

Willy felt silent tears streaming down his face as he pinched the sides of his head as hard as he could.

Fignataro sat down next to Willy and slowly put his hand on his shoulder.

"Willy, just slow down. Stop that kind of talk. Christ, I knew it was a bad idea to take you out on this. I thought it might help but you are not ready. You're still too close to this thing. Son, I'm sorry this happened to you.

I know a lot of the guys in the squad and on this job think that being involved in a shooting is badge of honor, and that it makes you a bad ass cop and all of that other John Wayne bullshit, but the truth is it just messes you up. Some cops bury it better than others, but this type of thing eats away at who you are and your already chipped faith in humanity.

I'm giving you some time off, starting now. Don't worry, I won't tell the head shrinkers at psyche services about it. I won't even tell the captain. You deserve a couple of days to get this right in your head, but it's just between you and me. As much as you annoy the crap out of me you are one of my guys, and it is my job to protect you, no matter what. Now, go back to the station house. Wait at your desk. When I get back you and me are going to get something to eat and then we can talk some more in my office if you need it."

Willy looked up at his Sergeant and wiped the tears from his face. Despite his anguish, he felt lucky to be sitting next to his Sergeant. Through all his pain and humiliation, he realized he was sitting next to a man who cared deeply about his soul.

*****

Hours later they all sat in the squad room with their bellies full of Chinese food. They were all exhausted and frustrated from the dead leads they had encountered. Willy scratched at the back of his right hand.

In the past Willy had always been an outcast. The only other Detective in the squad that had not mocked him on a regular basis was Colin, but now they all seemed to regard him with a careful reverence.

As Willy scratched and scratched and small bubbles of blood began to form on the back of his hand, he mused that this was the first time anyone on the job other than Colin had taken him seriously. He felt sad that the only reason it happened was because he had killed another human being.

He tried desperately to remember the man's face, but it was still a wavy and indistinct mass of features. Oddly enough, he could definitely remember the smell of the cordite in the air from his shots, and his mind kept playing flashes of the victim's body as it had spasmed with the force of the rounds.

He also felt a creeping fear that he was going to lose his job and end up in jail. If it came to that, he would leave the country. He knew he stood no chance of survival in jail. The day's failure to produce any credible leads depressed and terrified Willy all at the same time, and this dreadful thought ended with a huge and painful gas bubble in his stomach. Suddenly he felt claustrophobic. The squad room seemed small and dirty, and the walls looked grimier than he had ever remembered.

He silently nodded to the other Detectives and went down to the street. Fignataro was in his office, so he did not see Willy leave. Minutes later and without realizing how he had gotten there, he found himself across the street from the scene of the shooting. He stared at the storefront, as if his concentration on the door could change the past. He wished with everything he had in his being that it had never happened.

Why did Colin have to be away on that particular day? Why did he have to walk into that store at that moment? Why had he become a cop to begin with? He wasn't suited for this job. He worried about everything, was physically and emotionally weak, and did not fit in with any of the cops he had ever known except Colin. He knew he had a marginal talent for closing out cases, but so what?

So did half of the Detectives in the city. And now, he had actually taken another life and it looked like he was going to pay for it. He could almost see the judge banging the gavel and giving him a life sentence upstate where he would be torn apart by the cop haters and the gangs on his first day inside.

As he focused on the store's doorway, he suddenly saw a boy run into the street after a red ball. He also saw that the light had changed, and that traffic was moving south towards the boy and was not slowing down. The oncoming cars looked like a herd of large predators comprised of cheap steel and plastic, burying the boy in their oncoming shadow as they hungered for human flesh.

Willy ran out into the street, and just as the boy was about to be flattened by a skidding taxi, he pulled the boy to safety. The taxi screeched past and came so close to Willy that it tore the side pocket of his suit jacket off as it went by. Willy collapsed with the boy in his arms on the edge of the sidewalk.

The boy, who was still in shock, began crying as he stared up at Willy. He had short brown hair and a chubby body, but his face looked like that of an adult, and his portrait painted an odd picture.

The boy's mother came running over and hugged the child so tightly Willy thought she would crush him. Willy could see she was an attractive dark-haired woman with toned arms and legs. She looked tired and relieved as she hugged her boy.

"Thank you mister, thank you so much! You saved his life! "

As she said this, the woman began weeping and she grabbed Willy's hand. As she wiped way the tears, she looked at Willy and tilted her head at an angle as if she knew him.

"Wait a minute, you are that cop from the bodega the other day. I know you. You shot that guy!"

As if Willy were on fire the woman suddenly grabbed the boy and pulled him away and into the building directly across the street from the storefront, looking back at him as if he were a plague. Willy sighed and slowly trudged back up to the squad room.

*****

An hour later, as Willy dozed at his desk his phone rang. He was hoping it was Colin, but he heard a woman's whispering voice on the other end.

"Detective, go to this address-one forty-six West Forty-Fifth Street. On the second floor, in front of apartment two C and under the mat is a mailbox key. The key will open the mailbox for apartment two C in that same building. No one lives in that apartment, so no one will check the mailbox. There is something there you need."

The line went dead. The woman's voice sounded familiar, and then Willy realized it sounded very much like the woman he had met on the sidewalk after saving the child, but since she was whispering, he could not be sure and would never really know. He realized this could be a set up, but he really had nothing to lose.

He didn't tell anyone where he was going. If this was a way to arrange his death, he felt like he deserved it anyway. He removed his gun and his shield and locked them in his desk. Whatever was going to happen he was not going to try and fight it, and after the shooting he found the touch of his gun reprehensible.

As he walked to the address he was given on the phone by the mysterious caller he felt refreshed, and for the first time the violent visions of the shooting seemed to have left his mind. The building was a typical brownstone and matched the style of many others on both sides of the street. It was a tall narrow rectangle with five floors that touched the other buildings beside it so that they all looked like one very long house that covered an entire block.

As he entered the lobby he instinctively reached for his gun and shield and remembered they were locked in his desk. He smiled as he realized that whatever was about to happen, there was no possible way he could shoot someone. If he was cut down no one could claim he had acted too aggressively.

As he crept up the stairs a door suddenly swung open, and he was staring at a small man in his bathrobe. He looked at Willy like he was something foul and then slammed his door without a word. On the next floor he found the mat in front of apartment two C and the key was underneath, exactly as described.

He crept back down the stairs and found the mailbox the caller had mentioned. He stared at it for a full five minutes. Just as he was about to put the key in two young kids pulled open the door, glanced at Willy and then ran up the stairs. Willy waited until their rhythmic steps on the stairs stopped. Then he heard a door slam.

He quickly put the key in the mailbox and for a moment he thought it was all a sick joke, as the key did not turn the lock. He let out a large sigh and then tried again, this time putting a little more pressure into the turn of the key. The lock held for another moment and then he could feel the tumbler give in and the mailbox was open.

Inside was a white rag that was covering something black. Willy pulled on a pair of his hyper-allergenic gloves and removed the white cloth. Underneath was a small automatic. In a flash Willy suddenly recognized it as the gun the man had pointed at him in the robbery. Until this moment the details of the gun and the man's face had eluded him, but now they leapt into his brain the way a cat unexpectedly jumps up onto a windowsill.

His vision of the man's face was clear and so was the image of the gun he now held in his plastic gloved hand. He carefully wrapped it in the cloth and dropped it into his jacket pocket. He walked slowly out the lobby to the street. He pulled out his phone to dial his Sergeant. Before he placed the call he looked up at the dark sky and was astonished to see a weak and distant star.

He looked back down at the street at the motion of all of the cars and the people to a city that never stopped moving. He realized there was a chance he could be cleared of the shooting. If this was, in fact, the gun used by the man he shot, he would be okay.

He let out a deep sigh and felt a slight adulation creep through his stomach. He still did not know if he would ever reconcile what happened to him, and he was not sure he could ever fire his gun again, even at the shooting range. For today though, he at least had one thing left. He had hope. And for now, that would have to do.

Not the Dog
Madeleine McDonald

Lisbeth didn't mind for herself. What she minded, very much minded, was the killing of her beloved Patch.

At 86, Lisbeth had expected the Grim Reaper to come calling. On their daily tramps across the fields, whenever her knees ached more than usual, she shared her thoughts with the dog. 'You're walking as slow as I am today, Patch, old boy. We've done our time, and then some, haven't we? Let's get home before dark, and light the fire. A whisky to warm my old bones, and I've saved you some liver. Might as well make ourselves comfortable.'

Patch was greedy, and hoovered up more than his fair share of the home-made biscuits her great-niece Rachel gave her.

That his end had been unintentional was irrelevant. It was unnecessary and cruel. Unlike her self-centred niece, Patch had been a loyal presence since her husband died. Evenings were companionable with the dog stretched full length on the hearth rug, allowing her to tickle his backbone with her stockinged feet.

*****

A rage Lisbeth had not thought possible inhabited her bones. Her spirit hovered as her niece ransacked the cottage, throwing clothes, bedding, photographs and knick-knacks into bin bags, in a frenzy of activity.

'Why the hurry, Rachel? Some of this stuff might be valuable. Maybe you should ask an antiques dealer to take a look.'

Her friend Toby held a pair of blue glass candlesticks to the evening light that streamed through now uncurtained windows. 'Like these. They look Italian to me.'

'Shut up, Tobes. Lisbeth never went abroad. She'll have bought them in Scarborough, or Skegness, or some other godforsaken resort.'

Rachel snatched them out of his hands and tipped them into a bulging bin bag. There was a rattle of crockery as she dumped the bag alongside a pile of others. 'If you want to do something useful, pour me a drink.'

'No. You're driving, remember, and I want to get back to London in one piece. I'll make us a cup of tea instead.' Toby ignored Rachel's scowl and wandered into the kitchen.

Lisbeth floated behind.

'Look what I found,' he said when he came back with two mugs. 'I was looking for biscuits and this fell off a shelf. That's you. Same scowl, even when you were in pigtails. And is that your aunt and uncle?'

Rachel tore the faded photograph in half and threw it away.

'Temper, temper,' he reproved. 'If you don't want to take any mementoes, why not leave the job to the house clearance people?'

'Because I'm skint, as well you know. The house clearance man quoted me £1000 to clear the lot. £500 if all he has to shift is the piano and the furniture. He's got me over a barrel.'

'So?' Toby shrugged. 'Put it on your credit card and sort it out once you get probate. That can't be what's bugging you. You've been on edge all day. In fact, you've been acting funny since the old girl died. Anyone would think you were fond of her.' He went back to packing books into cardboard boxes, whistling under his breath.

'Do you have to be so cheerful?'

He swivelled round in surprise, then snapped his fingers. 'I know why. It's nothing to do with dear old Auntie Lisbeth. It's because your Josh won't commit. You're 30 this year, and he still won't tie the knot. That's it, isn't it?' He whistled louder.

Lisbeth knew why her niece wanted no mementoes. She watched her hands clench around a sheet. A guilty conscience drove Rachel to eliminate all reminders of her aunt's existence. Unease drove her to quarrel with Toby, her friend since primary school, and her one true friend.

Lisbeth's spirit floated back into the kitchen, where she knocked a cup off the draining board. She heard Rachel's gasp of shock. She watched Toby shut the kitchen window and attempt to soothe Rachel.

Lisbeth wanted her niece to suffer. Suffer as much as poor Patch had done.

My Dave told me you were a bad'un, she thought. You're my sister's only grandchild and I didn't want to believe him. But he saw through you alright.

Lisbeth undid the kitchen window catch again and knocked a pan to the floor. Over the metallic clang she heard Rachel swear.

*****

Unlike Toby, Lisbeth knew just what Rachel had done.

She knew now that Rachel had complained for years. *Why can't the old bat just die ... She's 86, she'll live forever, just to spite me ... It's ridiculous, someone her age chopping up firewood, I hope she chops her foot off and bleeds to death.*

Lisbeth also knew it was Toby who had pushed Rachel over the edge. Not deliberately. She absolved him of malice. He had simply made an unthinking quip about putting weedkiller in the coffee to finish her off.

Rachel worked in a museum – stuck at assistant curator level for the last five years because of spending cuts. That year the museum was hosting a special exhibition set in Victorian London, including waxwork figures in period dress. Along with the other staff, she was warned to wear gloves to handle the voluminous crinoline skirt, because of arsenic present in the dark green dye. One lunch hour, she slipped on gloves, knelt under the crinoline with a torch and snipped away part of the lining, fraying it again to leave no trace.

Lisbeth ate Rachel's home-made biscuits, and duly died. So did Patch. Rachel took the precaution of tipping the remainder of the arsenic solution into the outside well, which Lisbeth used to water the garden in the dry summer.

The coroner concluded it was an unfortunate accident.

Not so Lisbeth.

*****

Her spirit hovered in Rachel's kitchen, listening to her complain about Josh to her girlfriends. 'He takes me for granted. I was 30 last month.

30! He says there's no point discussing marriage yet. We're fine as we are, he says.' Her girlfriends murmured in sympathy, and contributed tales of their own partners' deficiencies.

'I found out he shagged that girl in the office,' one said, 'But he said it was only once, and what happens at work stays at work.'

'Men have it too easy,' another commiserated.

Lisbeth listened in disbelief. The young women talked of commitment, but did any of them know what that meant? *For better, for worse, for richer, for poorer, in sickness and in health.* Would any of them have the stamina for that?

She had grown up in rural Suffolk, with a dad who collected her at 11 pm prompt from dances in the village hall. She had married young and never regretted it. In 48 years of marriage they had the usual ups and downs, of course, but her beloved Dave had never taken her for granted, nor treated her with disrespect. They had been equal partners, each in their own way.

Not so Rachel's friends. For so-called independent young women, they all seemed preoccupied with dragging a man to the altar. Lisbeth longed to shake sense into them, all of them. Yet listening to their entitled, self-centred babble was her only chance of discovering a suitable way to punish Rachel.

The opportunity presented itself once probate had been granted. Lisbeth was amazed to hear that her cottage commanded such a high price at auction.

With the cash in her pocket, Rachel offered to finance 90% of a house deposit. She and Josh would have to move to the periphery of London to afford a proper house, but with Lisbeth's inheritance, it would be feasible.

Their feet crunched over fallen leaves as they viewed box-sized properties in unfashionable areas. The clocks had gone back and dank evenings made the properties seem even less appealing.

Josh became restive, focussing on the inconveniences of each new location.

Rachel became panicky, fearing they would be priced out of the market.

Eventually, they signed on the dotted line, unaware of Lisbeth's giddy whirl of triumph.

She stroked the solicitor's fingers just as he was entering the other solicitor's bank code. Startled, he scrutinised his fingers, and decided he really must get that draughty window in the corridor double-glazed before winter set in.

A single incorrect digit in the bank code meant that the deposit money was transferred to the wrong account. Although the payment bounced, the two banks involved took their time sorting out the tangle and returning the deposit to the first solicitor.

The vendor accepted a better offer. Rachel and Josh lost the house Rachel had set her heart on.

They quarrelled. 'It was your fault,' he argued. 'You were dancing with impatience in the solicitor's office. You rushed him, like you hassle me.'

'You're no fun any more,' he flung at her one night. Rachel went into meltdown, and he suggested a trial separation.

'She freaked out,' he told his mates in the pub. There were grunts of sympathy, before someone ordered another round.

Lisbeth considered Josh collateral damage. She had nothing against him, but nothing spoke in his favour either.

Josh decided to spend Christmas in Portugal, on a surfing holiday with his mates. Since he was no longer under pressure to save money, he treated himself to a new surfboard.

*****

On Christmas Eve, the shops were open late, and the streets lit up. For Rachel, Josh's treachery festered, and she was in no mood for festivities. When a Salvation Army band blocked the street, attracting a small crowd around them, her frustration reached boiling point. The happy faces and the chink of coins in the collection bucket conspired to mock her.

When Tobes started whistling along to *Hark the Herald Angels Sing*, it was the last straw.

Never a cautious driver, she put her foot down as soon as they left the band behind, heedless of pedestrians or other traffic. She jumped a red light, killing Tobes, her one true friend.

*****

Lisbeth hovered in the courtroom to see her great niece convicted of death by dangerous driving.

But she was not finished.

While Rachel tossed and turned in her chilly bunk, Lisbeth hovered in the cramped cell. She found it was best to wait until the lights were switched off for the night. The warders made their final round, locking gates as they went. Their footsteps faded and the prison settled into sullen silence.

'Patch,' Lisbeth called. Softly, insistently.

Rachel put her hands over her ears. The sound seared into her brain. There was no way to block it out.

Patch. Here, boy. Patch.

Ashes, Ashes
Joan Leotta

My mother pulled me close with the little strength she had left and whispered in my ear. "I'll always be with you." I smiled at those words. My mother was my only living relative which left me, at age twenty-six alone to face the world. She had always been my friend, protector, and ally in all that I did until recently. We argued a lot in the weeks before her car accident—over my new boyfriend, James. When I was called to the hospital, James was already there. He had seen her trying to cross the road and had given the police a description of the person who had pushed her down on the deserted sidewalk in front of her antique shop. She winced whenever I mentioned his name, even while she was unconscious, and again when she regained consciousness. She started to say, "JJJJ," But I interrupted and blurted out, "I love you, Mom, I'm sorry for arguing with you." She smiled, grabbed at my hand, and pulled me to her and spoke her those last words, "I'll always be with you."

I thought she meant those words in terms of a remembrance of her. Mother had always been fascinated by the Victorian idea of *momento mori*—mostly locks of hair from the dear departed set into a piece of jewelry. She sold them in her shop and was known for having a great collection. Many came and sought out her shop just for those bits of someone's beloved. As for her own beloved departed ones, my Mom had a small case with a lock of my father's hair.

Her parents and his had died escaping East Germany. He died when I was two. She was not afraid of death, in fact, a year or two ago, she said she wanted to become a different kind of *momento mori* when she died. She had read an article about a company that swirled a person's ashes into a glass globe—like a paperweight. For a few dollars more you could add sparkles to it or colored glass.

So, I obeyed her last wishes. My job as an accountant revealed that Mom's business was barely able to make rent, so I sold it, keeping only the jeweled *momento mori* with my Dad's lock of hair.

Before mom was cremated and stored in the glass, I had one lock of her hair cut and placed in the jewel case with my Dad's by her jeweler friend, the man who owned the store next to hers. I know he was a bit creeped out by the commission, but he did it because he knew my Mom. I didn't tell him about the snowball sized ball of glass swirled with the gray remains of my mother's body, that I now kept on my desk, my at-home workplace for my accounting business. The braided locks of hair in a locket I kept in my desk drawer.

James knew about it though. He hated it. He said, "Creeps me out, it's ghoulish, ghastly."

At first I simply laughed at his dislike of the paperweight. I liked having "mom" physically nearby. But then I noticed James was finding excuses not to come into my apartment, closing the door to my office when he did come in so that the glass ball was completely out of sight. And after he moved in, it seemed easier to leave Mom's *momento mori* paperweight in the drawer with the other one so James would not feel uncomfortable walking into my office.

Last night, I was working on a rush job for a client. James sauntered into the room. He's been out all day. Called to say he could not make it home in time for dinner. And the first words he spoke were, "Hey, Babe, I need some cash."

In the past months I'd seen letters from credit card companies to him, marked "final notice."

He had started to ask me for five or ten dollars before he went to work. But tonight he wanted a hundred dollars—cash. "Just a quick loan, Babe."

I'd already started to open the drawer where I kept a couple of tens in case I needed quick cash.

"Whoa! I don't have that kind of cash laying around. James, why do you need so much cash?"

His anger flashed. He stepped closer. "None of your business!" Then he leaned over the desk and struck me—hard, across the mouth. I fell backwards in my chair, my head hit the floor and I started to see stars. I heard James laughing. My head hurt so much. I could barely lift it. James kept laughing but then I saw Mom's paperweight fly out of the drawer, across the desk and strike James in the head. He began to bleed, screamed, and ran out.

I called the police. They took me to the hospital. I filed a complaint against James. When I got back to the apartment, before I took the pain pill, I went into my office to put the paperweight back into the drawer, but it was already there, sitting on the two ten dollar bills I kept for emergencies. Like always.

The next day I put all of James' things in a box in the hall outside the apartment. He tried to reconcile but I knew Mom had been right about him.

*****

One afternoon, a few months after, I was feeling sorry for myself and tempted to take James back into my life, to call him. I had convinced myself that I had imagined the incident with the paperweight (now back on top of my desk). As I reached for my phone to punch in James' number a "drunk dial" call buzzed in from James' best friend, Gregory. In general I always found Gregory rather loathsome and was sure he was the root cause of anything James did wrong—gambling, drinking, even that slap James gave me that was the impetus for me to throw James out.

"He did it, you know." Gregory was slurring his words. I was about to hang up but suddenly my Mom flashed in my head. Her stuttering when she regained consciousness—"jjj" Had she been trying to tell me that James had pushed her to the ground where she hit her head on the cement curb? I began to cry. I hung up on Gregory so he wouldn't hear me crying. After blotting my tears, I went to bed.

The next day, instead of calling James, I called the police station and asked to speak Detective Aldridge, the one who had handled Mom's case.

"It always bothered me that we couldn't find who pushed your Mom. I thought it was odd that no one had taken her purse or tried to break into the shop."

"Did you think it odd that James Fernlow was the one who found her?"

"Well, we did circle his name. But he told us he had arranged to meet your Mom at the store to help her with some of the larger pieces in the store—move them around to make a nicer display.

He said he had spoken to her the night before. We asked you about it, remember?"

I thought back. I'd been dating James for a few months at that time. I really didn't recall the detective asking me why James was there. "My memory is faulty about that time. I was so worried about Mom. I focused so much on her. We had been arguing and I wanted her to regain consciousness so I could apologize and tell her how much I loved her—still love her in fact."

Detective Aldridge spoke softly, "A mother's love never ends. I'm sure she knew you loved her."

"Well, she did regain consciousness for a minute before she passed. I don't think you every asked me about that."

"It's not in my notes. What did she say?"

"She started to stutter, jjjj and then I interrupted her and blurted out how sorry I was and how much I loved her."

I heard the detective take a deep breath. "My notes don't say that you confirmed her call to James."

"Well, at the time I was living in my own apartment—alone. After Mom died, James made himself indispensable, helping me with the sale of Mom's store. I do recall he was surprised when almost everything I got for the store and its contents went to settling debts, mostly made by the store. Buying more than she could sell was a weakness of Mom's.

I was still grieving when James told me he wanted us to move in together so he could take care of me. Not long after that he lost his job and began to borrow five and ten dollars at a time from me. The night I threw him out he wanted one hundred dollars in cash. When I said no, he struck me. That's when I threw him out. Last night a friend of his called me and told me James "did it." He didn't say what, but it made me start to think about my mom—what she might have been trying to tell me."

I stopped talking. I didn't tell the detective about the paperweight flying out of the drawer. The Detective then told me he had done a background check on James and found a long history of small theft and fraud claims, most dismissed for lack of evidence. "He was fired from several jobs for what the employers all called violent outbursts."

After a minute of silence, Aldridge added "I always thought he got there early, to the store to get your Mom to give him money. I don't think she was expecting him. Likely she said no, and he pushed her. He may not have meant to kill her, but she hit her head."

"Just like it happened with me." I was almost whispering into the phone. He asked for money, more than the usual ten or so and when I said I didn't have it, he hit me."

"That's true to type. The officers who handled your case when you pressed charges but then declined to follow up in court, they called me. They recognized the name on the case and knew it had been bothering me never to have caught the person who pushed your mom."

"I guess he thought Mom kept a lot of money in the store. After she died, I guess he thought I'd get a lot of money for the store and stock, but any money I got went to pay her debts. I guess there is nothing I can do about it though since no one saw anything. The jeweler next door wasn't at his shop yet and his cameras weren't working that day. He'd been having problems."

"It's more complicated than that. When I looked into it, I discovered that he hired your friend to fix the cameras and your friend just made it worse. He never said anything about it to you because he knew you were dating James."

I hung up and began to think about what could be done to get justice for my mother—and myself. The next day I called Detective Aldridge again. We devised a plan.

*****

The following Monday I called James. With a quiver in my voice, I told him I missed him and hoped he would come back. He was wary until I added this, "We can start our relationship off on a good footing by taking a trip, a weekend in New York. All the trimmings. I'm selling the last of my mother's pieces—the broach that has a lock of her hair and one of my dad's. A collector called me, and he is coming over today. He was talking to Mike, my jeweler friend who had the shop next to mom's and learned about it. Evidently it's a rare design and he wants to give me five thousand dollars in cash for it."

James began to laugh. "I'm not sure I want to start up again. You still have that crazy paperweight around?"

"It broke," I lied.

"Well, Babe, I'll have to give it some thought. You know, you hurt me pretty bad with that filing charges and all, even though you didn't follow up and let them put me in jail, not that I would have anyway After all, you were pretty awful to me. I'm sure a jury would have been on my side."

It was hard for me to control my own temper at this point, but instead I simpered, "I'm sure."

I told him I would meet him for coffee the next day and we could go together to get the train tickets for New York and decide on the hotel we wanted. "I'd meet you tonight, but I have to meet with a client and won't be home until nine or ten."

I called Detective Aldridge. "You think he will really try to break into my apartment tonight? I changed the locks from the time he lived here."

Aldridge replied, "I don't think the lock will be a problem for him. He actually did work for a security company for a while—that's how he knew enough about the cameras on the street to disrupt them so well. He can likely pick your lock easily. And he knows you like to keep money in the desk drawer, right?

I left the house around five and went to the police station to wait. The detective made me as comfortable as possible in his office and then went out to the stakeout arranged for my apartment.

At about eight thirty a call came into the station. A bloody man was stumbling down the steps of my building. The officers took him into custody. He was holding the marked bills from my desk drawer. It was James. They took him to the hospital and then charged him. The Detective went to the hospital and charged him. They called George, and brought him in. In exchange for dropping the charges on the coke they found on him, he agreed to spill all on James having pushed my mother. George had been with James and actually witnessed the attack, something he had not told me when he said he knew what James had done.

So, this time James was caught, for stealing the money and for pushing my Mom. The stakeout almost missed catching him though. Somehow he had slipped in through the service entrance but only came out through the front door when he got disoriented inside my apartment. "She told me it had broken but it was there, right on top of the money, that damned paperweight, and when I moved it, the thing flew up and hit me in the head, I tell you. All on its own."

No one believed him. There was blood on the paperweight, but they surmised he had put his head down and the paperweight had rolled out of the drawer onto his head. Well, that's not quite true. I believed him. Even though I now had the police on my side, and James was in jail, I knew it was my Mom who was still truly protecting me, just as she had promised.

A Missing Piece

H. E. Vogl

With a manicured finger Rudi Starowicz nudged the last print on the ledge an eighth of an inch, then he stepped back to admire his work.

"Excellent," he said.

Twenty perfect photographs all precisely arranged. And in the middle of the display his prize shot, a twelve by eighteen of the Empire State Building. Its sleek gray exterior and the surrounding blue sky formed a collage of triangles that converged to a point at the peak of the building. Satisfied, Rudi rolled his eyes down to the base of the photo and stopped.

"What's that?" he whispered.

Stuck to the window of the adjacent office building was a squashed bug. Rudi ran to the kitchen for a paper towel, came back and stretched over the couch to brush off the offending creature. But when he lowered the towel, it was still there. He leaned closer and pinched his fingers together to remove the intruder. That's when he realized that the defect wasn't on the print, it was in it.

Rudi jumped off the couch. He ran back to the kitchen and opened his laptop sitting on the table. After carefully wiping the screen to remove any trace of dust, he searched for the defect. Sure enough there was a small blob in the window of the office building. Frantically, he enlarged the errant scene, and what at first appeared to be an insect morphed into two people. A man and a woman positioned like marionettes. The man held an object and he appeared to be striking the woman. Rudi pinched the bridge of his nose and looked again. Only two people in animated conversation. And the object, nothing more than a folder raised over the woman's head. He slid the curser to the eraser tool, and three clicks later the couple in the window vanished into a pixelated netherworld.

"Another murder solved," he said and smiled.

*****

That night as the filter of consciousness gave way to sleep, Rudi dreamt. He was in New York walking down 34th Street on a sweltering September day. He stopped and ran his forearm over his brow. That's when he saw the façade of the building cutting through the sky like a knife.

He raised his camera to capture the moment before the light changed, and in a hushed voice he said, "No."

A stream of people flowed around him like water around a rock.

"Somebody look," he said pointing to the window.

"Nobody's gonna fall for that one buddy," a passer-by said.

"The window, he's going to kill her."

"Must see King Kong," a sarcastic voice said.

Rudi ran down thirty-fourth and smacked into his dresser. For a moment he stood there, dazed, soaked in sweat. Then he stripped off his pajamas and staggered into the shower. As a stream of cool water assaulted him, he realized it was only a dream. He toweled off, grabbed fresh pajamas, and went to the kitchen. At the table he opened his laptop and located the unedited version of the photo. It could be a murder, he thought.

Rudi picked up the phone and dialed. On the second ring the operator picked up.

"I'd like to report a murder."

"Sir, I'll connect you with emergency."

"No wait, it didn't just happen," Rudi said, his breath shortening to gasps.

"What do you mean?"

"It happened last year. I saw it in a photo on my wall."

"Sir, false reporting is a crime. Can I have your name and address?"

He hung up. Rudi went to the sink and choked down a glass of water. He regained his composure, but the possibility that a murder had been committed troubled him like a puzzle with a missing piece. And if he was going to find that piece, he'd need a plan. Rudi flopped on the couch hoping that sleep would bring the answer.

*****

The next morning cradling a mug of coffee, Rudi scoured a map of New York to obtain the name of the building where he saw the struggle. Then, he placed a call.

"Brisbane building, Security," a voice answered.

"Hello, name's Frank Boorman. I was in New York a few days ago looking for office space. I noticed that there was an empty window on the corner of the second floor facing thirty-fourth. Who could I talk to about leasing the space?"

"Sorry sir, that space is currently being leased."

"Might I ask by who?"

"Not sure, they just moved in."

"Who had it before?"

"That would be…" the security guard paused for a moment. "Rotary Insurance Company. Husband and wife team. Insured imported goods, I believe."

The guard was about to hang up when Rudi jumped in. "What a coincidence, I'm looking for insurance right now. Do you have their contact info."

"Can't say I do sir. Have a good day."

Rudi scratched his chin. He'd discovered a piece of the puzzle.

After a quick search he found the number for Rotary Insurance. On the third ring he heard a young woman's voice.

"My name's George Benson, I'm looking to insure a shipment."

"Sorry but he's no longer in business," the woman said.

"But the listing?"

"The owner retired. He must have forgotten to change it."

"Can I speak to him?"

"Why?"

"Um, I—I'd like a recommendation on who else I might contact."

She laid the phone down and swished away.

In the background he heard, "Sweetie, some man wants to talk to you about insurance."

"Tell him I retired."

"I did, but he wants to talk to you anyway."

"All right, just a minute."

The phone lifted and an impatient voice said, "Yeah."

"I'm looking for insurance for some cargo that I'm shipping to London, and I thought you might have an idea of someone I could contact."

"What are you shipping?"

"I rather not say, it's um...classified."

"Never heard of that. Can't help you there," he said.

"Listen, what was your name again?"

"Didn't say. Why?"

"Just keeping a record of who I called."

"Bill Farner. You have a good day." And the line went dead.

Another piece of the puzzle. Rudi picked up his pen and made a few notes. He knew the name of the company as well as the name of its former owner. He tapped his pen on the desk then made a note that the woman who answered the phone sounded too young to be married to a retiree. Now, he was certain. Farner murdered his wife.

Rudi checked the calendar and found that he was in New York the second week of September last year. He searched the obituaries for a woman with the last name of Farner but came up empty. Then he cross referenced every female who died that had a spouse named Farner. After an hour of searching, he found what he was looking for.

On September tenth, a Ms. Helen Wilson drowned while sailing with her husband William Farner. The couple had gone out on the bay early that morning. Shortly before noon Farner pulled into the dock, hysterical, saying that his wife had fallen overboard. He told the police that he couldn't call for help because his radio was out of commission. The authorities searched but never recovered the body. It was presumed that Wilson was washed out to sea when the tide receded. Helen Wilson, thirty-seven, was the daughter of Ryan Wilson, president of Wilson Importing. Yet, another piece to the puzzle. Rudi picked up his pen and jotted down. Farner had a motive. Money.

*****

Rudi stared at the antique brass placard on the face of the Wilson building. The previous week he had called to set up an appointment with Ryan Wilson, pretending to represent a clothing manufacturer from Vietnam. He walked across the marbled floor, admiring its cleanliness, then checked in with security. A minute later he was riding the elevator to the fifteenth floor and Wilson's office.

When the elevator opened Rudi showed his pass to a guard at the entrance.

"See him," the guard said pointing to a man sitting behind a desk at the end of the hallway.

"Name's Frank Connors. I have an appointment with Mr. Wilson.

Without looking up the secretary said, "Mr. Wilson's in a meeting, it will be a few minutes sir."

Rudi sat down and examined the waiting room. He felt the creased leather arm of his chair, dragged his foot along the sculpted rug, and fixed his eyes on a brass sconce attached to the wall. All spoke of Wilson's wealth. Rudi folded his hands and waited.

Twenty minutes later the secretary escorted him into a large wood paneled office.

"Mr. Wilson, Mr. Connors to see you."

Wilson waved Rudi to a chair to the left of a massive desk.

"Drink?" he said.

"No thanks."

"What can I do for you Mr. Connors?"

"I don't know how to go about this. I'm not here for the reason I stated. I'm here about your daughter."

"You better not be another insurance investigator," Wilson said clenching his fist.

"No, definitely not. I'm here because I believe your son in law murdered your daughter."

Rudi watched as a network of veins erupted on Wilson's forehead.

Wilson's hand moved to the intercom. "Security."

A Missing Piece

"Please, give me a moment.

Wilson pushed another button and said, "Have security wait outside my door."

"You've got two minutes Connors."

Rudi took out his laptop and showed Wilson the photo. He watched as Wilson's face drained of blood.

"At first I thought that the man standing over her was only holding a folder, but then I realized he was about to strike her with some blunt object."

Shaken, Wilson fell back in his chair. "Is this some trick?"

"Look at the date," Rudi said. "It's the day before your daughter was supposed to have drowned."

Wilson stroked his beard. "The location is correct, and the date makes sense. But how do I know that you didn't just invent this to shake me down?"

"For what reason?" Rudi said. "I'm only telling you the truth. I accidently photographed your daughter being murdered and I wanted to do the right thing."

Wilson swiveled to the window. When he came back around, Rudi could tell by the way Wilson's eyes softened that he believed him.

"I never trusted that son in law of mine. Right now he's shacked up with some woman half his age. Tell you what. Meet me at the marina tomorrow morning. I'll have my skipper take us out to the area where my daughter was supposed to have drowned. We'll start from there and backtrack. If there's anything to what you're telling me, they'll be a reward."

*****

It was shortly after seven when Rudi arrived at the dock. A thick gray fog hung over the bay. At the far end of the pier Wilson stood at the rail of a sleek cruiser and waved him onboard.

Coffee?" Wilson said, shoving a mug into Rudi's hands.

"It will take about an hour to get to the area. Then we'll circle. The water's deep, but this baby's got a hell of a sonar rig. If there's anything out there it will show up."

On schedule the skipper cut the engine and they drifted.

"Let's take a look," Wilson said motioning Rudi to a small screen at the right of the wheel.

"Most of what's on the bottom is debris," Wilson said pointing to the screen.

They trolled for a while when Wilson yelled to the skipper, "Cut the engines.

"Look," he said.

Rudi bent over to see a large rock resting on the sandy bottom.

"That's the spot where Bill was supposed to have dumped her," Wilson said.

"How do you know?"

Wilson straightened and put his hands in his pockets. "Because that's the story we agreed on."

Rudi's mind flipped to the next page. It was blank.

"You see, Mr. whoever you are, I'm broke, and I needed the insurance money from my daughter's death. Her alleged death that is. Right now, her butts on a beach in Costa Rica sipping a margarita."

A band snapped in Rudi's head, and he wobbled.

"It was supposed to have been an unfortunate accident, but you photographed them in the window and created this fiction that Bill murdered her. Now, we can't take the chance that someone might believe it, can we?"

A calloused hand let go of the wheel and cradled Rudi's elbow.

"Meet my skipper, Bill Farner."

Wilson looked at Rudi with eyes that were almost apologetic. "I imagine the coffee was a bit strong."

Rudi fell back onto the bench. And as the cruiser motored out to sea, Rudi snapped the last piece of the puzzle into place. It was him.

Killer on the Loose
Vinnie Hansen

On her last day as a teacher, Ms. Rose Goodwin was dwelling on death—one of the great themes of literature. Her long fingers rested on a dusty keyboard. She hunched toward a fifteen-inch monitor, but her mind rocked to Lucille Clifton's line "water waving forever." *Blessing the boats* was such a beautiful poem: "and may you in your innocence/sail through this to that." She would miss discussing such works.

"We came to pay our respects."

She blinked up at an inseparable trio of juniors, her favorite students, Charles, Sean and Abundio.

Abundio had delivered his statement with sincere dark eyes that both penetrated her heart and embarrassed her. If he wore a hat, it would be in his hands pressed to his thighs.

"Don't say that," Charles shoulder-bumped Abundio. "That makes it sound like Ms. Goodwin is dead."

Ms. Goodwin smiled up from her plastic chair. "That's right, Abundio. Don't jinx me."

Abundio shrugged back into his dignity. On one side Sean barely came up to Abundio's broad shoulders, and on the other, Charles Choi, as tall as Abundio, looked thin enough to fly away. He had not begun to fill out his wild high-school growth spurt.

"What do you mean, Ms. Goodwin?" Abundio asked.

Abundio always wanted to understand, which made him an exceptional student.

Sean and Charles bounced him back and forth between them like the pendulum of a clock.

Ms. Goodwin sighed. "You know those movies about the cop who gets killed his last day on the job?" One of her arms wrapped the waist of her black-and-white striped shirt while her free hand flipped to palm up. "It's a cliché."

Abundio nodded. The boys fully grasped cliché. But the three of them excelled in the Math, Engineering and Science Achievement program; they did not plan to be lit. majors. Probably for the best, but it made Ms. Goodwin wistful.

"Or the guy who retires and the next day drops dead of a heart attack?" she added.

"Oh," Abundio stepped quickly forward so Sean and Charles collided into each other. His friends laughed, but Abundio's black eyes didn't even blink. "So retirement could carry a curse?"

Sean tsked and dramatically threw his arms wide. "We're talking statistical probability here." An abnormally rational teen, Sean had once spent a patient half hour explaining black holes to Ms. Goodwin until she was hamstrung in his mixed metaphors. "It's like dying on your birthday." Sean clapped his hands together in a note of finality. "With over seven billion people on earth, millions of people will die on their birthday, and because retirees are old, a lot of them will die the day they retire."

"Geez, I feel better already," Ms. Goodwin said.

Charles rolled his eyes at the way his classmates were blowing it. "We just came to say goodbye."

Ms. Goodwin melodramatically clutched her hair and dropped her head. "That sounds even worse."

"You want a euphemism," Sean piped.

"Yes," she beamed, proud that he had used the word *euphemism*.

"We'll see you around," Sean offered. He reached up to tousle Abundio's straight black hair. Without losing his focus on Ms. Goodwin, Abundio swatted Sean as though he were a gnat. A dead one now.

To think she had once worried Sean and Charles might be harassing Abundio. Abundio could take care of himself, side-stepping them with grace.

"Yes," Ms. Goodwin said. "That's better. Let's not tempt fate. I'll see you around." She rose to give each boy a loose, back-patting hug.

*****

Three blocks away at the middle school, Bunny Fairhall recycled paper. She had not planned to retire, but the Golden Handshake was a good deal that wouldn't come around again soon. Retirement was the smart move, even if her heart ached, so that when Mitzi appeared in the classroom doorway, tears sprouted in Bunny's eyes.

"I came to say goodbye," Mitzi pronounced.

Ms. Fairhall stopped throwing reams of worksheets into an industrial-sized, rolling blue recycling cart. Although an English teacher for over thirty years, she found herself without words. She swiped at the dust bunnies clinging to the front of her pink blouse and the lap of her jeans.

Mitzi bailed her out. "Are you going to remember me?

"Indubitably."

Mitzi whispered a smile, so faint that if you didn't know her, you couldn't hear it, like the language of a secret sea creature. She loved Ms. Fairhall because she said words like that. They sounded like magic.

"No, you won't." Slightly pigeon-toed, Mitzi scratched the inside of her ankle with her red Converse. The other shoe was black.

Ms. Fairhall caught her lower lip with a tooth, one that Mitzi had pointed out wasn't "real."

"It's too big," she'd informed the whole class.

Kids were so delightfully honest.

Ms. Fairhall massaged her lower back with both sets of fingers, and inspected Mitzi there in the doorway, in her ripped jeans and Slayer tee-shirt, no breasts to speak of even though she was headed off to high school. Mitzi had cut her black hair herself, and it looked like it, poking every which way.

Early in the year, Mitzi had planted a plastic fly on the rim of Ms. Fairhall's tea mug, so whenever the teacher approached her drink, the students laughed with anticipation. But each time, their burst of excitement stopped Ms. Fairhall before she picked up her mug, as she cast about the room for the source of their amusement.

Finally, unable to bear the suspense, someone shouted, "Look at your cup!"

She'd peered at it. Nothing. Middle-school kids didn't know that folks her age needed glasses for such details.

Mitzi had marched up. She'd been wearing her jean jacket with all manner of things sewn to it and had been sporting a safety pin through her ear piercing. "I put a plastic fly on it." She pointed.

Ms. Fairhall bent close and laughed. She plucked up the fly and made it buzz. "Onomatopoeia." She had tossed it at Mitzi, who out of the air snatched the tiny plastic object into her fist.

Now, at the end of her career, Ms. Fairhall said, "I will remember you for the rest of my life."

"Why?"

"Because, my dear, you are full of beans." Ms. Fairhall could see Mitzi chewing on the words.

"Okay, then," Mitzi said. "I'm going to remember you for the rest of my life, too."

"You could sew that fly on your jacket."

Mitzi's delicate chin dipped a millimeter, a nod in the language of Mitzi. Then she smiled and vanished.

*****

Rose Goodwin was about partied out from school events, but she'd decided on one last retirement fling for personal friends. Twenty minutes before the guests were to arrive, Don Goodwin left to pick up the cake. Rose tied a bouquet of balloons to a metal, gold-star weight and took them to the porch steps. In spite of the helium, the breeze batted the bright orbs all the way to the ground. *Hmmm.* But the wind came in gusts, so at least part of the time the balloons floated upright. She didn't have time to second-guess the arrangement.

She was setting out the champagne flutes when Don's car rumbled into the driveway. Anxious to see the cake, she threw open the door for him. He entered with the large white box.

He smiled broadly. "It looks great. *Happy retirement, Rose.* In pink.

And they put a flower made from a strawberry on top to go with the strawberries in the cake."

Rose's face fell.

"Chocolate with strawberries? Whipped cream frosting? That's what you wanted, isn't it?"

"Did you move the balloons?"

He glanced in the direction of Rose's gaze—at the empty gold star on the step.

"I didn't do anything with them, Rose. They must have blown away. Did you tie them?"

Her heart dropped. "Of course." She ran into the street, looked both ways and into the sky, especially disappointed to lose the fish balloon Don had included, a nod to her love of the electric blue damsel in their aquarium.

"Rose," Don snapped, "they're gone. And even if you could see them, it's not like we could go catch them. It's not like we have a helicopter in the backyard."

She followed him into the kitchen and pulled champagne bottles from the refrigerator to make room for the cake.

"Did you double knot it?"

"No," she sighed. "Just a bow tie."

"Well," he shrugged. "They got away. Escaped."

"But they were only out there for five minutes."

"We'll ask our guests if they saw the fugitives."

"That's it," she brightened. "The damsel that got away. Did they see the outlaw swimming through the ocean of sky? Fleeing with her gang over Highway One?"

He laughed. "A perfect conversation starter. I can't wait to tell people how you ran into the street looking for them."

*****

HAPPY RETIREMENT—bright letters on silver Mylar—a wiggling fish and a half dozen traditional balloons sailed freely through the sky, trailing a tail of ribbon.

*****

That same Saturday, middle-school teacher Bunny Fairhall drove her Prius along the freeway, marveling at the power of word association. She didn't have to take anything to her school's potluck party for the five retirees, but almost immediately after telling Mitzi she was full of beans, Bunny had decided she would concoct a three-bean salad.

Now, a bag full of ingredients sat on the passenger seat, and she congratulated herself on the choice. *Easy and healthy.* The salad had enough time to marinate. *Marinate.* Now there was an interesting word, surely constructed from the Latin root mar, the sea.

*****

A downward gust blew Rose's bouquet of balloons into a towering liquid amber tree where a dried brown seed pod pricked the Happy Retirement balloon, the heart of the arrangement. Air seeped out, but the other balloons tugged it from the snag, towing the weight of the Mylar. With the new ballast, they floated low over the head of a short freeway exit. When the startling blue fish swooped over a gold Mercedes, blocking the driver's line of vision, she swerved. Three teenaged boys, waiting to cross at the end of the exit, jumped back at the sight of the car careening toward them.

*****

As Bunny Fairhall reached her exit, her hand searched the grocery bag on the passenger seat for the green onions. *Did I remember them?* Failing to feel any long, slick stalks, she tipped the bag, lifted out a can of beans, and peeked, and yes, there they were, flat against the bottom. She righted herself.

Before her, a gold Mercedes swung wildly. Bunny slammed on her brakes and cranked the steering wheel. Her car skidded sideways. A long-haired man in an old tan and brown Ford truck coming fast off the freeway, punched his boot into his brake, but still t-boned the passenger side of the Prius. The car spun so the front faced up the exit and the rear rammed into a guardrail post. The air bag of the Prius deployed. Exploding blackness engulfed Bunny Fairhall.

The three boys sprinted toward the accident. Sean pulled his cell from his pocket and thumbed 911.

"Where are we?" he shouted at his friends Charles and Abundio, not because he didn't know, but because he wanted to slow up their long legs, so they didn't see everything before he did.

The Mercedes had continued on its way as though nothing had happened behind it, but a skinny man with stringy, dirty blond hair and wearing shit-kickers climbed, shaking, from his dented pick-up. Behind the Prius and truck, traffic clogged back onto the freeway. A white Honda Fit eased its way around the scene. On the far side of the exit, balloons lodged in an oleander bush.

Even with the pick-up providing a barrier, Charles watched for cars trying to edge around the accident the way the small Fit had. He creaked open the door of the Prius. A woman's head sank toward the steering wheel as the air bag deflated.

"She looks dead," Abundio said over his shoulder.

Pocketing his cell phone, Sean hopped to see around the wall of Charles and Abundio. "She was slowed up for the exit," Sean said. "She couldn't have been going more than maybe forty miles per hour tops. She has an air bag." Because he was small, Sean had mastered stoicism in fourth grade. He had disciplined his voice never to quaver and his eyes never to tear. "She's probably just unconscious."

With a trembling hand, the man from the pick-up brusquely motioned cars forward. They crawled around the accident, their tires in the gutter or up on the berm, the drivers peering at the scene, trying to absorb all the details in a passing moment.

Charles nudged Abundio. "Feel for a pulse."

In the distance a siren shrieked. "Really," Sean insisted, "she can't be dead." He wondered if he should take a picture with his phone as some kind of evidence.

"Dead?" the man said. The boys whirled, startled that he'd moved so close. "You kids saw the accident, right? You know it wasn't my fault."

"Maybe she had a heart attack." Charles' shirt flapped around his thin torso. The random, piercing wind chilled him. "The crazy way that Mercedes was driving could have freaked her out."

Abundio nervously touched the woman's neck. "I don't feel

anything."

The siren slowed, stuck in the freeway traffic jam.

Abundio bent over, searching for signs of life, such as a moving finger. There were no protruding bones or oozing blood. Maybe Charles was right about a heart attack. The frizzy hair and the bit of face he could see looked familiar. "Maybe we should try to pull her out and start CPR."

Another siren approached from the opposite direction, coming up the surface streets.

"No," Sean said. "Didn't we learn in P.E. *not* to move an injured person?" Sean circled the car to the safer side and cracked the groaning, caved-in passenger door. He peered into the grocery bag.

Charles followed him. "Anything good?" He had to say something funny—or vomit. His body trembled like a reed.

Sean dropped to his knees and fished around on the floor and under the seat. He came up with a can of kidney beans. "Remember what we learned in physics?"

"What?" Abundio said from the other side of the car. "Are you insane? Help me get this woman out!" He peeled the deflated air bag away from the woman's face and recoiled.

Sean replaced the can on the floor, sank one knee into the seat, leaned across, and parted the woman's hair this way and that as though searching for lice.

"What are you doing?" Abundio shrieked.

"Yup." Sean pointed to her temple. "Right there. She was hit with a flying can of beans." He extracted himself from the car and spoke over it to Abundio and the hippy-ish man. "Car stops, but the objects inside don't."

Abundio gaped. "Do you know who she is?" A burst of wind blew back his dark hair and whipped his shirt against his ribs.

Sean stared at Abundio, who had his knuckles in his mouth. The sirens on the surface street closed in. Thank God. Everything indicated that Abundio's first impression had been right. The woman was stone cold dead.

Abundio nodded toward the body. "That's Ms. Fairhall. From middle school."

"Oh my God. Wasn't she retiring, too?" Charles said. "Like Ms. Goodwin?"

"Holy shit." Abundio jumped back as though the car contained an asp. The curse of retirement was real.

On the other side of the vehicle, Sean's mouth rounded into a screech of alarm, but the sound didn't come out. A big, low, chromed-out motorcycle was charging down the tunnel between the accident and the line of cars crawling down the other side of the exit. The rider wore a leather vest and army-style helmet and planned to zip through the narrow passageway. He was a juggernaut aimed straight at Abundio.

Loud pipes alerted Abundio before Charles' shout. He turned to meet the roaring metal.

The biker veered and hit a car.

Metal machine and man scraped and pancaked and bounced down the exit. The fire truck screeched, bucking to avoid the sudden appearance of the old Indian motorcycle and its rider sliding down the asphalt like a landing Frisbee.

The balloons tugged free from the oleander and drifted away in the capricious breeze.

*****

Rose stared out the glass panes of the front door. "Maybe I should put the champagne back in the 'fridge."

Don waved a hand by his ear. "No one but you, Rose, thinks he should arrive on time to these things." Still he checked his watch, ten minutes after four, and peered over Rose's shoulder.

"Hatsue," Rose fretted. "Hatsue is always on time." Another English teacher, Hatsue was noted for running a tight ship.

On cue, Hatsue's Honda Element turned the corner and pulled into the driveway. Hatsue reached over to the passenger seat and jumped down, bottle of wine in hand, the breeze playing with her gossamer sea green dress. "Traffic was horrible," she said. "Must have been an accident." She extended her gift. "Happy retirement!"

Accepting the bottle, Rose asked, "When you were sitting in traffic, did you see my balloons sail by?"

As the wind rustled leaves and spit dirt at the women's legs, Don pointed out the vacant star to Hatsue. She understood immediately and laughed. "Off into the wild blue yonder."

Regret pinged through Rose. She'd miss seeing Hatsue on a regular basis. Would miss mulling over works like Clifton's poem. Would miss students like Sean, Abundio and Charles. She looked to the sky, thinking of her untethered balloons swimming through the blue expanse from "this to that." *In the end, aren't we all unmoored, transported on a breath from here to there?*

Rose sighed wistfully, thankful to be alive for her first day of retirement. "Let's go have some champagne." She opened the door.

The Usual Unusual Suspects

Gerald Elias leads a double life. He is the author of the critically acclaimed Daniel Jacobus mystery series that takes place in the dark corners of the classical music world, other novels, and many short stories and essays.

Elias is also an internationally recognized musician who has been a violinist with the Boston Symphony and music director of the Vivaldi by Candlelight concert series in Salt Lake City since 2004. He divides his time between the shores of Puget Sound in Washington and the Berkshire Hills of western Massachusetts, where he continues to expand his literary and musical horizons.

https://geraldeliasmanofmystery.wordpress.com/

Bob Richie wonders why author bios are always in the third person, and wonders why he cannot instead write the following: "I'm Bob Ritchie. Originally from California, I now live (and write) in Puerto Rico (Check out that sky!) My work has appeared in *Unlikely*, *Penumbric Speculative Fiction Magazine*, *Triangle Writers Magazine*, *Crimeucopia—We'll Be Right Back – After This!*, and others. I am a musician, as well, and have had the privilege of collaborating with Jon Anderson. Now, if I could just occupy a room containing a guitar, a piano, and a Paul McCartney, my life would surely be complete." He supposes we'll never know.

Michele Bazan Reed's short stories have appeared in *Woman's World* magazine and several anthologies, most recently *Detective Mysteries Short Stories*, *Mid-Century Murder*, *Malice Domestic 15: Mystery Most Theatrical*, *Masthead: Best New England Mysteries 2020*, *The Fish that Got Away*, *Crazy Christmas Capers* and *The Big Fang* (2022).

A member of Sisters in Crime and its Guppy Chapter, Private Eye Writers of America, and the Short Mystery Fiction Society, she won a 2017 Daphne Award in the unpublished mainstream mystery category.

Michele's Crimeucopia appearances have been in *The I's Have It*, *Tales From The Back Porch*, and most recently *We'll Be Right Back – After This!*

Terry Wijesuriya has been a published author since the age of seven, though admittedly it was a plotless short story about a butterfly, which appeared in the local children's newspaper....

She reads anything interesting that she comes across, with her favourite genre of fiction being Orientalist adventure. She also runs a very sporadic fan blog dedicated to JT Edson's Floating Outfit series—https://www.theysabelkid.wordpress.com. She lives just outside Colombo with her family and other animals.

Aran Myracle is a US Army veteran and current youth social worker. He firmly believes that what doesn't kill you makes you weirder, and many things have failed to kill him. He resides in Washington State, USA, with his partner, their dog and cat, and a fair amount of pet fur tumbleweeds. *Chinese Submarines* is Aran's first, but hopefully not his last, Crimeucopia appearance.

Alexei J. Slater from London, England studied English Literature and had poetry published in the university magazine. He worked for seven years at former Beatle, George Harrison's famed production company *HandMade Films* (known for *The Life of Brian* and other classics). He has written and produced many award-winning short films including '82' based on his own short story and still writes 'spec' tv and film screenplays. Recent stories include *Dubois, Wyoming* which was a Quarter Finalist in ScreenCraft's Cinematic Short Story Competition 2022 and he is preparing to query agents with his debut crime novel. More at www.alexeijslater.com.

Nikki Knight describes herself as an Author/Anchor/Mom…not in that order. An award-winning weekend anchor at 1010 WINS Radio in New York, she writes mysteries including *LIVE, LOCAL, AND DEAD*, a Vermont Radio Mystery from Crooked Lane, and as Kathleen Marple Kalb, the Ella Shane and Old Stuff series. Her short stories appear online and in anthologies, including *CRIMEUCOPIA: Tales From The Back Porch*, and *DEADLY NIGHTSHADE: Best New England Crime Stories 2022*. *Bad Apples* won an Honorable Mention in the 2021 Black Orchid Novella Award Contest.

She, her husband and son live in a Connecticut house owned by their cat.

Issy Jinarmo is a pen name of writing trio Jill Baggett, Narelle Noppert and Maureen Kelly OAM. Never having met each other – living thousands of miles apart in Australia – they first 'met' through The Fellowship of Australian Writers NSW Inc.

From there they began their collaboration and started writing as a group by email in 2020 when Life as the world knew it took a sudden shift, and online pastimes became a way of keeping friends in touch. And from that collaboration, Issy Jinarmo was born.

Her successes have included Specul8's resent supernatural anthology (https://www.specul8.com.au/product/haunted-an-anthology/36), the Australian magazine Mona (https://www.monamagazine.com/), and is involved with the Fellowship of Australian Writers NSW (https://fawnsw.org.au/membership/bulletin/back-issues/)

N. M. Cedeño is a member of the Short Mystery Fiction Society and Sisters in Crime: Heart of Texas Chapter. Her stories have appeared in anthologies and magazines, including *Analog: Science Fiction and Fact*, *After Dinner Conversation*, *Black Cat Weekly*, and *Black Cat Mystery Magazine*. She blogs at https://inkstainedwretches.home.blog/. For more information visit http://nmcedeno.com/.

Wendy Harrison is a retired prosecutor who turned to short mystery fiction during the pandemic. Her stories have been published in numerous anthologies including *Peace, Love & Crime, Autumn Noir, Crimeucopia, The Big Fang, Gargoylicon,* and *Death of a Bad Neighbour* as well as in *Shotgun Honey*. When Hurricane Ian destroyed her home in Florida, she moved to Washington State, as far from Florida as she could get.

Andrew Darlington has been regularly published since the 1960s in all manner of strange and obscure places, magazines, websites, anthologies and books. He has also worked as a Stand-Up Poet on the 'Alternative Cabaret Circuit', and also has a phenomenal back catalogue of published interviews with many people from the worlds of Literature, SF-Fantasy, Art and Rock-Music for a variety of publications (a selection of his favourite interviews have been collected into the Headpress book *I Was Elvis Presley's Bastard Love-Child*).

His latest poetry collection is *Tweak Vision* (Alien Buddha Press), and a new fiction collection *A Saucerful Of Secrets* is now available from Parallel Universe Publications, and a Scientifiction novel *In The Time Of The Breaking* (Alien Buddha Press) was published in January 2019. Catch up with him at http://andrewdarlington.blogspot.com/.

Larry Lefkowitz was born in Trenton, New Jersey (motto: Trenton Makes, the World Takes), became a lawyer, immigrated to Israel, got married (finally at age 39) and became a freelance writer. His writing is aided by the fact that he does not possess a cellphone nor does he belong to Facebook because, to quote him, "My face does not belong in a book."

His stories, poetry, and humor have been widely published. The latter, the humor, he finds hard to keep out of even his serious writing. He had a number of Sherlock Holmes stories published, including one which takes place in a nudist colony, which of course tests Holmes' powers of identification to its limits.

Along with other successfully published detective stories, Larry's story collection Enigmatic Tales is published by Fomite Press (https://www.fomitepress.com/enigmatic-tales.html). It is a collection of

Jewish stories whose characters live in the world but strive to understand it, faithful to the saying that if Jews don't know the answer, they answer with a question. His new detective novella, Trouble in Jades, is looking for a publisher. Lefkowitz admits that he is an old guy, but his writing keeps him young (relatively).

Jesse Aaron served as a police officer in New York City and Connecticut for over five years and also worked in the field of private security/investigations. His first novel, *Shafer City Stories* is available on Amazon.com (https://www.amazon.com/Shafer-City-Stories-Tales-NYPD-Harlem/dp/1518853137/). Jesse's short story *The Leaky Faucet* was featured in *Crimeucopia – It's Always Raining in Noir City*. Jesse has two more short stories on the way to publication and is currently at work on his upcoming serial killer thriller *Harlem Hipster Homicides*. Jesse's style is dark and gritty, and his stories focus on the underside of the police and private detective worlds. Jesse has a love of all things Noir, Science Fiction, and Fantasy.

Madeleine McDonald finds inspiration walking on the chilly, windswept beach of her Yorkshire home. As a former precis-writer, she enjoys the challenge of writing flash fiction. Her short stories have been broadcast on BBC radio, and published in various anthologies and journals. Her latest novel, *A Shackled Inheritance*, is available from Amazon Kindle. Her most recent win is the *Press 53* contest for November2022, https://www.press53.com/53word-story-contest.

Joan Leotta plays with words on page and stage. She performs tales featuring food, family, and strong women. Internationally published, she's a 2021 and 2022 Pushcart nominee, a Best of the Net 2022 nominee, and a 2022 runner-up in the Robert Frost Competition. Her essays, poems, and fiction are in *Ekphrastic Review, When Women Write, The Lake, Verse Visual, Verse Virtual,* anti-heroin chic, *Gargoyle, Silver Birch, The Wild, Ovunquesiamo, MacQueen's Quinterly,* and *Yellow Mama*, among others. Her chapbooks are *Languid Lusciousness*

with Lemon (Finishing Line Press) and *Feathers on Stone* (Main Street Rag).
https://mainstreetragbookstore.com/product/feathers-on-stone-joan-leotta/

H.E. Vogl is a retired professor who has turned to writing fiction. His stories, occasionally dark but always absurd, explore the quirks in the fabric of everyday life. Vogl's work has appeared in *Fiction on the Web*, *Bewildering Stories*, *Every Day Fiction*, and *Fabula Argentea*.
His *Only a Cannoli* appears in *Crimeucopia – It's Always Raining In Noir City*.

Vinnie Hansen fled the winds of the South Dakota prairie and headed for the California coast the day after high school graduation.
A two-time Claymore Award finalist, she is the author of the Carol Sabala mystery series, the novels *Lostart Street* and *One Gun*, as well as over fifty published short works.
Still sane(ish) after 27 years of teaching high school English, Vinnie has retired and plays keyboards with ukulele groups in Santa Cruz, California, where she lives with her husband and the requisite cat.
For more information, go to https://www.vinniehansen.com/ for news and updates.

CRIMEUCOPIA
WE'LL BE RIGHT BACK —
— AFTER THIS!

FEATURING:
JIM GUIGLI, GLEN BUSH, EDWARD LODI, CATE MOYLE,
JAY ANDREW CONNOR, BOB RITCHIE, MICHELE BAZAN REED,
EVE FISHER, MICHAEL WILEY, JOAN HALL HOVEY, J. T. SEATE,
AND MADELEINE MCDONALD

This is the first of several 'Free 4 All' collections that was supposed to be themeless. However, with the number of submissions that came in, it seems that this could be called an *Angels & Devils* collection, mixing PI & Police alongside tales from the Devil's dining table. Mind you, that's not to say that all the PIs & Police are on the side of the Angels....

Also this time around has not only seen a move to a larger paperback format size, but also in regard to the length of the fiction as well. Followers of the somewhat bent and twisted Crimeucopia path will know that although we don't deal with Flash fiction as a rule, it is a rule that we have sometimes broken. And let's face it, if you cannot break your own rules now and again, whose rules can you break?

Oh, wait, isn't breaking the rules the foundation of the crime fiction genre?

Oh dear....

CRIMEUCOPIA
The Cosy Nostra

A Crimeucopia Family Gathering

17 writers take us on Cosy journeys - some more traditional, while others are very much up to date.
Eve Fisher, Alexander Frew, Tom Johnstone, John M. Floyd, Andrew Humphrey, Joan Leotta, Gary Thomson, Eamonn Murphey, Matias Travieso-Diaz, Madeline McEwen, Lyn Fraser, Ella Moon, Gina L. Grandi, Louise Taylor, Judy Penz Sheluk, Joan Hall Hovey and Judy Upton.
Paperback Edition ISBN: 9781909498242
eBook Edition ISBN: 9781909498259

CRIMEUCOPIA

As In Funny Ha-Ha

Or Just Peculiar

Putting the Outré back into OMG are
Jesse Hilson, Gabriel Stevenson, Maddi Davidson,
Brandon Barrows, Robb T. White, Regina Clarke,
Martin Zeigler, K. G. Anderson, Andrew Hook,
Ed Nobody, Jody Smith, Michael Grimala,
W. T. Paterson, James Blakey, Emilian Wojnowski,
Andrew Darlington, Lawrence Allan, Ricky Sprague,
Bethany Maines, John M. Floyd and Julie Richards

Paperback Edition ISBN: 9781909498266
eBook Edition ISBN: 9781909498273

CRIMEUCOPIA
CARELESS ♥ LOVE

You're driving me crazy
You're making me mad
'Cos the only way of lovin' you
Is with a good love gone bad...
(Vicky LaPerso – The 1956 Ventura Tapes)

Fifteen writers tell us about affairs of the heart – some with humour, some with a darker intent, and others that are never quite exactly what they seem. Is it all about manipulation? Can there be more than one agenda? And does Love really conquer all, even when it's supposedly blind? Or maybe Love is just an old Devil, looking for mischief?

Steve Sneyd, Ange Morrissey, James Roth, Michael Wiley, Gustavo Bondoni, Matthew Wilson, Peter W. J. Hayes, Wil A. Emerson, Brandon Barrows, Bern Sy Moss, Michael Anthony Dioguardi, Russell Richardson, Robert Petyo, Sam Westcott, Bryn Fortey and *Vicky LaPerso* – all of whom take us on roller coaster rides through a fictional Tunnel of Love.

Paperback Edition ISBN: 9781909498303
eBook Edition ISBN: 9781909498310

CRIMEUCOPIA
The I's Have It

Featuring: Mike Job, Jill Hand, Joe Giordano, Michael Thomét, Michele Bazan Reed, Paul R. Paradise, M. C. Tuggle, Edward Lodi, Lynn Hesse, Kelly Zimmer, John M. Floyd and Shannon Lawrence

Investigators and investigations are the mainstay of most Crime fiction sub-genres. Everything from the original *Golden Age* of country houses and the amateur sleuth, through to the high tech ultra-modern 21st Century – a place where the cyber investigators sometimes appear to be baffled by old-fashioned motivations of power and greed, and human foibles such as love and revenge.

So is there any real difference between the Private and the Public Sector investigators? Not much, if writers are to be believed, and the two can often be found straddling both sides of the 'what's legal procedure?' fence.

Of the twelve authors contained within, eleven are voices new to the world of Crimeucopia - and although the theme is *Investigators*, the material ranges from Cosy, through to not too Hardboiled - and most are touched with a vein of humour, be it light or dark. Rather like a box of chocolates...

Paperback ISBN: 9781909498327 eBook ISBN: 9781909498334

CRIMEUCOPIA

It's Always Raining In Noir City

Where even the cat beats you at chess

Featuring:
Laurence Raphael Brothers
Shannon Hollinger
Lillie Franks
H. E. Vogl
Allison Whittenberg
Bruce Harris
Robert J. Mendenhall
Shawn Kobb
Dan Meyers
James Roth
Jesse Aaron
Julian Grant
E. James Wilson
Brandon Barrows
Hollis Miller
and Joe Giordano

Is the Noir Crime sub-genre always dark and downbeat? Is there a time when Bad has a change of conscience, flips sides and takes on the Good role?

Noir is almost always a dish served up raw and bloody - Fiction bleu if you will. So maybe this is a chance to see if Noir can be served sunny side up - with the aid of these fifteen short order authors.

All fifteen give us dark tales from the stormy side of life - which is probably why it's *always* raining in Noir City....

Paperback Edition ISBN: 9781909498341
eBook Edition ISBN: 9781909498358

CRIMEUCOPIA

Tales From The Back Porch

Telling tales are:
Penny Hurrell, Teresa Trent, Wendy Harrison, Maroula Blades, Tom Sheehan, Jan Christensen, Bryn Fortey, Michele Bazan Reed, Carol Willis, Madeleine McDonald, Adam Meyer, Nikki Knight, Regina Clarke, J. W. Wood, Deb Merino and Alison McDonald

Small town, big city, watercooler or the back of that 1950s beat-up Chevy Bel Air with the leather back seat that your parents told you never to get familiar with. It doesn't matter where you hear it, gossip is 100% pure ear addiction – and knowledge is, after all, power when all's said and done.

So why don't you settle down, get yourself comfy, and pour yourself a drink – long and tall, or just short and nasty, the choice is yours – and let these 16 story tellers spin their tales as only they know how.

Paperback Edition ISBN: 9781909498365
eBook Edition ISBN: 9781909498372

CRIMEUCOPIA

When the theme is no theme at all, you've just got to ask the question

Say What Now?

Featuring:
Peter Ullian,
S. E. Bailey,
N. M. Cedeño,
Edward St Boniface,
Jan Glaz,
Eleanor Luke,
Momodou Bah,
Eve Fisher,
John M. Floyd,
Joan Leotta,
Glen Bush
and DL Shirey

Sometimes editors are forced to reject submissions through no fault of the author. It could be a wonderfully written manuscript, but if the editor cannot place it, then what do they do?

MIP has been lucky in its flexibility and its "Can we start a new project with this?" attitude. Some of the dozen authors contained within are seasoned professionals, having been published in the likes of Alfred Hitchcock's, Ellery Queen's, or other notable publications, while some are making their publishing debuts as Crimeucopians. And while the quality throughout remains exceedingly high, the subject spectrum is the widest we've published so far. But that's only fitting when you consider that the theme of this Crimeucopa is that of No Theme At All.

And in true Murderous Ink fashion, with a dozen authors to choose from, you're bound to find something you'll like, and something you didn't know you'd like until you've read it.

Paperback Edition ISBN: 9781909498389
eBook Edition ISBN: 9781909498396

Printed in Great Britain
by Amazon